PRAISE FOR THE
STEEL BROTHERS SAGA

D11158756

CHERISHED

CHERISHED

STEEL BROTHERS SAGA
BOOK SEVENTEEN

HELEN HARDT

WATERHOUSE PRESS

For my mother

PROLOGUE

The sun rises over the Rockies and casts light on my vines.

I won't stay long.

I have to get home to feed Penny and let her out.

But for a moment, this is where I need to be.

Away from the chaos.

Away from the fear.

I let her in.

I fucking let her in.

What's worse? She let *me* in.

Now, I have to hurt her, and though I'd rather burn in flames from the inside out than hurt Ashley White—the woman I love—I have no choice. It can't be avoided. Once you're steering toward the cliff, it's too late to stop the catastrophe.

She awakened me.

Made me want something I have no business wanting, made me want to confront the demons hiding somewhere inside me.

She awakened emotions left dormant for decades.

And though it led to the best and most profound moment of my life, the price is too high. Far too high.

For I know the truth. The problem with letting the good feelings out is that the bad feelings must come along for the ride. There's no escape.

The monster inside me is loose now. Loose in the midst of the chaos.

And I'm on that ride into hell.

CHAPTER ONE

Ashley

I was no longer afraid.

My mother was gone most of the day, looking for work or begging for money to feed us for another twenty-four hours. I sat alone in the tent. I wasn't supposed to leave our sanctuary, but I disobeyed today. It was so hot, and I could barely breathe.

I opened the flap, and then the stench hit.

The smell of tent city.

Pee, poop, puke.

I felt funny, and saliva pooled in my mouth. That feeling right before you hurl. Smell was the one sense I had that didn't seem to collide with the others very often, and I was thankful.

The stink alone was enough.

Mom and I had learned to walk carefully among the tents, avoiding the piles of poop and the used syringes. Once I asked Mom how people who lived on the streets could afford to get drugs. Her answer was, "That's why they're on the streets."

Still, I was confused.

Why were we on the streets, then?

I never got a straight answer from her. Only that she was doing her best.

And she was. I never doubted it. I knew only that my father died when I was too young to remember, and she'd lost her job soon after that. We were eventually evicted from our apartment, and with nowhere else to go, we packed up and headed for tent city.

This was home now.

In the tent to our right lived a nice old man. He was a Vietnam veteran, though I didn't know exactly what that meant, other than he'd fought in a war a long time ago. Maybe we'd learn about Vietnam when I went back to school in the fall. I'd be in third grade.

Mom made sure I went to school.

I hated it.

I couldn't have friends over, and I couldn't accept any invitations from friends—the few who actually offered them. Most of the other kids looked down on me. Sometimes I had to go to school in the same clothes because nothing else was clean. Sometimes we had to use the little money we had for food instead of the laundromat.

On our other side lived a brother and a sister. They were teenagers. Mom said they'd been "lost in the system." Their parents were either dead or had abandoned them, and instead of going into the system, they chose to live here.

Were there beds in the system? Showers? Food every day? If so, the system didn't sound too bad to me.

We were lucky that a nearby building let us use their bathrooms. They allowed single women with children inside, but no one else. Mom had taught me how to thoroughly cleanse my body using hand soap. Being homeless was no excuse to be dirty, she said.

Still, I remembered the warm pelting glory of an actual shower. One day, I'd experience that heaven again.

I took three trips to the building each day to use the toilet as well. I'd learned not to drink anything before going to sleep. It wasn't difficult. We conserved what water we had. Mom said we were never to relieve ourselves outside. Homelessness was also not an excuse for being disgusting.

"How are you today, Ashley?"

I turned to see Mr. Davis, the veteran, sitting in his lawn chair and reading.

"I'm okay. How are you, Mr. D?"

He coughs.

Gray smoke. That's the color of his cough. It turns grayish green when he hocks up a loogie.

"Been better. But it's a beautiful day, so who's complaining?"

"What are you reading?"

He held up his tattered paperback so I could see the title.

"Kidnapped. What's it about?"

"It's a classic," he said. "It takes place in historical Scotland and is about a young man's adventures."

"He's kidnapped? That doesn't seem like a good adventure."

"He gets away. And then gets into trouble. But what young man doesn't?" He laughs but ends up choking again. "Don't ever start smoking," he says when he finally catches his breath.

"I won't."

"It's a nasty habit."

"I've never seen you smoke."

"I don't. Not anymore. But I still have the aftereffects."

"Maybe you should see a doctor."

"Most doctors don't welcome patients who can't pay their bills."

"What about the free clinic?"

He coughs again. "Nothing free about it. Besides, there's nothing wrong with me. I may cough a little, but I always stop eventually."

I cocked my head. "I guess that makes sense. Do you have any other books?"

"A few. They're in a box inside my tent. You can take a look if you want."

"Okay. Thanks." I scrambled into his tent.

I breathed through my nose. Mr. Davis's tent smelled... icky. Like phlegm and puke. Blech. The box of books sat in the corner, and I pawed through it. They were all paperbacks and all well used. I didn't see anything that interested me until—

Little House in the Big Woods by Laura Ingalls Wilder. It looked like a children's book, but why would Mr. D have a children's book? I grabbed it and scrambled out of the tent, leaving the flap open. His tent needed to air out.

"Find something?" he asked.

"Yeah, what's this one?"

"It belonged to my daughter. She had the whole set."

"You have a daughter?"

"Had," he said. "She died a few years ago. Leukemia."

"What's that?"

"It's a form of cancer. Cancer of the blood."

"Oh." I frowned. "I'm very sorry."

"Me too. She was way too young to die. But let's not talk about sad things. There's enough to be sad about. Read the book. I hope you like it. If you do, maybe you can get the rest of them from the library."

"What happened to the others?"

"Who knows? This was the only one left after Melissa died."

"Do you know what this one is about?"

He nodded. "I read it to Melissa when she was about your age. Maybe younger. It's about a little girl who lived in the eighteen hundreds with her pioneer parents."

"What does she do?"

"Well . . . she helps her mother churn butter. She sews. She has a corncob for a doll."

I wrinkled my nose. "That sounds boring. Can I read yours instead?"

"This one?" He holds up Kidnapped.

"Yeah. I'd rather read about someone who's kidnapped and has adventures than some girl who has a corncob for a doll."

"Tell you what," Mr. D said. "You read that one, and when you're done, I'll give you Kidnapped. Deal?"

"Okay. That's a deal." I took the book back into my tent and opened it.

★ ★ ★

I jerk my eyes open.

I'm still in the hotel room at the Carlton, clutching the horrible note Dale left for me.

I read it once more.

This will get you back to the ranch. Take today off.

Dale

I wasn't asleep, just in a kind of meditative state. I'm so numb, and my senses . . . It's so strange to not sense anything.

So what do I do?

I return to my childhood. My childhood, where my best friend was a Vietnam vet who lived in the tent next to ours. He introduced me to literature that day. I was always a good reader, and I turned into a voracious one after that day. I devoured *Little House in the Big Woods*, and after that, *Kidnapped*. Then

Treasure Island and *Little House on the Prairie* and everything else both Laura Ingalls Wilder and Robert Louis Stevenson wrote. I moved on to C.S. Lewis, J. K. Rowling, Judy Blume, and J.R.R. Tolkien. Then, as I got older, Jane Austen, Charles Dickens, George Orwell, Margaret Mitchell, Harper Lee, and contemporary authors like John Grisham and Nora Roberts.

But *Kidnapped* still holds a special place in my heart.

After that day, I was never without a book in my hand.

Why this memory? Why now?

I rise and regard my phone on the nightstand. It's eight a.m. Dale told me to take today off, but I will not. I scramble to the bathroom and take a quick shower. Then I don my red sundress and order a cab. By the time I reach the lobby, my taxi is waiting. I hastily give the cabbie the address.

"That's a ninety-dollar fare, ma'am."

I flash him the bills Dale left on my nightstand. "Just get me there quickly and you can have both." I'll be glad to be rid of them. I don't want the reminder of Dale's crudeness.

His eyes morph into circles, and he nods. "You got it."

CHAPTER TWO

Dale

"So the tasting went well."

I look up from the pile of reports I'm eyeing. Uncle Ryan stands in the doorway to my office.

"Yeah. It went okay."

"I hear our intern was a smash."

I look back down at the papers in front of me. I haven't actually read any words. It's all a gray blur. "She did well."

"Looks like she did more than well," Ryan says. "She sold the hell out of the apple wine and your Cab Franc."

I sigh and meet his gaze. "Yes. She's a talent."

He cocks his head. "Does that bother you?"

"Why should it? I'd expect nothing less from a doctor of wine."

"She's not a doctor yet."

I resist rolling my eyes. "Whatever."

"I haven't seen her yet this morning," Ryan says. "What do you have her working on?"

"I gave her the day off."

He lifts his eyebrows. "Oh?"

"Yeah. As a reward. You know, for the tasting." The tasting that I just refused to give her any credit for other than "she did well." Uncle Ry is going to see right through this crap.

"A reward for doing her job after one day?"

I sigh. *No, I gave her the day off because I can't face her. In fact, I don't know whether I'll ever be able to face her again.*

"Yes. She's not being paid. It seemed . . . appropriate."

Ryan inhales. "All right. Good enough. Not the way I'd have handled it, but I gave her to you. She's your responsibility." He turns to leave.

"Uncle Ry?"

He looks over his shoulder. "Yeah?"

"She'll be back tomorrow."

"I expect so." Then he leaves.

I throw the papers back into their manila folder. I won't be good for anything today. At least I won't have to see Ashley since she won't be here. I'll stay away from the main house when I get home. In fact, I'll just grab Penny and spend tonight in the vineyards.

"Damn it," I mutter under my breath.

"Good morning."

That voice. That sweet and soft voice.

I look up.

The object of my affection stands in my doorway.

God, she's even more beautiful this morning. She wears skinny jeans and a pink T-shirt. Her hair is still damp and hangs around her shoulders in a golden cascade. Her lips, pink and full and slightly glossy.

No makeup. She doesn't need it.

Just Ashley.

"What are you doing here?" I ask, my voice taking an edge I don't expect.

"I work here, remember?"

"I gave you the day off."

"I chose not to take it."

I look down at the folder. "I'm deluged with paperwork today. I don't have time to deal with . . . "

"With what? With me? Or with *us*?"

I draw in a breath, trying to stop the wildebeests stampeding across my heart. "There is no us, Ashley."

"There was last night."

"Last night was a mistake."

The words taste bitter on my tongue.

Because they're a lie. A big-ass lie. Last night was the most wonderful time of my life. More wonderful even than watching the stars alone among my vines. It was heaven.

All my life I've avoided heaven.

If I acknowledge heaven, I also have to acknowledge hell.

And now hell is coming for me.

My intercom buzzes. Saved by the bell. I press the button. "Yeah?"

"Dale, I have Bridget from Qwest Labs for you."

"Qwest Labs?"

"Yeah. You know them?"

Then it hits me. Qwest Labs. That's where I had my blood drawn for the paternity test. Dad and I put a rush on it.

"Put her through." Pause. "This is Dale Steel."

"Mr. Steel, this is Bridget Miles from Qwest Labs."

"Yes?"

"I have your DNA test results."

I clear my throat. "Go ahead."

"Both the blood test and the cheek swab show a 99.9 percent chance of paternity with the subject Floyd Jolly."

I shouldn't be surprised. I already knew. Floyd's eyes told the tale better than DNA ever could.

Still, it's a jolt to my psyche.

After all these years, I have a biological father. One I know. One who's a drunk and a derelict.

I have to call Dad. Then we have to tell Donny. He doesn't know anything about Floyd Jolly yet. Dad and I decided to wait until we had actual proof.

Fuck.

"Thank you for getting back to me so promptly," I say in a robotic monotone.

"You're very welcome. Is there anything else I can do for you?"

"No, there isn't. Bye." I lay my phone down and look up.

Ashley.

She's still here, standing in my office, looking like a feast for all senses.

Here comes that ride into hell.

"Close the door," I tell her, my voice still monotone.

She lifts her eyebrows but doesn't move.

"Close the door," I say again.

She edges backward, never dropping her gaze from mine, reaches behind her for the doorknob, and pulls the door shut.

"Come here," I say.

"What do you want?"

"I think you know."

"Wait, wait, wait… You leave me in a hotel room with money on the night table. Make me feel like nothing more than a common whore, and then you—"

"You want to talk? Fine. Go talk to someone else. If you want to fuck, you can stay here."

"Dale, I—"

"It's a simple question, Ashley."

"It's anything but simple. We need to figure out—"

"I don't need to figure anything out. I already know what's happening. I'm on a ride into hell. You want to come along?"

She wrinkles her forehead. "What?"

"I can't explain it. I don't want to anyway. If you want to be with me, you have to take the bad with the good. Otherwise, there's the door." I gesture.

She bites her lower lip, and all I can think about is how much I wish those were my teeth instead of hers. I want to bite her there gently.

I want to bite her there not so gently.

A cool rush of breeze flows over my flesh.

There are things... Things I've let linger in the dark recesses of my mind. Things that I think I might like to try in the bedroom. Or here. In my office.

I never let my mind go there, but now it's been unleashed.

I gave myself permission to experience pleasure. Fuck. It was more than pleasure. I was...

Dare I say it?

I was happy.

Happy during those hours with Ashley in that hotel room less than twelve hours ago.

Fucking happy.

A smile tugs at my lips at the memory.

A smile.

"Go ahead," Ashley says.

"Go ahead with what?"

"You want to smile. Do it. Why do you resist it so much? Especially with me?"

"You don't want to know."

"Maybe I do want to know. I care about you, Dale."

"I don't *want* you to care about me."

Her pretty face falls. I've hurt her. I don't want to hurt her, but my words are no less true.

She whips her hands to her hips. "Maybe life isn't always about what *you* want. I care for you, and you can't stop me. In fact, I ... "

No, Ashley. Please, don't say it. If you say it, I'll have to say it back, and I can't. I'm not ready. I'll never be ready.

" ... admire you," she says.

Thank God. She didn't say the L-word.

And though I'm relieved, another emotion supersedes it. I'm disappointed.

I wanted to hear her say she loves me.

Because I love *her*.

I love her so much it hurts. It's like my heart is being squeezed so hard it may explode at any minute. And it's ice on the back of my neck, tingles across my flesh. And that tightness in my groin, only it's different, because the physical now has an emotional component.

I'm a mass of fucked-up feelings, a kaleidoscope of chaos.

Yes, I gave myself permission to experience happiness.

Now, without permission, my darker side comes along with it.

And I want Ashley White so much, I may just walk through fire to have her.

CHAPTER THREE

Ashley

I love you.

In the end, I couldn't say the words, because I couldn't bear the possibility—the *probability*—that Dale wouldn't return them.

I admire you.

True, no doubt. The man's a genius with wine. Probably with other things too, if he'd only let me in.

Don't push.

Jade's words echo in my head.

But it's not in my personality *not* to go after what I want. I had to. My mother taught me that a long time ago when she scrimped and scraped to get us out of tent city. In the end, though, I defied her. She wanted me to go after a sure thing.

I chose to go further. It wasn't enough to be out of tent city and in an actual dwelling. It wasn't enough to go to beauty school like my mother did. No, I wanted college. And when my interest in wine surfaced during undergrad, I wanted grad school too.

I got it. Full scholarships and all.

Now there's something else I want.

I want Dale Steel.

And what's truly frightening?

I want him more than I've ever wanted anything. In fact, I may give up wine and my doctorate and everything I've worked for if it means one more night with Dale.

A chill sweeps over me.

I don't mean that.

Yet I do.

My feelings for this man are that intense. That consuming. That frightening.

He still hasn't replied.

He doesn't have to. I've seen that look in his fiery green eyes. He wants me as much as I want him. I take a step toward his desk.

He lowers his eyelids slightly, and a soft groan emerges from his throat.

That dark-red beauty flows over me. Around me.

Around us.

Then his intercom buzzes.

Damn.

He moves out of his trance. "Yeah?"

"Dale, your father's on the line."

"Weird. Why didn't he call my cell?"

"He says he tried. You didn't answer."

"Oh." Dale pulls his phone out of his pocket. "I guess it's still on silent. Put him through."

Still on silent.

From last night. Our time together.

"Hey, Dad."

I don't listen to Dale's side of the conversation. I'm still awash in the dark Syrah beauty of his voice. Of us.

Because we're one now, in a way.

The burgundy darkness is Dale, yes, but it's also Dale and me.

The first time I've felt such a oneness with someone.

The first time I've felt this kind of all-consuming love.

Funny. The numbness from early this morning has vanished now that I'm in Dale's presence again.

Dale hangs up the phone. "I have to go."

I jolt out of my reverie, though his voice is still coating me in dark red. "Oh?"

"Yeah. My dad and I have to go to Denver. To see Donny."

"Why?"

"It's personal. I'll tell Uncle Ryan, and he'll see that you have stuff to do for the next day or two. I won't be gone longer than that."

"But—"

"It's personal, Ashley. That's all I can say." He walks to the door and opens it.

And though the room still pulses with the dark and beautiful burgundy, something has changed.

Our connection is severed, in some strange way.

Because Dale has something on his mind. Something he won't share with me.

Something I hope to uncover on my own.

★ ★ ★

I sit across from Ryan in the tasting room, where we nosh on a lunch provided by some of the staff. Steel beef, of course, on pumpernickel with kalamata olive pesto and a salad of heirloom tomatoes and baby greens. Steel peach cobbler for dessert.

"I'm going to take you out to the slopes this afternoon. Harvest is beginning."

"Without Dale?"

"Grapes don't stop growing just because Dale has personal business to attend to."

"Do you know what's going on?" I ask. "With Dale, I mean."

He pauses a moment before replying. "My brother and his sons have to take care of some stuff. That's all I can say. I'm sorry."

That's all I can say.

Dale used those same words.

"It's okay. But I'm concerned. Is Dale okay?"

"Of course. He's fine. As are Talon and Donny. Just a few things that need tending."

"But he'll hate missing the harvest."

"Dale's seen dozens of harvests, Ashley. And he'll be back long before it's done. No need to worry."

I nod. Ryan's right. But I do worry. Dale is so... I want to say distant, but that's not quite right. Because though he is distant, he's also not. We've been as close as two people can be.

He was all in during our lovemaking. *All* in.

We both were.

Leaving the vines right now to go to Denver must be killing Dale. I want more than anything to take away whatever pain he's bearing inside.

I know it's there. I just don't know what it is.

"We've been monitoring the growth and the weather reports daily," Ryan continues. "It's time to begin. The hand harvesters started this morning."

"Hand harvesters?"

"We're still a relatively small operation. Harvesting by hand is best, though we do use machine harvesting after the grapes for our flagship wines are picked." He smiles. "Want to tell me why we use hand harvesting when machines are cheaper?"

"Of course. Harvesters only pick perfectly ripened and healthy bunches, and they're also able to handle them gently to prohibit bruising of the fruit. Damaged fruit can lead to oxidation."

"Good."

"Did you know that in Champagne, hand harvesting is required?" I ask.

"Is it?" He winks.

He's giving me a chance to show off my knowledge, and I decide to take him up on it. Why not? Dale may not be impressed with my education, but Ryan is. Or at least he's doing a good job pretending.

"It is, by law," I continue. "One day I'd love to visit the region and take part in the harvest. They need over a hundred thousand pickers each season."

"You'd really like to take part?" he asks.

"Does that surprise you?"

"Somewhat. I understood you to be most interested in tasting and sales, not in production."

"I am. But what wine scholar wouldn't want to experience harvest time in Champagne? Or Bordeaux or Bourgogne, for that matter. Or the northern Rhône. Or southern. Heck, anywhere in France. Or Italy."

"You haven't had the pleasure?"

"No. Not yet." Not really on the radar for someone who grew up homeless and relies on scholarships for her education.

"Would you believe I've never been to France either?"

I stop my jaw from dropping to the floor. "You haven't?"

He shakes his head. "Never felt the need. I've been a few places. Jamaica, for one. Key West. The US and British Virgin Islands."

"You like tropical places."

He laughs. "True enough."

"Why not travel more, though? I mean . . . you have the means."

"We do. But we Steels are homebodies, for the most part. There's no more beautiful place on the planet than the Colorado western slope."

"I've always been partial to the coast," I say, "but this is a beautiful place."

"My brother Joe would move to the coast in a minute if he could," Ryan says. "I swear that man is part fish."

"Brock's father?"

"Yeah. Brock got his love of the water and his swimming talent from Joe. But Joe also loves ranching. He loves working with the animals. Plus he's a born businessman. He and Bryce—he's married to Marjorie—handle all the finances and investments for us. The two of them have been best friends since we were kids, and I swear, together they're unstoppable."

"Brock said he works with his dad."

"Yeah, definitely. Brock is Joe's mini-me. His older brother, Bradley, is much more like their mother, Melanie."

"Brock told me his brother runs the Steel Foundation."

"He does. Well, he and Henry—he's Bryce and Marj's oldest—run it together."

"What does the foundation do?"

"Mostly fundraising. Our two biggest projects are mental health research and child trafficking rescue."

I widen my eyes. "Interesting. Why those two?"

"Our mother, Daphne Steel, suffered from mental illness her whole life. It's an homage to her." He looks down at his plate. "As for the other, it's just something we as a family feel strongly about."

"Two very worthy causes." I take a sip of my water.

And I wonder why Ryan doesn't meet my gaze.

CHAPTER FOUR

Dale

Dad and I meet Donny at his apartment in Denver.

He's his usual jovial self. "Great to see you!" He pulls first Dad and then me into his patented man-hug. "What's so important that you had to drive all the way out here?"

We already told him everyone was fine when we announced our visit, so he had no reason to be fearful.

He still has no reason to be fearful. So our father appeared out of nowhere. So what? We always knew he existed. Someone sired us. I always hoped he'd be better than what we got, but who was I kidding? Anyone who ran out on two children could never be close to a saint.

"Can I get you a Peach Street?" Donny asks Dad.

"Maybe in a minute."

"Shit," Donny says. "Must be serious."

"It's serious," Dad says, "but it's not a big deal. Not really."

"O . . . kay." Donny raises his eyebrows. "Mind if *I* have a Peach Street?"

"You don't need it," I say. "Here's the thing, Don. We found our father. Our birth father. Or rather, he found us."

Donny's already raised eyebrows nearly fly off his face. "Say what?"

"He got in touch with me—well, a PI got in touch with

me on his behalf. Dad and I went to meet him a few days ago, the day you drove back to Denver with Dee."

"And you're only telling me this now?"

"We wanted to get the DNA results first," Dad says. "There wasn't any point in upsetting you before we knew for sure."

"I had a right to know."

"You did. And now you know." Dad rakes his hand through his dark hair streaked with silver.

"So . . . what's he like?"

"About what you'd expect," Dad says. "For a guy who abandoned a girlfriend with two kids."

"So they weren't married."

"We never found any evidence that they were," Dad says, "and he confirmed it."

"What's his name?"

I scoff out a laugh. "Floyd Jolly."

Donny shakes his head. "My name is Donovan Jolly?"

"Your name is Donovan Steel." Dad regards him sternly. "It's been Donovan Steel for twenty-five years. Before that it was Robertson. It's never been Jolly. He isn't even on your birth certificate."

"Which is weird," I say, "since he's obviously the father of both of us."

Dad wrinkles his forehead. "Hmm. I wonder . . ."

"What?" we both ask in unison.

Dad chuckles softly. "You two are so in sync sometimes it's scary. Diana and Brianna were never like that."

We've been through a lot together.

I don't say this out loud, of course. Donny has long gotten past the past. He's a better man than I.

"What are you wondering?" I ask Dad.

He brushes off my query. "Nothing. Never mind."

"When do I meet this esteemed father of ours?" Donny asks.

"Whenever you want, I guess," Dad replies. "He lives in Grand Junction."

"In a run-down cracker box," I add.

"Oh? I suppose I didn't think he was some virtuous stranger."

"No," I say. "He's a drunk. A doper too, from what we saw. And he likes cats."

"Fuck, really? A cat person?"

"Crazy, right?"

"What's he look like?"

"Tall. Balding a little, I'm sorry to say, but I hear the gene for male pattern baldness is carried on the X chromosome, which means we don't have it."

"Thank God." Donny smiles. "Especially for you and that man bun worthy mess of yours."

I ignore my brother's comment. We're alike in some ways. Nothing alike in others, like our personalities, for instance. And the way we prefer to wear our hair. He's always favored a more clean-cut look. Especially now, working as a Denver attorney.

"Honestly," I say, "I knew he was our father before the DNA results came back. He has our eyes. The same shape, and the color is the same as mine."

Donny sighs. "So what now?"

"Nothing," Dad says, "unless you want to do something. He's the man who fathered you. Who brought you into the world, along with your mother. So in that vein, I'm pretty damned grateful to him."

"Should we help him?" my brother asks.

"He hasn't asked for our help," I say.

"No, he hasn't," Dad agrees. "But I'd be willing to offer to pay for rehab. Get him off the sauce."

"Why?" I say. "He abandoned us. And he was kind of a dick to you. You punched him, if I remember correctly."

"You punched him?" Donny chuckles. "Go, Dad!"

Dad resists smiling. "He's still your biological father."

"Would you do the same for yours?"

Dad's face goes pale. His own father, Bradford Steel, passed away in a prison cell not too long after Donny and I came to Steel Acres.

Neither Dad nor his siblings ever talked about him. The most we ever got out of anyone was that he'd made some bad decisions and had to pay the price. We knew his wife, our grandmother, was mentally ill and institutionalized for most of her adult life. The two of them died within forty-eight hours of each other, though in different places. The only information we've been able to find indicated Bradford Steel tampered with federal evidence.

Donny and I are the only grandchildren old enough to even remember them, and we never met either of them.

"*My* father is not the issue here," Dad finally says.

Donny and I are both stunned into silence.

We've known it all along. Want to get our dad—or his brothers and sister—to go silent?

Mention Bradford Steel.

No other records exist of him. Nothing. Donny and I did our share of snooping when we were teenagers. The other kids, to my knowledge, never did. Our grandfather is a nonentity to them. Henry, Brad, Dee, and Ava were babies when it all happened, and the others weren't born yet.

Finally, I clear my throat. "Until he asks for our help, I see no reason to give it."

"I agree with Dale," Donny says. "Though I guess I should meet the guy."

"You don't have to," I say.

"It's curiosity, mostly," he admits. "I'll drive home in a few days."

"Your call," Dad says. "We just didn't want to tell you this news in a phone call."

"To be truthful," Donny says, "I'm not sure how I feel about it. I should be angry, I guess. But I'm not."

"I'm angry enough for both of us." I clench my hands into fists without meaning to.

"It's in the past, bro," Donny says.

"A lot of things are in the past." I grit my teeth.

"Requisite words are 'in the past,'" Dad says. "I don't want this having a negative effect on you boys. Anger is okay. But let it pass."

"Exactly what do *you* know about it?" I ask. It's a valid question.

"More than you know," Dad says. "More than you'll *ever* know."

CHAPTER FIVE

Ashley

Jade sent Darla home early as it's just the two of us for dinner.

"I thought we could go into Snow Creek and try that new Italian place," Jade says to me.

"There's a new Italian place?"

She nods. "They opened up over the weekend. Have you been into town yet?"

I shake my head. "When would I have the time?"

She laughs. "Touché. Let's go. We'll take a walk before dinner, and I'll show you around."

★ ★ ★

A half hour later, Jade parks her Mercedes on a side street. "Small-town parking is always a challenge. I never learned to parallel park until I moved here."

I laugh. "I can't parallel park to save my soul."

"I once had to do it in Talon's pickup. It was at least a hundred maneuvers. I swear!"

We laugh together.

I like Jade Steel. I like her a lot. Already, I know we have a lot in common. She came to Steel Acres when she was twenty-five, like me.

And she fell for a Steel heir who seemed unattainable at the time.

Things worked out for her.

Will they work out for me as well?

Who knows? Right now, the object of my affection is in Denver with his father and brother. I have no idea why, and I know better than to ask Jade. She clammed up when I asked why she called Talon a "broken man."

We walk off the side street onto the main thoroughfare. "This is Main Street. Colloquial, huh?"

"Does every small town have a Main Street?" I ask, laughing.

"Pretty much. There was a petition years back to change to the name to Steel Avenue, but Talon and the others wouldn't hear of it."

"Why?"

"It's not their thing. They're not in any of this for the glory."

Interesting. Dale said the same thing about his winemaking. He does it for the joy of the art, not for the glory.

He was raised well by his father, and also by this remarkable woman walking next to me.

She stops at a brick building. From the outside, it looks like a saloon straight out of the nineteenth century, with a green-and-white awning and the name of the establishment painted on a wooden sign.

"This is Murphy's Bar. The owner is Sean Murphy. Apparently he's a nephew of a friend of my father-in-law. His uncle, also named Sean Murphy, died here in Snow Creek when he was young, and his namesake came here to pay his respects and never left. Murphy's is a Snow Creek institution. Sean retired a few years ago, and his son Brendan runs it now. He's about Dale's age. They went to school together." She touches the handle. "Feel like a pre-dinner drink?"

"If you'd like."

"Sounds good to me. We have no idea if the new restaurant even serves alcohol." She opens the door.

A bell jingles, and I follow her in.

"Jade Steel!" A man behind the bar greets her. His voice is low but jubilant—a bright orange like the sun welcoming a new day. Very different from Dale's.

"Hello, Brendan."

"Who's that with you?"

"This is Ashley White. She's interning with Ryan and Dale at the vineyards this fall. Ashley, Brendan Murphy."

Brendan Murphy is a tall and handsome ginger with vibrant blue eyes. His hair is long like Dale's but not as full. Still, the flamboyant auburn makes quite a statement, along with his masculine jawline and aquiline nose. No mistaking him for anything but an Irishman.

"Great to meet you, Ashley White," Brendan says. "What can I get for you lovely ladies?"

"Do you have my son's Cab Franc?" Jade asks.

Brendan lets out a guffaw. "I've watched you Steels come in here for years and order wine you can drink for free at home. It does a heart good."

"We believe in supporting local businesses."

"So do we. That's why we serve your wine."

"I thought you served our wine because it's the best."

Brendan winks. "It is, at that. How about you, love?"

"I can't think of anything better than Dale's Cab Franc," I say. "I did a tasting yesterday where it was featured, and it was very well received."

"They've got you doing tastings, huh?" Brendan grabs

two cocktail napkins and sets them on the bar in front of us. "You must have gotten on someone's good side. Ryan and Dale don't let just anyone handle those."

"They don't?" Then I berate myself. I'm not even slightly surprised. I don't know Ryan well, but Dale? He didn't want me anywhere near his baby.

"Ashley's more than qualified," Jade offers. "She's working on her PhD in oenology at UCLA."

Brendan's eyes brighten. "A wine doctor? Impressive."

The words "wine doctor" from Brendan's mouth don't sound nearly as judgmental as they do coming from Dale. Brendan truly is impressed.

I smile. "It's what I love."

"Hmm." He pulls a bottle of the Steel Cab Frank from his shelf, uncorks it with ease, and pours us each a glass. "I have a nice Bordeaux I've been saving for a special occasion. You might be just the person to appreciate it with me. We don't get a lot of wine connoisseurs here in Snow Creek."

"You have Dale and Ryan," I say.

He nods, winking. "For sure. But neither of them is really my type."

"Oh." I stop myself from jerking backward. He's coming on to me. Asking me out. Sort of. I glance at Jade. She knows how I feel about her son. Does this bother her?

"It's a Château Latour," he says.

"Wow." I try not to look overly surprised. The guy runs a bar. Of course he comes in contact with seven-hundred-dollar bottles of wine. "We tasted some premier crus in tasting class, but I've never been able to afford a bottle."

"Then you should join me. Later this evening, maybe?"

"Actually," Jade says, "Ashley and I were going to have

dinner over at the new Italian place."

"Lorenzo's," Brendan says. "Try the veal piccata. It's wonderful."

"So you've been there already?"

"Last week, on opening night. Chicken cacciatore is the specialty of the house, though, so maybe you should order that. I'm just not a huge chicken fan."

Somehow I wasn't surprised. Brendan—much like the Steel men—looks like he was raised on red meat and potatoes. Bangers and mash, in his case.

"I'll try it," Jade says. "I love chicken. It's nice to have a break from beef now and then."

"Do they have any seafood on the menu?"

"I believe there's a linguine with clam sauce," Brendan says. "Probably not what you're looking for though, California girl."

I laugh in spite of myself. "I haven't been here yet a week, and I'm missing my sushi and fresh catch of the day."

"There are some great seafood restaurants in Denver," Brendan says. "And one in Grand Junction that's pretty good too. It's not too far from here."

A restaurant in Grand Junction... I was just at a restaurant in Grand Junction last evening...

And then... I had the most amazing few hours of my life.

Which won't ever be repeated, it seems.

"Talon and I can take you into the city anytime you're craving seafood," Jade says. "I'm afraid fish isn't really on Darla's repertoire. She's a wonderful cook, though. I'm sure she wouldn't mind learning to cook seafood for you."

"Oh, no. You don't need to go to that kind of trouble. Every meal I've had since I got here has been delicious."

My wine is nearly gone already. Dale's Cab Franc glides down my throat so easily.

Jade finishes hers. "Please put these on our tab, Brendan. Are you ready, Ashley?"

I polish off the small amount left in my glass. "Yes."

"Now wait," Brendan says. "I can't let you go until you agree to share my bottle of Latour."

Both Brendan and Jade stare at me.

And I don't have a clue what to say.

CHAPTER SIX

Dale

"What's that supposed to mean?" I demand of my father.

"It means I get it."

"How can you possibly?" I pace across Donny's living room. "I just went through this shit with Ashley, Dad. She tried to lecture me about my privilege. Apparently she went to bed hungry once when she was a kid."

Or many times. I don't know. I didn't ask.

"I'm sorry to hear that," Dad says.

"I am too, but that's not my point. My point is she doesn't know what Donny and I went through before we came to Steel Acres. But you ... You've always lived there. How the hell do you know anything about keeping the past in the past?"

My father waits a moment before answering, but his nostrils are flaring. He's trying to maintain control. He's good at it. He rarely raised his voice to us when we were kids. Almost as if—

"I don't owe you any explanation, Dale," he says. "I'm still your father, and I've been around a lot longer than you have."

"Yeah, Jesus, Dale." Donny shoves his hands into the pockets of his dress pants.

No big surprise. Donny always takes Dad's side. Donny also likes to pretend those horrible months never happened.

Sometimes I wish I were more like him.

"What aren't you telling us?" I demand. "Why the hell did you take us into your home all those years ago?"

"We've been through this."

"I know. I know. Because you could give us what we needed. What the fuck does that mean, Dad?"

Dad pauses again, getting control of his nostrils. "Your aunt Mel gave you the help you needed. And I had the resources to get you the best child psychologist in Denver, as well. Wouldn't you do the same thing?"

Interesting question, and my anger subsides for a moment while I actually consider it.

Yes.

Of course, yes.

I'd help any child who needed my help. Like Dad said, I have the resources. But further, I'd also understand, having been through it myself.

I nod. "Absolutely. I will always help anyone in need."

"Then you have your answer," Dad says.

I don't, but that's his way of saying the conversation is over.

A look passes between Donny and me. A look that says we know Dad is hiding something. A look that says we'll probably never know the truth because we've searched before to no avail.

"So will you help your birth father?" Dad finally says, his dark gaze meeting mine.

"Why should I?"

"You just said, and I quote, 'I will always help anyone in need.'"

I scoff. "I meant children. You know exactly what I meant."

"I know exactly what you *said*."

"We were talking about kids. About Donny and me and why you helped us."

"So if your father were a child, you'd help him?"

"Hell, Dad, if my father wasn't a child and he needed help through no fault of his own, I'd help him. But he abandoned us."

Dad nods. "It's your choice. I'm willing to help him if the two of you are willing. But I won't if you tell me not to."

"Wait a minute, Dale," Donny says.

"What?" My tone is harsher than I mean it to be.

"He *is* our father."

I point to Dad. "That's our father."

"For God's sake, you know what I mean. But for him, you and I wouldn't be here. And frankly, we both have pretty damned good lives, all things considered."

"*All* things considered?"

"Yeah, Dale, *all* things."

I soften my gaze. For a moment, Donny is seven years old again, and that need to protect him coils tight in my belly.

I protected him then.

And I protect him now.

But there are things he still doesn't know.

★ ★ ★

My little brother cries in my arms.

I push my own pain and horror into the back of my mind and focus on his.

Only Donny is important. He's mine to protect.

I haven't done a very good job so far.

I vow to do better.

Donny sobs against my shoulder, his nose running and wetting the dirty T-shirt I wear.

We don't wear pants. The T-shirts are long enough that they cover our privates when we get up to use the makeshift toilet in the corner of the room.

I'm used to the smell now.

It no longer nauseates me.

I force myself to be used to most of it.

But I'll never get used to listening to my brother sob. I'll never get used to his cries for help. I'll never get used to the image of masked men brutalizing his small body.

From now on, I vow, they won't touch him.

I'll do anything to make sure I take the brunt of what they have to give.

I tamp down my emotions and sniff back a tear.

I'm done crying.

No more.

I'm done.

CHAPTER SEVEN

Ashley

"Sure," I finally say. "I'd love to taste the wine with you."

"Wonderful. How about dinner tomorrow? My place?" He points to the ceiling.

"You live here?" I ask.

"Right above the bar. My father lived there until he married, and then he rented it out. I've been hanging my hat up there for the last ten years, since I moved out of my parents' house."

"All right. I work until six."

"Seven, then?"

"Sure. No, wait. Let's say seven thirty. It's a half-hour drive, and I'll need to clean up. I worked in the vineyards today."

"You don't look like it."

"I had a shower, goofball."

"I'm looking forward to it." He winks.

"Who'll be manning the bar?"

"I do have employees, you know."

"Right." Dumb question. Several waitresses and another bartender are here.

I turn to Jade. What must she be thinking? She knows how I feel about Dale. "Time for dinner?" I say.

"Yes. Thanks, Brendan. See you soon."

"Absolutely. Tell Talon I said hi."

"I will."

I follow Jade out of the bar and back onto Main Street. Should I say something? I bite my lower lip. I'm at a loss for words, which is unlike me.

Finally, I open my mouth, when—

"It's okay, Ashley," Jade says.

"You don't even know what I was going to say."

"Of course I do. We both know how you feel about Dale. But there's no reason why you can't share a bottle of wine with another young man."

"It doesn't feel quite right."

"Would you be interested in Brendan if not for Dale?"

"Well . . . yeah. I think. I mean, he's handsome and funny. And he runs a bar, which means he knows a few things about wine, so we have that in common. But . . . "

She laughs.

"What's so funny?"

"Again, you remind me of myself all those years ago."

"It's like only Dale exists to me," I say. "It doesn't make any sense. Brendan is clearly a great guy, and any other time I'd be flattered by his attention."

She shakes her head. "Oh, Ashley, I know exactly what you mean."

★ ★ ★

Lorenzo's is an adorable little Italian place. We walk in, and I'm suddenly transported to 1950s Little Italy in New York. Or at least what I assume 1950s Little Italy would be. Dean Martin croons through the sound system, and the tables are covered with red-checkered cloth.

Our server brings a carafe of Chianti and a loaf of crisp Italian white bread.

"This is lovely," Jade says.

"I agree. I feel like we've traveled back in time."

"Lisa Lorenzo is a second-generation Italian American. Her parents moved to Snow Creek when she was in high school. I believe she graduated with Donny." Jade wrinkles her forehead. "No, she was a few years younger. She graduated with Henry. With so many offspring, it's hard to keep them all straight sometimes."

"Everyone knows everyone around here," I say. "A far cry from LA."

"Yes, but you get used to it, and once you do, you'll never want to live anywhere else."

"Snow Creek does have its charm."

"I'm afraid I didn't give you the tour I promised. We ended up having that drink, and then you and Brendan hit it off."

I look down at the piece of bread I'm swirling in olive oil.

"Ashley," Jade says after a few minutes of me swirling and being mesmerized by the darkness of the balsamic vinegar making images in the light-green olive oil.

I look up. "Hmm?"

"It's okay that you hit it off with Brendan."

"I know." I force out a chuckle. "It's so strange . . . "

"What?"

"You're Dale's mom. And here I am talking about seeing someone else, when you and I both know . . . "

"I love my son," she says. "More than you'll ever know, at least until you have children of your own. But . . . he gets in his own way sometimes."

"Meaning?"

She swallows the bite of bread she was chewing and then sighs. "Dale has never been able to open up. Especially not to me."

I nod. "I'm sorry you're not as close as you'd like to be."

"Don't get me wrong. He and I have a wonderful relationship. But he has a few walls built up, and I fear no one will ever be able to knock them down."

"That sounds like a challenge," I say.

"Oh, it's not. When I say he gets in his own way, I mean a lot of things, but mostly I think he gets in his own way of being happy."

"Do you think he could be happy with me?"

"How could he not? You're smart and lovely, and you have so much in common. If he'd just let himself *feel* something."

"You don't think he feels?"

She shakes her head. "I'm not explaining this very well. He loves us all. Especially his father and sisters. Yes, he feels for all of us and would do anything for us. For any of his cousins as well. He's a good man."

"I know that."

"But he's built a wall around himself. It's been there since he came to us, and it seems to grow taller with each passing year. Sometimes I want to bulldoze it down and yell at him to just unmask his feelings. But it won't do any good. Men like Dale need to come to the realization on their own."

"Men like Dale?"

She nods. "He's a lot like his father, as I've told you before. He can't be pushed, Ashley. And believe me, I know how it feels to want to push."

"I haven't pushed him."

I don't feel my words are untrue. Maybe I've pushed

him a little, but mostly I've just conversed with him, maybe played devil's advocate a bit. And I haven't discouraged his physical attentions. Should I have? It's not really in my nature. I like sex. A lot. I don't apologize for that.

None of this is suitable conversation to have with his mother, though.

"I'm not saying you have."

"I know it was a mistake to go into his house that day Penny ran off. If he'd been home, I'm not sure what I would have said or done."

"Doesn't matter, because it's over. I'll keep your secret. There's no harm done anyway." She smiles, takes a sip of the Chianti, and then grimaces. "Oh, my. I used to love Chianti, but I'm spoiled now, with my brother-in-law's and my son's wines."

I haven't tasted the wine yet, so I bring the goblet to my lips. I let the liquid rest on my tongue for a few minutes. It's a little too acidic for my tastes, but it's a basic table wine. "This isn't Chianti Classico," I say. "You'll find it better once our food arrives, especially if you order something with a tomato base."

She smiles. "You just sounded a lot like Dale."

"He does know his wine."

"As do you."

I can't help a laugh. "Well, I am almost a doctor of wine!"

Her tone becomes serious again. "If you're able to get through to my son, you have my blessing. You're a wonderful young woman."

My cheeks warm. Jade has no way of knowing how much her words mean to me, and I can't begin to express the thought in mere words myself. So I say simply, "Thank you."

"If I had it my way, you'd be together," she says. "I want happiness for my son, and if he'd let himself feel something,

I think he could find happiness with you."

"Dale knows he's loved," I say. "I can tell that just by my limited interaction with him."

I force myself not to wince at the use of the term "limited interaction." Our interaction has hardly been limited physically. But emotionally? It's been very limited. Nonexistent, even.

"I believe you're right," Jade says. "Dale knows how much we all love him. What he doesn't know, though—and may never be able to grasp as long as he lives within those walls he's erected around himself—is how much he's cherished."

CHAPTER EIGHT

Dale

I turn to my father. "It's your money. If you want to help him, help him."

"I'd like to have the support of his biological sons."

"You have mine," Donny says.

Begrudgingly, I finally say, "Fine. You have mine as well."

Why so much anger? So he abandoned his kids. He's not the first lowlife to do that. And he bears no blame for what happened to us.

Except that maybe he does. We were alone in our house the day we were taken. If he hadn't abandoned us, maybe our mother could have been there with us instead of working all the time.

But many single mothers leave their children home alone, and they grow up just fine without ever experiencing what my brother and I did.

Still, the rage claws at the back of my neck.

Rage I never let myself feel before. I tamped down all emotions long ago to survive.

I had to.

For if I'd allowed myself to feel, I wouldn't have been able to deal with what happened to me. The horror and torture I endured to spare my brother.

It was worth it. It still is. My brother is a fine young man, and though he may have his struggles, he's put the past behind him in a way I'll never be able to.

I'd do it all again to protect him. I have no regrets.

Which is a lie. That thing buried inside me is pawing at its cage, determined to escape.

I ignore it and focus on my conscious regret.

Allowing emotion to overtake me.

I'm in love.

I'm in love with Ashley White, and the feelings are so overwhelming I can't make sense of them.

They're beautiful but chaotic. Like all the perfect notes of a symphony but with discordant undertones that keep it from its pureness.

And those feelings have also given rise to the intense anger that consumes me now.

"I want to meet him," Donny says once again.

"All right," Dad says.

"And just so you know, he'll never be my real dad." Donny smiles.

"I know that." Dad returns his smile. "Trust me, I'm not in any way feeling displaced."

"Good," I say. "You'll never be displaced."

"Are you boys hungry?" he asks. "We can hit up one of Denver's fine restaurants."

"Starved," Donny says.

I regard my brother. He just had news that could have upended his life, but he's jovial as ever, starving as usual.

I worry about him sometimes. Though I took the brunt of abuse while we were in captivity, he still took a lot. Yes, we had the finest therapy money could buy once we came to the ranch, but I fear something remains in my brother that he doesn't let anyone else see.

And I fear it could come out with a vengeance.

If it does, I'll no longer be able to protect him.

★ ★ ★

Dad and I return to the ranch at noon the next day. We eat a quick lunch with Mom at the house.

"I had the pleasure of dining with Ashley last night," Mom offers.

"Oh?" Dad says.

I say nothing. Of course she ate with Ashley last night. Ashley lives here, Dad and I were in Denver, so they ate together. I fail to see the point in my mother's assertion.

"Yes," she continues. "We went into town and ate at Lorenzo's."

"Lisa Lorenzo's new place?" Dad says.

Mom nods.

Lisa Lorenzo is several years younger than I am. I remember her, as she hung out with Henry and Brad sometimes.

"We stopped at Murphy's for a drink first," Mom continues.

Dad nods. "How's Sean?"

"We didn't see him."

"I suppose not, now that he's retired."

"He's around sometimes, but last night Brendan was manning the bar."

"How's Brendan, then?"

"He's good. Busy. He seemed quite taken with Ashley."

The bite I just took of my sandwich lodges in my throat. I can't respond. I wouldn't anyway, but I physically can't.

"That's not surprising," Dad says.

"Not at all," Mom agrees. "She's a lovely girl. Like a ray of sunshine around here."

I take a drink of water and swallow hard, dislodging the ball of bread and meat from my throat.

A ray of sunshine.

Everything I'm not.

God, I have no business dragging her into my life, especially now that I've let loose the hell inside me.

Ironically, she was the catalyst.

Or rather, the feelings she brought out in me that I can't control—those are the catalyst.

I like Brendan Murphy. He and I went to school together from fifth grade on. We weren't best friends, but then I wasn't best friends with anyone. He's a good guy—smart, nice, hardworking.

And right now I want to fucking pummel his face into the ground. Punch his nose until an artery spurts blood.

"Both she and Brendan could do a lot worse," Dad says. "Though I think Ashley should be focused on her internship."

"I agree," I say gruffly.

"What makes you think she's not?" Mom queries.

"I didn't say that," Dad argues.

"She's certainly entitled to a social life."

Dad stiffens slightly. Only slightly, but I see it in his facial muscles. This bothers him, and I don't have a clue why.

It bothers me too. A lot. But why should it bother Dad?

I wipe my lips with my napkin and rise. "I need to get back to work."

"You left half your sandwich," Mom says.

"Not that hungry." No lie there. The thought of Ashley and Brendan Murphy effectively killed my appetite.

"Honey . . . " Mom begins.

"Let him go, blue eyes."

Yeah, Dad gets me. He knows when I need to leave a situation.

He knows when I need to think, or when I need to be alone.

And now, more than ever, I want to know exactly *how* he knows.

I'll figure it out. Somehow. But at the moment?

I'm going to find Ashley and do whatever I must to make sure she never sees Brendan Murphy again.

CHAPTER NINE

Ashley

Cutting clusters of ripe grapes from a vine is harder than I imagined it could be. I didn't realize how sore I was from yesterday's work until I began doing it again this morning. Now, having just finished lunch, I'm at it again, sweat dripping from my brow even though it's not even seventy degrees outside.

Dale's still in Denver. What would he think if he knew I'm having dinner with another guy tonight? Dinner and a bottle of Château Latour?

I wipe my forehead with the back of my leather-gloved hand.

He won't care.

As much as it hurts, I have to face reality.

He won't freaking care.

I hold the cluster of grapes gently in my hand and then cut the stem with my sharp pruning shears. Next, I lay the fruit gently in the trays sitting next to me.

Other harvesters work diligently—and a lot faster than I do. I'm all theory and no practice as far as this step in winemaking goes. Sure, I've had classes about what I'm doing, but I've never actually participated in the process until now.

I hold back a chuckle. Dale would be loving this. He'd

expect much more from a *doctor* of wine.

Is he back from Denver yet? I have no idea. Jade told me at breakfast that she expected them back today, but she didn't say when. Then she and I both went off to work, and I've heard nothing since.

Does Dale ever participate in the harvesting? He must. As far as he's concerned, these vines are his.

Of course, these aren't the Syrah vines. I'm cutting Cabernet Sauvignon grapes today. I remove another cluster from the vine and lay it gently alongside the others. I wipe the sweat from my forehead with my forearm and begin again.

"Good work."

I nearly jump out of my jeans. That gruff low voice. I know it better than I know my own. The dark-red color of it warms me and chills me simultaneously.

I turn and meet Dale's green gaze. "Thank you. It's more difficult than I imagined."

"Some things you can't learn from a book," he counters.

I don't reply. He's right. I simply nod and turn back toward the vines.

"You're done here," he says.

I turn back to face him. "Oh?"

"Yeah. I need you for the tasting."

"There's no tasting today."

"No, but tomorrow we're doing the lunch and tasting, and I have to get you prepped."

"Can't we do that tomorrow morning?"

Dale draws in a breath and then exhales slowly. His nostrils flare slightly. Is he angry? Angry that I'm questioning him?

Finally, "No. We'll do it now."

"All right, then." I set my cutting tool down, remove my gloves, and place them in the bucket with the others. Then I follow Dale out of the vineyards to his truck.

He opens the passenger door for me. "Get in."

I smile more sweetly than I'm feeling. "Thank you."

He starts the engine, and we drive for a few moments in silence.

Then I turn to him. "How was Denver?"

"Fine."

"And your brother?"

"Also fine."

"Your dad?"

"What is this? Some grand inquisition?"

"Just making conversation."

"We're all fine."

But the tension in his jawline says otherwise. Talon and Donny may be fine, but Dale most certainly isn't.

My instinct is to ask what's wrong. Already, though, I know he won't answer.

Don't push.

I hear the words in Jade's voice.

I pull my phone out of my pocket to check the time. Three p.m. I'll need to be done here by six to get back to the house, clean up, and then meet Brendan for our dinner at seven thirty.

I'm looking forward to it.

Not because I want anything to happen between Brendan and me. In fact, I want the opposite.

But damn, I'm yearning for some actual conversation. With Diana gone, the only person I have to talk to is Jade. I adore Jade, but she's a generation older than I am and she works full-time in Snow Creek so she's not around a lot.

So yeah. I'm looking forward to good food, good wine, and good conversation. Nothing at all wrong with that.

Dale pulls into the winery parking lot. He turns to me, and his eyes soften.

"What?" I can't help asking.

"You have a smudge of dirt on your nose."

"I've been harvesting. I'd be surprised if I didn't."

"It's . . ."

"For God's sake. What?"

"It's cute." He pulls a red bandana out of his pocket and reaches toward me, gently erasing the smudge.

Yes, gently. His touch is so gentle, and I warm instantly.

"If it's so cute, why did you remove it?"

He doesn't reply. Simply folds the bandana and shoves it back into his pocket. Then he leaves the truck and walks to the passenger side, where he opens the door for me. I get out and follow him into the building to the tasting room.

"So what do I need to know for tomorrow?"

He clears his throat. "We serve lunch in here. My cousin Ava caters it. Have you met her?"

"Briefly, at the pool party before Dee left."

"She'll deliver the food by eleven thirty, and lunch is at noon."

"Do you want me to set up or something?" I ask.

He shakes his head. "We have people to do that."

"Okay. What should I do, then?"

"You need to be here during lunch to answer questions from the tasters. Of course, we'll provide lunch for you as well."

"Won't you be here?"

"Yes. So will Uncle Ryan."

"I'm sure the tasters will direct their questions to the two of you," I say.

"They may, but I'll be deferring to you."

My eyebrows shoot upward. "You will?"

"You're a doctor of wine, after all."

Is he being sarcastic? I honestly can't tell at this point. He liked what I did at my first tasting.

I say once more, "Not yet. I only have my master's in wine."

"Good enough. Neither Uncle Ryan nor I possess a master's or doctorate of wine, so you're ahead of us. You're the expert."

Again, is he making fun of me? Being sarcastic? Or just being an asshole?

So hard to tell.

But two can play this silly game.

"Of course. I'll answer whatever questions you feel are appropriate. Which wines will we be tasting tomorrow?"

"The red table blend, the fine Cab, the Meritage, and the Syrah."

Excitement roars through me. The Syrah. I haven't had the pleasure yet of tasting the Steel Syrah myself. I can't wait.

"Which ones will I be doing?"

"The table blend and the Meritage."

Disappointment aches. But Syrah is Dale's favorite grape. Of course he'll take that one for himself.

Doesn't matter. I'll wow them with the red and the Meritage. I've already tasted the table blend, and it's wonderfully simple in its complexity.

"May I have a taste of the Meritage?" I ask.

"Why?"

"Uh . . . so I know what I'm dealing with tomorrow."

"You didn't taste the Cab Franc in advance, and you did fine."

My cheeks warm. "That's nice of you to say, but you know as well as I do that I'll do even better if I taste the wine ahead of time."

His lips quirk up at one corner. Just a little. "Maybe I like seeing how good you are on your feet."

I shake my head. "No one does a tasting without sampling the wine first."

"You did."

"Yeah, and I shouldn't have had to."

"A doctor of wine should be able to do anything."

Anger boils in my belly. "You're so determined to make me fail. Why, Dale?"

"Make you fail? Didn't I just compliment you on your first tasting?"

"Yeah. But at the risk of patting myself on the back, you'd be hard-pressed not to. I kicked that tasting's ass. We both know it. But why make it harder on me? Why do you want me going in blind?"

He opens his mouth, but I gesture him to be quiet.

"Don't even say something ridiculous like a doctor of wine should go in blind."

He lets out a laugh.

A real, honest-to-goodness laugh, the likes of which I've never heard from Dale Steel.

It's beautiful. It's uplifting. It's a gorgeous cloak of dark-red magnificence.

And already, it's a new addiction.

CHAPTER TEN

Dale

I'm laughing. Truly laughing.

This woman makes me laugh, and damn, it feels good. It feels fucking fabulous.

She joins in, and her sweet giggle is more than I can take.

I love her. I love everything about her. Every damned thing. It's a foregone conclusion. I will never *not* love Ashley White.

I'll just have to learn to live with it.

With that thought, my laughter wanes.

And my libido kicks in.

Not that it wasn't already kicked in. I'm always on high horny alert when I'm near Ashley, and many times even when I'm not. The memory of her smile, of something amusing she said, of the feel of her lips upon mine—all those things trigger a tightness in my groin.

She doesn't have to be anywhere near me to make me want her. I always want her.

Always.

And right now, as she suppresses her joyful giggles, her lips parted just so, I can't help myself.

I grab her and pull her into my arms.

She looks up at me, her blue eyes slightly guarded and

her lips still glossy and parted.

If only we could hold this gaze forever. Just looking at her—the sheer beauty of her—could keep me content forever.

But my body kicks in, and I lower my mouth to hers.

Her lips stay parted, and I swoop my tongue between them.

Delicious. Simply delicious. Nothing tastes sweeter than Ashley's kisses. No trace of sugar or fruit or wine. It's simply Ashley, her natural sweetness that extends to all parts of her body. Especially that paradise between her legs.

Is she wet for me?

I advance, taking her with me until her back hits the wall. I lean into her, let her feel my erection as I push into her belly.

I deepen the kiss, my lips firm upon hers. I want to inhale her. Breathe every part of her into every part of me. I've been joined to her once, in sex. It was amazing. Life changing. But still not enough. Never fucking enough.

I'm drowning now, drowning in the sea of lust that is Ashley White. Her beauty, her intelligence, her wonderful sense of humor.

Drowning, and God help me, I don't want to be saved.

But just as I'm falling deeper underwater, she pushes against me and breaks the kiss.

"Are you insane?" she says. "Employees are everywhere. Your uncle could walk in here."

She's not wrong.

I know that. And at the moment, I absolutely don't give a damn.

I take her lips once more.

And once more she shoves me away.

"Dale!"

I look into her sapphire-blue eyes. Such fire and passion in her soul. I see it, and I know it's reflected in my own.

"I want you," I say gruffly. "I want you more than I've ever wanted anything."

She shakes her head, trembling. "You don't. You just want sex."

I rake my fingers through my hair. "Of course I want sex. I'm not a fucking rock. But it's more than that."

"If it were more than that, you wouldn't have left me in that hotel room. Bills on the nightstand. You made me feel like a . . ." She shakes her head. "No. No, no, no. You did not. No one can make me feel inferior without my consent."

"Eleanor Roosevelt," I say.

"Yes. I'm not a whore, Dale."

"I never said you were."

"You left money on the nightstand."

"So you could get home."

"Yeah? Well, you didn't live up to your end of the bargain."

"What the hell are you talking about?"

"You said you were going to use me up that night. But instead, we fell asleep. In the morning, instead of facing me, you ran. You *ran*, Dale."

Again, she's not wrong. What can I say? I have no excuse. Only that I knew what had happened. That my emotions were no longer suppressed, and that meant . . .

That meant the rage would surface.

I already experienced the rage last night, talking about my birth father.

The rage.

The fucking rage.

But right now?

My love for this woman—this passionate, striking woman—overpowers the rage.

"You want me to use you up?"

"That's what you said you'd do."

"Fine. Tonight. My place. Seven."

She parts her lips and then brings one hand to her face, her eyes wide. She says nothing.

"I'll take your silence as your consent. See you then." I turn, still hard, still raging with lust and passion.

"Dale..."

I turn. Her cheeks are ruddy, her lips pink and swollen. The top of her chest is a lovely pinkish gold.

"Yes?"

"I... I can't. Not tonight."

"Why not?"

"I have... a date."

CHAPTER ELEVEN

Ashley

As the words leave my mouth, I expect one of two things to happen.

Either he'll kiss me again in anger, or he'll turn and leave with no further response.

I'm completely unprepared for what ultimately happens.

After he stares into my eyes for seconds that seem like eternity, he smiles.

He fucking smiles!

And as much as I love his smile—will do almost anything short of murder to experience it—I don't want to see it now.

Is the smile real?

I've seen his smile so seldom that I'm not sure.

The laughter, though—that raucous jubilation that melted like hot burgundy toffee over me only moments earlier—that was real.

This?

I have no idea how to respond, and it occurs to me that may be exactly what he's going for.

I clear my throat. "So you see, I can't possibly meet you at your place tonight."

More waiting.

Now his smile is definitely forced. The tension around his lips and jaw is palpable.

Finally, he speaks. "After, then. Nine o'clock."

What? He's *not* going to demand that I break the date? He's *not* going to demand to know who I'm seeing? He's not going to demand . . . *anything*?

I may love Dale Steel to within an inch of my life, but I don't know him.

I don't know him at all.

I want to go to his place more than I want my next breath. I'd gladly break the date with Brendan if I thought Dale and I had a future. But I don't know how Dale feels about me. I know only that—despite his initial criticism of my hair out of a bottle—he's attracted to me physically and he wants me. That much is more than obvious.

But emotionally? He's a closed book. He may feel nothing at all for me other than lust.

I like being lusted over. I like sex.

With Dale, though?

I want more.

I want it all.

And I have to face the fact that he may never be able to give me the love I desire.

The love I deserve.

Do I give up a date with a man I like, but don't love, for a night of passion with a man I do love but who may never love me back?

Do I follow my head or my heart?

I've never had to make a decision like this, for although I've had my share of dates with men I like, I've never been in love before. My head and heart have always been in sync.

Until now.

I inhale. Exhale slowly.

I've made my decision.

"I'm sorry," I say. "The answer is no."

His tense smile erodes on his face. His green eyes burn with... Is it anger? I can't tell, except that it's not anything positive.

I wait.

And I wait.

When I'm convinced he won't respond, he finally does.

"Change your answer," he says, his jaw clenched.

God, I want to. I'm ready to sell my soul to the devil himself to have Dale kiss me, touch me, make love to me.

But I have to think with my head, not my heart.

"I'm sorry, Dale. I can't."

"You *can*."

That voice. That rich Syrah voice. I inhale once more. Exhale. Try to ease the sweet pain in my nipples, the throbbing between my legs.

"I can't. I'll see you tomorrow for the tasting." I turn and leave the tasting room.

I leave the winery and walk to the office building where I parked the car—loaned to me by Talon and Jade—this morning.

Dale didn't tell me I could leave for the day, but I do anyway. It's nearly four, and my body is betraying me. I wanted so much to say yes. I wanted so much to cancel my date.

I wanted...

But wanting is no longer enough.

I've spent my life taking what I want from men. Being content with sex alone. They were, so why shouldn't I be?

But now that want has turned to love.

And as much as I yearn for Dale, for his body touching mine, it will no longer suffice.

I sigh.

I'll give in.

Eventually.

If he keeps trying, that is.

But today, I stand my ground. I show him that I'm not that easy. That though we're as physically compatible as any two people can be, I need more.

I will no longer settle.

CHAPTER TWELVE

Dale

I want to run after her, tell her I love her. That I'll do anything to have her.

But I can't.

Because right now, my rage consumes me, overtakes me, and if I go after her, I'll take it out on her.

On the woman I love.

The woman I love who'll be kissing another man tonight.

Darkness surges inside me. I grab a handful of my hair and tug. Hard.

Focus. Have to focus.

Just need to get home, and then I can blow like a fucking volcano. A hurricane. A tornado. Every act of God that destroys ...

That's what I am right now.

I know it deep within my soul.

If only those who tormented me still lived. I'd have an outlet for my wrath.

But they don't.

That ring was shut down long ago, and those who tortured me are either dead or imprisoned.

So where do I focus my rage?

Where?

Not my family.

And as angry as I am, not Ashley.

I love her. I wish her no harm.

But on her date . . .

Who is she seeing?

And where did she meet him? She's been here for little more than a week.

Fuck.

Last night. She and Mom went into town. Mom said Brendan Murphy was taken with her.

That's it. It's got to be.

Her plans tonight are with Brendan Murphy.

Fuck him. I wanted to break his nose just hearing Mom say he was taken with Ashley.

Now?

I want to break *him.*

My fists clench. I want to punch him, kick him, fucking *end* him.

And as much as I know these feelings are irrational, I don't care.

I drive home quickly, paying no attention to the road, so blinded am I with rage.

I screech into my driveway, leave the truck, and enter the house. Penny paws at me, but I let her out quickly, making sure she has ample water. She's only a dog, but I don't want any witness, human or canine, to what I'm about to do.

I head to the basement of the guesthouse. I've converted part of it into a home gym. It gets little use, as the physical nature of my work—and my good genes from Cheri Robertson and Floyd Jolly—*who knew?*—keeps me in good shape.

Today, though, I'm glad for the Century BOB torso

training bag I purchased a while ago when I was studying taekwondo on my own.

Bob's face is plain and his painted-on hair is blond, but instead I see Brendan Murphy's red hair and blue eyes staring at me, his strong Irish jaw taunting me, jeering at me.

She's mine.

She'll never be yours.

You don't deserve her.

You'll never love her.

His last silent words ring untrue. The truth is that I *do* love Ashley.

But my love for her is what unleashed this wrath in me. Unleashed it on the world.

And Ashley *is* my world.

I strip off my shirt and shake my head, letting my hair tickle my shoulders and neck.

Then I pounce.

Boom! A punch to Brendan's perfect nose.

Then an uppercut under his chin.

A knife hand to his neck and one more to his shoulder.

My jeans aren't the easiest garments to move in, but I pull one leg upward and land a roundhouse kick to Brendan's flank and then to his head. A perfect double kick. I'll feel it tomorrow, but tonight I don't care.

A hook kick is next, to his other flank, and then I jump and execute a perfect axe kick to the top of his head.

The real Brendan would be writhing on the ground about now.

But still I punch.

Still I kick.

Still I grunt, sweat pouring off me.

And still Brendan taunts me, standing tall, blow after blow.

Fuck you! Fuck you! Fuck you!

I plow forward into Brendan, tackling him to the ground. Fist to face, fist to face, fist to face—

I jerk. Did I hear something? Someone calling me?

Composure. I need composure.

I grasp and grasp and grasp but can't find it. Still I pummel fake Brendan's face. The face that magically regains its shape no matter how much pain I inflict.

You can't have her! You can't have her! You can't have her!

The click of the basement door opening. "Dale? You down there?"

You can't have her! You can't have her! You can't have her!

Footsteps from somewhere in the back of my mind.

Someone's coming.

Still I punch, punch, punch.

"Dale!"

Strong arms try to grapple me away, but no . . . I won't give up. Not until Brendan Murphy is gone. Reduced to roadkill mush.

"Dale, what's the matter with you?"

I turn, but instead of my father's dark eyes, I see Brendan's blue ones.

I've got her. I'm going to fuck her.

In a blind rage, I pull my fist back and land a perfect punch to his smarmy expression.

"Damn! That smarts! What the fuck is wrong with you?"

As if on its own, my elbow pulls back, my fingers curl, and I'm ready to execute another blow—

My back hits the floor, and someone hovers over me, his blue eyes angry.

Except the eyes aren't blue.

They're dark brown.

My father's eyes.

My father.

His cheek is red, and blood oozes from a small wound near his eye.

I punched my father.

"What the fuck is wrong with you?" he demands again.

I close my eyes.

I can't answer him.

If I answer him, he'll know.

He'll know the monster has been unleashed.

He'll know I'm not who I seem to be.

And he'll no longer want to be my father.

CHAPTER THIRTEEN

Ashley

Brendan's apartment over the bar is small and cozy—just a living area, kitchen, and bedroom. He's broiling burgers when I arrive, and I can't help a laugh. Burgers will work great with the Latour, but most connoisseurs enjoy such a premier wine with classier fare.

"I know, I know," he says with a laugh. "But I know how to make burgers. And they're perfect, if I do say so myself. Thick and juicy and medium rare. Add a slice of cheddar jack and some tomato, and you've got something as good as any gourmet meal I can think of."

"I can't disagree," I say. "I may be studying to be a sommelier, but I live pretty frugally back home in LA. Burgers are sometimes a luxury."

"Oh?"

Crap. I've just opened the door into my life in Cali, including my childhood. Something I didn't mean to do.

I choose to laugh it off. "Oh, you know. I've been a starving student for nearly eight years now."

"I get it. When I first moved out of my parents' house, I ate my share of ramen."

"Haven't you always had a job here?" I ask.

"Of course, but this is a small town. Tending bar isn't

exactly lucrative, and I didn't do it full-time while my father was in charge. He and my mom couldn't afford college, so I was on my own, and with student loan payments and all . . . You know the drill."

Indeed I do. Except for the loan payments. Because my mother and I had basically nothing, I got most of my college paid for by grants, and I received full scholarships for all my grad school. I don't want to invite any more inquiries about my past, though, so I simply nod.

Brendan puts the hamburgers on a platter and sets them on his small table, where the Latour already sits.

I gesture to it. "May I?"

"Of course."

I pick up the bottle. The label is understated, with the red logo showing a lion atop a castle and the lettering in a slightly ornate serif font. "Where did you get this?" I ask.

"I appropriated it from a case my dad got about ten years ago."

"You *appropriated* it?"

"Yeah." He smiles. "But then Dad said I could have it."

The mention of Brendan's dad triggers a memory. "Jade told me that your dad had an uncle who died here in Snow Creek."

"Yeah. At a wedding, of all things."

I lift my brows. "A wedding?"

He nods. "A wedding at Steel Acres, actually."

My heart plummets to my stomach. When Jade spoke of her beginnings with Talon, she kept mum about certain things.

What kind of secrets is she keeping?

"At the ranch?"

"Yeah. The wedding of Talon's dad, Brad Steel."

"Brad Steel. The name is familiar. Oh, yeah. One of Dale's cousins is named Brad."

He nods again. "Joe's kid. Named after his grandpa, I guess."

"So what happened at the grandfather's wedding?"

"Man, that was long before my time, and no one talks about it anymore, but basically my great-uncle was Brad Steel's best man. The way I hear it, he passed out while giving his toast, and he never woke back up."

Icicles grab at the back of my neck. "What happened? I mean, how did it happen?"

"No one knows. For a while, there were rumors of a drug overdose or poisoning. Like I said, this happened over sixty years ago."

"Surely there are records."

"Weirdly enough, there aren't. I only know what's been passed down by my family."

"How old was your uncle?"

"Great-uncle. He was young. Twenty-two or twenty-three."

Acid churns in my gut. "That's awful."

"Yeah. I always wondered why my dad wanted to come here."

"Why did he?"

"He was trying to figure out what happened. He hit dead end after dead end, but he loved this place, so he stayed and opened up the bar."

"Did he even know his uncle?"

"That's just it. He didn't. But he was named after him, so I guess he felt close to the situation or something."

I nod. "I guess I get it."

"Then you're ahead of me. I don't get it at all. But I love Snow Creek. My mom's a local. They met when Dad first got here, so she probably had a hand in why he stayed as well."

"It is a charming little town."

"It's home."

I nod once more. I could easily hang my hat here.

But I won't.

I'll see my internship to its end, but after that, I need to leave.

I need to get away from Dale Steel.

And then a lightbulb shines above me. Brendan and Dale went to school together. They're the same age. Maybe Brendan has some insight.

I clear my throat. "Jade tells me you and Dale went to school together."

"We did."

"So . . . are you friends?"

He pauses a moment, wrinkling his forehead. "That's an interesting question."

"It's a yes or no question," I counter.

"For most people, yeah, it is. For Dale?" He sighs. "It's kind of hard to answer."

"Why?"

"Because I'm not sure Dale *has* friends."

"What do you mean by that? Is he not friendly?"

"No, he's perfectly friendly. He's a good guy. He's just . . . I'm not sure I can describe it. We hung out sometimes. We had fun. But something doesn't quite fit. It's like he's got a shield around him or something."

"He doesn't let people in," I say, more to myself than to Brendan.

"Yeah. That's it. And we were in high school, you know? And we were guys. It wasn't like we had slumber parties and pillow fights."

"I hate to rain on your parade, but not all high school girls have slumber parties and pillow fights. I think I went to one slumber party in my life, and I've never been in a pillow fight."

He gasps in mock surprise. "Say it's not so!"

I can't help a giggle. "Some high school girls are very social, but so are some high school guys. But I get what you mean. It's different."

"Yeah. Snow Creek is hardly a thriving metropolis, so the guys in our class were all friends. Everyone liked Dale, and he liked everyone else as far as I know. But there was something different about him."

"He's closed off," I say.

"Yeah. Exactly."

"I know. I've been working with him since I got here." *And sleeping with him . . .*

"So you've experienced it."

"Yeah, which is weird, because his brother doesn't seem that way at all. Of course I've hardly said two words to him. He was here for one day before Diana left for Denver."

Brendan nods. "Donny's definitely different."

"I wonder why he still goes by Donny."

"His real name is Donovan. It's what he prefers, I guess."

"Do you remember when Dale and Donny came to the ranch?"

"Yeah. They were both quiet at first. We were still in elementary school. Donny opened up pretty quickly."

"But not Dale."

"Right. Not Dale."

I can't imagine Dale ever opening up to anyone, so what Brendan says next surprises me.

"He and Donny went through a lot of therapy, or so I heard."

Therapy requires a lot of opening up. "Why would they need therapy?"

He shakes his head. "Beats me. Maybe they came from an abusive home or something. I mean, why else would two brothers be adopted when they were ten and seven? They were probably in the social services system, and Talon and Jade adopted them from there."

Why? Good question. From what I've learned, the Steels are generous people, but taking on two young boys who probably came from less than optimal circumstances... But did they? Dale himself told me he never went hungry.

Of course, not going hungry and being abused aren't mutually exclusive.

An ache squeezes at my heart. I can't bear the thought of Dale enduring any kind of abusive situation.

"What happened to their parents?" I ask.

"No one really knows. The Steels kept the whole thing pretty quiet. I probably shouldn't say this..."

"Say what?"

"I like the Steels. They're great. They do a ton for this town, and they support all the local businesses. And I like Dale and Donny. But public records have a way of disappearing sometimes, if you get my drift."

"I'm afraid I don't."

"You're not the first person to wonder about Dale and Donny's past. Most people in town have at one time or another. But there's nothing out there. *Nothing.*"

"Maybe you're not looking in the right places."

"It's not like anyone's hired a PI or anything. It's not our business, and most of us can't afford it anyway. But people wonder, you know?"

I nod. I know. I'm probably more curious than anyone in Snow Creek, because I'm in love with one of them.

"Then with Jade being the city attorney, and all," Brendan continues. "She has access to all local and state records. Probably even federal records."

"That doesn't mean she can make them disappear."

"No, but the Steels can pay for just about anything they want. If they want something—or someone—to disappear, they can make it happen."

Shivers crawl across my back. "Some*one*? Are you kidding me? They could make some*one* disappear?"

Brendan twists his lips. "I can see you bring out things in me that I don't normally talk about. We haven't even started the wine yet."

I smile coyly. "By all means, let's taste it. I've been looking forward to it all day."

CHAPTER FOURTEEN

Dale

Dad shakes me this time, gripping my shoulders. "Dale! What the hell is going on? Open your fucking eyes!"

I hesitate, but only for a split second.

This is my dad. The man who rescued me. The man who loves me and whom I love.

My eyelids flutter open. He's blurry at first—dark hair, flesh, and the pinkness of his cheek and eye.

He'll have a black eye tomorrow. A black eye that I gave him.

"What is it, son?"

Son.

The word cascades over me. I'm still his son. I just punched him, and I'm still his son.

"Dale! For God's sake, talk to me."

I part my trembling lips. "I'm sorry. I'm so sorry."

"Never mind about that," he says. "What's wrong? What do you need?"

"You're . . ."

"What? Answer me!"

"You're concerned about what *I* need?"

"Of course I am. You're my son."

My son. Not for long. Not when he discovers who I truly am.

"But I just . . . "

"You sure as hell did. Where'd you learn to punch like that?"

Dad taught Donny and me how to fight. The father and son talk about how to turn the other cheek whenever possible but to defend yourself if you have to.

I gave him a martial arts punch, though. Something I learned on my own.

"An . . . app," I say. True story.

"It's a damned good app." He loosens his hold on me. "I'm going to get up now. And then you're going to tell me what's going on."

I inhale and hold the air in my lungs for several seconds before I let it out slowly.

I need to regain control. Difficult, now that my emotions— which I've held captive inside me for so long—are running rampant, as if they're whooshing through my veins along with my blood.

I know my father. He won't leave me until he's convinced he knows what's going on and that I'm okay.

Which means I need to focus.

Focus, so I can pretend.

I'm not a good actor. I never have been. But I've never had to be, as long as the feelings stayed buried deep inside my soul.

I inhale and exhale several more times.

"You okay?" Dad asks.

I nod.

It's a lie, but I nod.

"Good. We're going to go upstairs and sit down. Then you're going to tell me what the hell just happened here."

I nod again.

Another lie. But at least I have a few minutes to compose a viable story.

I rise, wearing only my jeans and boots. I follow my father up the basement stairs, through the hallway, and into the kitchen.

"Drink?" he asks.

"Sure." It'll give me more time.

He heads to the bar in the adjacent room and returns a few minutes later with two bourbons. He sits down at the kitchen table and gestures me to sit next to him. I plunk down in the chair, and he slides a lowball glass of amber liquid toward me.

"Drink," he says.

Reluctantly, I pick up the glass and watch the bourbon swirl.

What sounds does this color conjure up in Ashley's mind? I bring the glass to my lips and take a small sip, letting it sit on my tongue for a moment as if I'm tasting wine.

So different from wine, yet no less alluring. This, my father's favorite bourbon, is smooth as silk and smoky as a forest fire.

Delicious all around.

I swallow. It doesn't burn. It simply melts my throat with its heat.

Finally, I meet my father's gaze. I haven't come up with an alibi, so I'm going to have to go with my gut. He'll ask me something, and I'll answer.

Dad takes a drink and sets his glass down. "I'm ready."

"For what?"

"For your explanation of why you did this." He points to his cheek and eye.

"I'm sorry."

"I know you are. What I want to know is what precipitated it."

"I was working out." I pick up my glass. "I guess I lost control. I'm sorry."

"That's twice now. You don't have to say you're sorry again. What's going on, Dale?"

A loaded question if ever one existed.

A loaded question my father doesn't actually want the answer to.

"I haven't worked out in a while. I decided to today, and I lost control."

"That was more than losing control. You weren't punching and kicking that bag. You were punching and kicking a person."

I say nothing. I can't deny his words, so I don't even try.

So much for pretending.

"I understand," he says.

Does he? Does he really?

I shake my head. "You can't."

He stays silent for a moment. A moment that seems like an hour or two while I wait for the Talon Steel wisdom to cross his lips.

My father always has wisdom on occasions like these.

"As a matter of fact," he finally says, "I can."

CHAPTER FIFTEEN

Ashley

Brendan hands me the bottle of Latour. "Would you like to do the honors?"

I smile. "That's kind of you, but being an almost doctor of wine doesn't give me any special way of uncorking. As a bartender, you probably do it more often than I do. At least for now. When I'm a sommelier, I'll do it a lot."

"Fair enough." He uncorks the Latour with an expert hand and then pours it into a glass carafe. "Let's give it a few minutes."

"Good call. Grand crus need their breathing time."

Though I'm anxious to taste the wine. Because it's an excellent cru and vintage, of course, but also because it may loosen Brendan's tongue even more.

My curiosity is warranted, as I'm in love with Dale. But I'm also being nosy for the sake of being nosy, like when I walked into Dale's unlocked home.

I should know better.

The chance to find out details the Steels won't tell me has fallen into my lap, though. Details that may help me understand the man I love better. I can't walk away from this chance.

"Help yourself to a burger," he says, "before they get cold."

I smile and load my plate.

"Those buns are from Ava Steel's bakery," Brendan says. "She makes the best bread I've ever tasted."

"Oh?" I squirt ketchup on top of my burger. "I've only met her briefly."

"She's awesome. Really down-to-earth. If you met her and didn't know who she was, you'd never guess she was a Steel."

"Really? I think the Steels are pretty down-to-earth."

"They're nice folks," he says. "But I wouldn't call them down-to-earth. They live in the lap of luxury."

I let out a laugh. "Well, that's true enough."

"Ava doesn't, though. She lives above her bakery, in a place kind of like this. She lives off the money she makes herself."

"That's pretty cool," I say.

"It is. She's amazing." He smiles slightly.

"Methinks you might have a little crush on Ms. Ava Steel."

"Oh? No, not really. She's way too young for me."

"How old is she?"

"Twenty-four."

I burst into laughter.

"What's so funny?"

"I'm only twenty-five!" Then I stop myself. Maybe Brendan doesn't think this is a date. To him, it may be a couple of people who appreciate wine sharing a nice bottle.

"Are you?"

"If you tell me I look older, I'm walking right out that door."

"Of course not. You look amazing. I guess I just thought, with your knowledge of wine and all . . . "

"That I must be ancient?"

"No." His cheeks turn ruddy. "I'm not scoring a lot of points here, am I?"

I give him a good-natured punch in the arm. "I went straight through college to get my masters and now my doctorate." I deliberately ignore his "scoring points" comment because scoring points with me is impossible. I'm in love with another man.

Somehow we've gotten off the subject of the Steels, which is what I want to be talking about.

"The Latour is probably ready now." I reach for the bottle.

"Yeah. You do the tasting honors."

"Happy to." I pour myself a small portion of the dark-red liquid. "Beautiful color. Deep red with a tinge of brownish orange. Like any good aged Bordeaux."

So far from the color of Dale's voice, though. Syrah is much different.

"A lot of the vines in Pauillac are over a hundred years old." I swirl the wine around in the glass, watching the wavy shapes it forms against the crystal. "They also use biodynamic farming, just like the Steels do."

"Do they? I didn't know that."

I continue swirling the wine, releasing its bouquet. "Yeah. Biodynamic farming tends to make the wine a purer reflection of the terroir."

"Interesting."

I'm not sure Brendan finds it interesting at all. He's a bartender, not a sommelier. Still, in his profession, he needs to know a fair amount about wine.

"It's lovely on the nose. I'm getting black fruit, of course, and then cedar and a touch of coffee." I pour him a tasting portion. "See if you agree."

Brendan picks up his glass and swirls the wine expertly. Then he lowers his nose into the glass and inhales. "Hmm.

Dark plum, I think. Blackberry. And yes, the cedar. I'm not getting coffee."

"It's subtle. Try to push the dark fruit to the side and concentrate on what's left."

He sniffs the wine again. "Still not getting it, but I'll defer to the expert."

"Not all noses work the same," I say. "I think mine goes on overdrive sometimes because of my synesthesia."

"No kidding? You have that?"

"I do. Don't tell me you actually know what it is."

He nods. "One of my aunts has it. She sees letters and numbers in colors."

"That's the most common kind," I tell him. "Mine's a little more complex. Sounds have colors and colors have sounds. Sometimes tastes have colors. My senses are really intermingled. I'm used to it for the most part, until something really jumps out at me."

"Like what?"

Like Dale Steel's voice. But I'm not about to share that with Brendan, who's still a virtual stranger to me.

And I've successfully managed to stray off topic again.

I bring the goblet of Latour to my lips and take a sip, letting the lush liquid sit on my tongue. It's so full and vibrant that it almost feels gelatinous against the inside of my mouth. I swallow, relishing the warmth in my throat.

"It's wonderful," I say after swallowing. "The tannins have softened with time, but they're there, and they're exquisite. But they pale in comparison to the black fruit. Currants are forefront, with some pepper and coffee on the finish." I take another taste. "Delicious. Beautifully delicious. Thank you so much for sharing this with me."

Brendan takes a sip as well. "Yes, it's wonderful. I doubt I appreciate it as much as you do, but I swear it goes down like mother's milk."

"It does." I pour us each a full glass and raise mine. "To a lovely dinner, a wonderful wine, and good company."

He clinks his glass to mine. "I'd hardly call burgers lovely, but I'll take it. To many more dinners together."

I smile. Perhaps he wants more from me. More than I can't give, as I'm in love with someone else. But we can be friends, for sure.

And friends talk.

Something I'm counting on.

CHAPTER SIXTEEN

Dale

Silence looms between us for a while.

Maybe, just maybe, my father will level with me. Tell me why he adopted Donny and me all those years ago.

He rescued us, for sure, but why was he there on that remote island where we were held captive? He and Uncle Ryan carried us to safety, and we ended up...

My God.

We ended up in a house. A house that looked just like the main ranch house—the house I grew up in.

Images form in my head—images I've tried my hardest to forget.

Thoughts. Talks with my brother.

Our...

Fuck.

Our suicide pact.

Donny almost drowned in that replica house. Aunt Ruby performed CPR and saved him.

Why was *she* there? Why were my dad and uncle there? And that older guy...? And the lady...? The baby she carried...?

These were things I never shared with Aunt Mel or any of my other therapists.

These were things I didn't even recall until this moment.

Fragmented pictures—like looking in a broken mirror—fly through my consciousness.

"Dad . . . "

"Yeah?"

"Are you going to say anything more? Or leave me hanging?"

He clears his throat. "I don't know, son. First, I should tell you why I came over here."

I nod. "Okay."

"I made arrangements for your father to go into rehab in Grand Junction."

"You're my father."

"I know that, and you know what I mean."

"Call him Floyd, then. Not my father."

"Of course. Floyd has agreed to the treatment. It begins tomorrow. It's a three-month in-house program."

I feel nothing. Not a damned thing.

"It's nice of you to help," I force myself to say.

"He gave me my sons. I owe him."

I shake my head. "You owe him nothing. *I* owe him nothing."

"You owe him your life."

"So he shot sperm at the right time. It doesn't take a genius to do that."

Dad laughs. "I don't blame you, Dale. I have no love lost for my own father, but I recognize what he did for me, and the first thing he did for me was give me life."

"He didn't do it alone," I retort.

"No, he didn't. I owe the same to my mother."

I nod. I know so little about my grandfather, and even less about my grandmother.

"Your father died in prison."

"He did. And he deserved to be there. But he also did a lot for me before then, when I was growing up."

A touch of sadness laces Dad's tone, and I'm unsure what to make of it.

"My father denied me things I needed at certain times in my life, but he did teach me how to run the ranch, taught me the value of money and a hard day's work. I owe him for that."

"Those are things fathers are *supposed* to do. You did them for me."

"I did. I've tried very hard to be the father my own father wasn't."

"You're a great father."

"Thank you. That means the world to me. But I've kept things from you. I had my reasons at the time, and I'm too old now to second-guess my actions."

I stare at him, our gazes meeting.

"I expected you to look surprised," he says, "but you don't."

"I didn't question much when I was a kid," I say. "I was just glad to be out of that horrendous situation and living in a wonderful place with people who cared about me. But as an adult . . . "

"As an adult, you question my motives."

"Not so much your motives. I mean, what you did was amazing, and Donny and I can never hope to repay you."

"Children don't have to repay their parents."

"But we *weren't* your children, Dad. You *made* us your children, and while I'm ecstatic that you did, I never quite understood why."

"I cared about you. Grew to love you."

"Of course you did. I'm not questioning that. But you were newly married with a baby on the way, and you took in two troubled boys. Not the easiest thing to cope with. You didn't have to do it."

"What might have happened to you if I hadn't? Your mother was gone, and we couldn't find your father."

I sigh. "You had resources most don't. You could have found Floyd Jolly."

"We tried, son."

"Did you?"

He smiles weakly. "Maybe not very hard. Since his name didn't appear on your birth certificate, we didn't need his permission for the adoption."

"And it would have made the adoption process more difficult if he showed up."

Dad nods. "I doubt he'd have resisted, since he abandoned you years before, but it was one less thing we had to deal with to finalize the adoption."

"He might have asked for money," I say.

Dad wrinkles his forehead. "He might have, but has it occurred to you that he hasn't asked us for anything since he found us?"

I part my lips but then realize I can't refute his claim. He didn't ask us for anything when we showed up at his home. He didn't ask us for anything when we dragged him to a lab the next day for the DNA test. And he didn't ask for rehab. Dad offered it.

"Doesn't change what he did in the past," I finally say.

"You're right. It absolutely doesn't."

"I can't forgive the abandonment."

"I understand."

"I mean, do you forgive your father for everything?"

Dad's lips form a flat line. He shakes his head. "No, I can't. I never did."

"Then why—"

He gestures me to stop talking. "I'm not forgiving your father—sorry, Floyd—for anything, but he needs help. He didn't ask us for it. He hasn't asked us for anything. All he's done is try to find his biological sons."

"Why now?" I ask. "The whole thing perplexes me to no end."

"It does me as well," he agrees. "Maybe, once he's sober, we can find out."

"Maybe. Honestly, I don't care one way or the other. I'm more interested in the motives of my *real* father. You. You said you've kept things from Donny and me. Maybe it's time I know the whole story."

He sighs. "Haven't you guessed by now?"

"No."

But it's a lie. Things occur to me from time to time—things I can't bear to bring to the forefront of my consciousness.

Things I've gone through. Things my brother has gone through. Things countless others have gone through.

Things that maybe . . .

Possibly . . .

God, I don't want to go there.

But I must. Maybe the truth will help set me free.

"I haven't allowed myself to think of reasons that might make sense," I say with a sigh. "I don't want to acknowledge them."

"Then you already know."

"How? How is it even possible?"

"It's a long story," he says. "Long and complicated. My brothers and I have covered things up as best we can. It took a lot of money and connections, but we buried that part of our past for our children's sake."

"Part of me doesn't want to know. Never wants to know. I can't bear the thought of something so heinous happening to you or anyone else."

"You wonder why I couldn't forgive my father," he says. "My father played a significant role in what happened to me, and when it was over, he covered it up as I did, but with one difference. He didn't get me the help I needed when I was young. I was determined not to make that same error in judgment."

Briny bile crawls up my throat. I swallow down a dry heave.

It's true, then. Everything I could never allow myself to face.

Because I could give you what you needed.

Those words Dad uttered meant more than just the best therapy money could buy.

He could also give Donny and me his understanding. Practical understanding.

"How?" I ask again. Then, "I'm so sorry, Dad. I'm so fucking sorry." I bury my head in my hands.

Tears don't come. I'm dry. My throat is like a hot desert.

"I'll tell you. You and Donny both."

"No." I shake my head vehemently. "Leave Donny out of it. I spared him all I could when we were in captivity, and I'll spare him this now."

"Oh, Dale," Dad says, his tone laced with sadness. "It's not up to you to save your brother. You can only save yourself."

CHAPTER SEVENTEEN

Ashley

Small talk.

I'm so sick of small talk, but that's all that's happening as Brendan and I finish our dinner and the Latour. Somehow, I've got to get him back on the subject of Dale and the Steels.

It doesn't happen, so I check my watch. "It's getting late, and I've got work early."

"You can't leave yet," he says. "There's dessert."

"Oh?" I clutch my stomach. "I'm sure I couldn't eat another bite."

"I'm sure you can. I bought a peach pie from Ava's bakery. Made with Steel peaches."

Steel peaches are the bomb, but I wasn't fabricating. I am actually pretty full. Still . . . this is a chance to get him talking again. The pie itself is a segue back to the Steels.

I smile. "You've convinced me. Her hamburger buns were excellent, and I already know I love Steel peaches."

He rises and pulls the pie out of the refrigerator. He slices two pieces, plates them, and brings them back to the small table, sliding one in front of me. "You'll love it. I've never had anything from Ava that isn't top notch."

"Tell me more about Ava," I say, spearing a piece of the pie with my fork. "How did she leave the Steel family?"

He laughs. "She didn't leave. She's still very much a part of the family. She just wants to do things on her own, and she's not interested in any of the Steel ventures."

"Not all the Steels work on the ranch. Donny and Diana don't."

"No, but they've still got the Steel money behind them. Who do you think paid for their education and training? Donny wouldn't be a lawyer and Diana wouldn't be a budding architect without the Steel money."

"I don't think you can say that," I say. "Scholarships are readily available for qualified applicants." *I should know*, I add in my head. But I'm still not ready to divulge too much of my past to Brendan.

"But who needs to qualify when the Steels can just pay?"

"Are you saying Donny and Dee aren't qualified?"

"You're putting words in my mouth. That's not what I'm saying at all. They're both bright. All the Steels are. But they were spared the pain in the ass of applying for aid."

I can't disagree. Applying for financial aid and scholarships *was* a giant pain. By the end, my fingers nearly filled in all the information on autopilot. My perseverance paid off, though, in free college and grad school.

"I see," is all I add to his comment.

"Nothing against being loaded," Brendan says. "I'd love having no student loan payments."

I say nothing this time. I'm spared student loan payments because Mom and I were so financially destitute that I received grants as well as scholarships for my undergrad. What was left, Mom and I both worked hard to pay. Mom doing hair, and I waiting tables on weekends.

The fact that Brendan has student loan payments means

only that he was better off than I was during his college years—
something I'm still not willing to share.

Yet I get it. He's not begrudging the Steels their fortune,
or Donny and Dee their lack of student loan repayment. He's
simply stating fact. I perceive no purple envy in his tone.
Yes, to me envy is purple, not green—something that always
astonished my mother.

"The luck of the draw," I say simply. "We can't all be born
into ultrarich families."

"Or adopted into them," Brendan says.

Hmm. *Now* there's a little purple in his tone. He's Dale's
age, went to school with Dale. The envy is understandable. I
don't hear any resentment, really. Just a little "gee, it'd be nice
if I'd had his luck."

Indeed, it'd be nice if I'd had a little of his luck as well.

But I turned out okay, and by the looks of things, so did
Brendan.

"So we're back to Dale," I say. Which is exactly where I
want to be. "Tell me more."

"About Dale?"

"Yeah."

"I've told you all I know. He's a good guy, but he's...
unreachable in a way."

"Did he have a girlfriend in high school?" Already I'm
smacking myself in my mind. That question sounded really
immature, but there's no taking it back now.

"Not really. He dated now and then, went to dances. But
never anything serious."

"Dale went to dances?" My jaw drops. I can't even imagine
Dale dancing in a gym full of students.

"Sure. We all did. Remember, Snow Creek is a tiny little

town. Everyone knows everyone, and everyone participates in the social activities."

"He just doesn't seem the type."

Brendan laughs. "I can't disagree, but he was there. We all were."

"But he never dated seriously?"

"To my knowledge, he still hasn't. Some of us wondered if he might be gay, but we abandoned that theory a long time ago when a friend of mine who *is* gay debunked it."

No, definitely not gay. I simply nod.

"Tell me more about why you think the Steels covered something up," I say.

"I've pretty much told you all I know. Grandpa Steel died in prison, and his wife killed herself when Talon and the others were young."

I gasp. "She *killed* herself?"

"Yeah. But there's no record of that either."

"No death certificate?"

"Oh, there's a death certificate. But people wonder if it was forged."

"Why would anyone forge a death certificate?"

"I don't know, but the Steels can do it."

"What makes you think that?"

"Because they forged one for Brad Steel himself. He faked his own death."

Colors, sounds, emotions descend around me in a psychedelic, discordant waterfall. What kind of family have I wandered into?

"Shocked?" Brendan asks.

"Of course I am. Who the hell fakes their own death?"

"Brad Steel, apparently. And he probably faked his wife's too."

"But you said Brad Steel died in prison."

"He did. But before he went to prison, he came back from the dead, so to speak. Twice."

I'm incredulous. "Twice? Why?"

"No one knows."

"There are prison records. Court documents."

"There should be, but there aren't."

"When did Brad Steel die?"

"About twenty-five years ago."

"Ample time for all records to be covered."

"Exactly."

"But didn't anyone ask at that time?"

"Probably."

"But no one got an answer?"

"The only answers," Brendan says, "lie with the Steels themselves. If anyone else still lives who knows the truth, they've probably been handsomely paid to keep quiet."

"Does this have anything to do with your uncle? Great-uncle, I mean, who died at Brad's wedding?"

"If I knew, I'd tell you. Just watch your step around the Steels. They're good people, but if you cross them, you may just disappear."

CHAPTER EIGHTEEN

Dale

Save myself?

That ship sailed as soon as I fell in love with Ashley White. I let loose a thunderstorm that can never be contained.

"I tried to save Donny," I say, "all those years ago."

"You were a child yourself, Dale."

"But he was my responsibility. I was older."

"I understand."

"Do you? Does that mean—"

"No," he says. "Only I have been through something similar to you. My brothers and sister were spared."

"I just can't—" My breath catches, and for a moment I wonder if I'll be able to take in another gulp of air.

"Breathe, Dale. Breathe."

My father's voice soothes me. It always has. Those nights I'd wake up in terror, it was he who calmed me. When my mother tried, I cried and cried until she brought my father to me. Only he could chase away the nightmares when I was young.

Now, I'm forced to chase them away myself. I've grown stronger. Indeed, I was stable.

Until Ashley.

Now, the chaos of unchecked emotion lives within me

daily, and each day, those feelings are harder and harder to control.

"I'll grant your request," Dad finally says. "But only for now. Donny will eventually come to me—or to you—and demand the truth. Frankly, I'm surprised it took you both this long."

"I'm not," I say.

"Oh?"

"Donny deals with things in a different way than I do. He keeps busy with work, friends, and women. He doesn't give himself time to dwell on anything unpleasant."

"And you?"

"I buried it. Buried it along with my emotions, but..."

"But what?"

I exhale, trying to slow the beat of my tumbling heart. "That's no longer possible."

Dad smiles. "From where I'm standing, that's a good thing. Emotion isn't something to be feared, son."

"Isn't it?"

"The bad may be bad," he says, "but the good... The good is unlike anything you can imagine."

"But you can't have one without the other."

"No, you can't," he agrees. "The universe has a duality to it. You can't escape it."

"How well I know."

Dad cocks his head, lifts one eyebrow slightly. He wants to ask me how I know this. I can almost see the words coming together inside his head. But he won't. He knows better. Dad will never push me. If I want to tell him anything further, it will be on my own terms.

But then he'll know...

He'll know the darkness inside me, the demons that have haunted me and that are now close to my surface.

But maybe . . . just maybe . . . he's the one person who will understand.

"I'm in love."

The words rush out, devoid of emotion.

He smiles. "That's wonderful."

"But it's not." I grab a fistful of my hair. "Don't you see? I never let myself feel those things before. I could get close to you, to Donny, the girls. Even Mom to a certain extent. Aunt Mel. But none of those relationships required the all-consuming passion I'm feeling now. That visceral emotion that I kept buried deep. And now that it's out . . . "

"You're afraid of the other side of the coin."

"Oh, I'm *not* afraid," I say. "That's what terrifies me."

"Let's concentrate on the bright side first," Dad says. "Ashley is the object of your love, I take it?"

I nod. "Ridiculous, I know. I've barely known her for a couple of weeks."

"Does she know how you feel?"

"No. I've been . . . I haven't been the nicest to her."

He laughs. My father fucking laughs! But it's a different kind of laugh. He's not making fun of me. He's . . . Is he understanding me?

"What the hell is funny about this?" I finally say.

"Nothing. Nothing at all. I just see so much of myself in you." He shakes his head. "We may not share blood, but you're the most like me of all four of my children. Somehow, I've always known this. Now do you see why I had to adopt you and your brother? I had to give you what no one else could."

The love a son can feel only for a father overwhelms me

in that moment. I'll never be able to repay this man. I can't even try. The beauty is he doesn't expect it. Doesn't want it. He only wants my happiness. Mine and my brother's and sisters'.

Questions for my father are jumbled in my mind. *How did you get through this? How did you make a relationship work? How? How? How?*

But I don't ask them. I'm not sure his answer would help anyway. He and I are two different people.

"Something you need to realize," he continues, "is that your mother made the same commitment to you that I did."

"I know that."

"But you've never felt close to her."

I sigh. "It's not the way I want it. We're just . . . different, I guess. Aunt Mel says it's okay. You've told me it's okay."

"It is. Even your mother has accepted it now."

"I'm sorry I was hard on her. You're right. I owe her as much as I owe you."

"You owe neither of us anything. I just wanted to make sure you understood that it wasn't just me. If your mother hadn't been all in with the idea of adopting you and Donny, I wouldn't have pushed it."

My eyes widen.

"Don't get me wrong," he goes on. "I wanted you two more than anything. But marriage is a two-way street. I couldn't have given you what you needed without Jade's full support."

"I never doubted her love for me."

"No, I don't think you have. She *has* doubted your love for her, though. She doesn't anymore. Jade was young, only twenty-five, when we took you boys in. She was still a child herself in some ways. Sure, she was ready to have an infant, but maybe not quite ready to have a troubled ten-year-old."

I sigh. "I know, Dad. I've been over and over this in my own mind. Believe me."

"I believe you have. Your mother rose to the occasion. She has a strength inside her that is tougher than anything. In her way, she's stronger than I am."

I lift my eyebrows. "I find that difficult to believe."

"I don't think you've ever really seen the truth of who your mother actually is. She's brilliant."

"I know that."

"Do you? The two of you don't click, and that's not the fault of either of you. It happens with parents and children sometimes. I'm not asking that you change your relationship with her. Just look beyond what you know of her. See what's inside."

"And then . . . " My mind whirls. "And then I'll understand why you love her so much. Which will . . . "

Dad's dark eyes light up. "You read me better than I read myself sometimes, Dale. You're right. It will help you understand your love for Ashley."

I scoff. "It's incomprehensible."

"Is it? She's beautiful. Brilliant. A lot like your mother in many ways."

"She's nothing like Mom."

"Not in looks, no. But think about who she is inside. Understand why I was so drawn to your mother, and you'll understand better why you're drawn to Ashley."

"It's completely different. Mom was . . . Well, she'd been left at the altar."

"True. Which made her resistant to another relationship so soon."

"Then how . . . ?"

"It was a bumpy ride at first. But the heart wants what the heart wants, Dale. There's not a lot of rhyme and reason to it in the beginning sometimes. If you dig deeper, you'll see that the heart and head can be in agreement."

I shake my head. "I hardly know Ashley."

"You know her better than you think you do."

"How can you say that?"

"Because you're very stingy with your affection, Dale, but you're giving it to her. Somewhere inside you, you know she's worth it."

I rub at my temples, trying to soothe the headache that erupts whenever I try to make sense of my emotions. "I'm still being stingy with my affection. And damn, it's difficult with her. I want to give her everything."

"What's stopping you?"

The monster inside me. The chaos. The ride into hell.

But I don't say any of this to my father. Instead, "What do I do now?"

"My best advice?" He smiles. "Don't fuck it up."

My father, as usual, doesn't mince words, but it's advice I fear I won't be able to heed. I don't know how to love Ashley. Not the way she wants me to.

And what I want from her . . . She won't know how to give her love to someone like me.

The buzz of my phone interrupts my thoughts. It's a group text from Brock.

Dad and I are heading into town for a drink at Murphy's. Anyone want to join?

Dad glances at his phone, presumably at the same text.

"I could use a cold one." He points to his eye. "You up for it?"

Given that Ashley is no doubt out with Brendan Murphy this very minute, I'm up for it.

"Absolutely." I shove my phone back into my pocket after texting that Dad and I will join. "Let's go."

CHAPTER NINETEEN

Ashley

Chills skitter over my flesh.

If you cross them, you may just disappear.

Brendan's warning doesn't sound like any of the Steels I know. Everyone's been perfectly kind to me. All except the one I'm in love with, that is.

Faked deaths? Faked documents?

What the actual fuck?

I drop my fork onto my plate with a clatter.

"You're kidding, right?" I finally say.

"In a manner of speaking. I like the Steels. But I can't deny the fact that there are a lot of secrets about them that no one knows."

"So you don't think I'm in any danger?"

"No, of course not. Just stay on their good side."

"Was your great-uncle ever on their bad side?" I ask with wide eyes.

"I honestly don't know. I don't think so. I mean, he was Brad Steel's best man."

"Then his death was an accident."

"Maybe. But he was a healthy and robust twenty-two-year-old. How many healthy and robust twenty-two-year-olds drop dead at weddings?"

I don't have an answer for him. So I decide to change the subject back to my own person of interest.

"Tell me more about Dale in high school."

"He was bright. Really smart. But he hated sitting in a classroom. He was fidgety all the time. In the earlier years, the teachers were pretty lenient with him. I'm not sure why. Any of the rest of us would have gotten detention for what he pulled."

"What exactly did he pull?"

"Nothing horrible, but he distracted the class a lot. He tapped his pencil on the desk nonstop. Or he squirmed in his seat. Stuff like that."

"That hardly sounds like anything abnormal."

"It's not abnormal . . . for a five-year-old. An eleven-year-old should be able to sit still."

"Maybe he had ADHD," I say, but I know already Dale doesn't have ADHD. If he did, it would have been diagnosed and treated long ago.

"I remember talking to my mom at the time, and that was her response as well. But he didn't have the other symptoms of ADHD. He didn't have problems focusing, just sitting still."

"Did it get better?"

"Eventually. By high school he was able to sit through classes. But during passing periods he ran laps around the school building. Seriously."

I widen my eyes. "Wow. Really?"

"Yeah. It was the strangest thing. He never stayed for any extracurricular activities."

"You just said he attended dances."

"He did. But he didn't help plan them. Didn't play any sports. Didn't participate in any clubs. Not that we had a lot of options at Snow Creek High."

"He didn't go to college..." I murmur, more to myself than to Brendan.

"He did for a semester," Brendan says. "We went to Mesa together in Grand Junction. But it wasn't for him."

"He needed to be outdoors," I say.

"Maybe. But like I said, he didn't play any sports at school, despite being built like a tree trunk. The football coach was after him since he was a freshman. Football would have given him a lot of time outdoors."

Except not the kind of time he craved. I know this already. Dale couldn't be part of a team. Couldn't depend on others. He needed the solitude of his vineyards. Of the vast acreage of the ranch.

I take another bite of my pie and chew it slowly, my mind racing.

"He's a strange bird," Brendan continues. "Strange, but a good guy."

I swallow the peach goodness. "Did you ever try to find out why he was the way he was?"

"Not really. He wouldn't let anyone close enough to even venture to ask that question."

Sounds like Dale, all right. "What about his younger brother?"

"Donny was different. Much more outgoing. He was three years younger than me, so I never knew him very well, but he was a star tight end on the football team his senior year."

"Snow Creek High actually had enough students to put together a football team?"

"Barely," he laughs. "That's why Coach was so adamant about Dale playing. He's a natural athlete, but he wanted no part of it."

I nod, taking another bite of the flaky peach pie.

"He comes to the bar every now and then."

I swallow. "Who? Dale?"

"Yeah. Sometimes with his dad. With Donny, if he's in town. Occasionally with one of his cousins. He always orders his own wine."

"Like Jade did last night."

"Yeah. I've said before, the Steels do a lot for this community."

"Yet the community still gossips about them."

He laughs raucously. "Touché. But you're doing your share of gossiping tonight too."

"I'm not," I say with mock sincerity. "I'm just listening."

"Why all the questions about Dale?" Brendan asks.

My cheeks heat instantly. "I work with him. That's all."

"How is he to work with?"

"Good." I take another bite of pie.

"That doesn't sound too convincing," Brendan says after swallowing.

"He knows a ton about wine. He may know more than I do, which is strange given I've studied wine for years."

"He's worked with wine, though. And he learned from Ryan. My dad always said Ryan was a genius."

"He is, but Dale is no less so." I gouge the last piece of pie crust with my fork.

"You think?"

I nod. "I know. He understands the process in an almost intimate way, beginning with each bud on the grapevine and ending with award-winning wine in a bottle. It's like … It's like it's all part of him, in a way."

"I can see that," Brendan agrees. "Dale was always kind

of cerebral. He didn't like school, but he was good at it, if that makes sense."

"He didn't like being stuck in a classroom," I say. "The ranch is his classroom now. The vineyards. The winery. The tasting room. All where he can stretch out and move to his heart's content."

"How do you know all this about Dale?" he asks. "You ask so many questions, but you seem to know him a lot better than I do after twenty-five years."

An unintended smile edges onto my face. "He and I are . . . We're just . . . alike in some ways."

Brendan rolls his eyes. "Fuck."

"What?" I raise my eyebrows.

"I don't have a chance with you, do I?"

My mouth drops open. Am I that obvious?

"I know the look of a woman whose heart belongs to someone else. I've seen it a few times before."

This time I smile again, though embarrassment is the cause. "Dale and I aren't involved."

"But you'd like to be."

"He's made it clear that it won't happen."

Brendan shakes his head. "He's nuts, then."

I sigh once more, still playing with the last piece of pie crust on my plate. I've reduced it to crumbs. "I think I'm the one who's nuts. You're a nice guy, Brendan."

He clutches his chest, teasing. "Always my fate. I'm the nice guy."

"I mean it as a compliment. You're smart and good-looking as all get-out. Plus, you're baggage-free, from what I can tell."

"Maybe not free, but a lot less than Dale Steel, I'd wager."

"See?" I finally rest my fork on the pie plate. "I'm nuts. And for the record, if Dale weren't a factor, I'd be all over you."

No lie there.

"I suppose you're going to tell me we can be friends."

"I'd like that."

He laughs. "I'll take what I can get. It was fun getting to know you, Ashley."

"You too." I stand. "I suppose I should be going." I actually want to stay, to try to get more information about Dale, but that's not fair to Brendan.

He stands as well. "I'll walk you down to your car."

"Thanks. And thanks so much for sharing the Latour with me. It was lovely."

"I only share good wine with people who appreciate it," he says, "and you're certainly in that category."

I smile. In that moment, Brendan Murphy is very attractive, and I wonder what kissing him might be like.

But the thought drifts away when Dale's image surfaces in my mind.

And I know I don't want to kiss anyone but him. Ever.

CHAPTER TWENTY

Dale

Maryanne is tending bar tonight. She's a local girl, barely twenty-one, and Brock is in womanizing mode. I'm used to his behavior—hell, my little brother does the same thing—but I'm a little pissed, since merely a week or so ago, Brock was pulling his games on Ashley.

Better Maryanne than Ashley, though. Why the hell am I pissed on Ashley's behalf? I don't want her with Brock any more than I want her with Brendan Murphy or anyone else.

I want her with *me*.

Except I don't.

I don't *want* to want her.

I have no business dragging her into my chaos.

Maryanne slides my glass of wine in front of me, laughing. "Ruby for you. You and your uncle crack me up, coming in here and ordering your own wine."

"Why not drink the best?" I say.

She giggles at me. "You're so funny, Dale."

I wasn't being funny, but whatever.

Brock chimes in then. "Dale and Uncle Ry are like two peas in a pod, except for their personalities."

This gets a laugh from everyone at the bar, which is mostly my family. Dad and me—he said an accident in the orchard caused his black eye—Uncle Joe and Brock, and Uncle Bryce, Henry, and Dave. No women chose to join us. Usually Mom or Aunt Ruby will bite, but apparently not tonight.

My body tingles in a strange way that I've come to know.

Ashley is near.

At least I hope she is. Brendan Murphy lives above the bar in the studio apartment. I've been there a few times.

There's a bed.

A bed right out in the open.

Where he may be, right at this moment, with Ashley.

The thought consumes me, and I absently curl my fingers into fists.

The rest of my family converses and laughs, but it's all white noise to me. I'm clutching my glass of wine with a white-knuckled grip.

Ashley.

Ashley is here.

Ashley is upstairs in bed with Brendan.

Ashley.

My Ashley.

"Dale." My father grasps my arm. "You okay here?"

"Fine," I say gruffly.

"Good." He moves his eyes toward the stairway leading to Brendan's place.

Ashley is descending, looking as beautiful as ever in a light-blue camisole and skinny jeans, her hair piled on her head in a messy bun. A silver chain hangs around her neck, luminous against her tanned skin.

Our gazes meet, but she doesn't react.

Brendan walks behind her.

At least she's not in his bed.

But *was* she? I grip the stem of my goblet this time. I could break it so easily, watch the shards of glass hit the wooden bar.

"Ashley!" Brock calls. "Come join us at the bar!"

"Thanks," she says, "but Brendan was just going to walk me to my car."

My car. It's not her car. It belongs to my mom and dad. She's borrowing it.

Why do her words irk me so?

Why does everything irk me?

Brendan Murphy irks me more than anything else. Is that a smug grin on his face? Did he bed the woman I'm in love with?

Brendan's no womanizer, but who can resist Ashley White?

"Just one drink," Brock urges.

Ashley laughs.

What a joyful sound!

Makes me want to retch. Not the laugh, itself. No. The fact that I find it joyful. That it makes me want to smile. To take her in my arms and declare my love for her.

That's what makes me want to retch.

"Brendan and I just shared a bottle of Château Latour," she says. "No more drinking for me this evening."

Château Latour. She names the wine for my benefit. No one else here knows a Latour from a Gallo. Okay, my family knows a little more than that, but Ashley doesn't know that.

Yeah, she mentioned the Bordeaux name for my benefit.

"There's such a thing as a nonalcoholic drink, babe," Brock chides.

She smiles at him. Smiles at him! And then walks toward the bar. "Why not? The night is young."

But you have work tomorrow.

Of course, so do the rest of us.

It's not even that late. Only nine thirty.

She looks toward me. What does she want? My approval? I look away . . . and meet Dad's gaze.

Dad's disapproving gaze.

An empty barstool sits at my right. Am I supposed to offer it to Ashley? The problem is . . . Brock sits on the other side of that stool.

Instead, Ashley chooses a seat at the end of the bar and Brendan sits beside her. Hmm . . . I don't recall anyone inviting *him* to join us.

Of course, it's his bar. His father's anyway.

"Go talk to her," Dad says under his breath.

"I can't."

"You can."

"She's with Brendan."

"So?"

I polish off what's left in my wineglass and shove it across the bar to Maryanne.

"Want another, Dale?" she asks.

"No. No thanks." I rise and grab Brock's arm. "Let's play some pool."

"Not in the mood," he says.

"I'll play you." My cousin Henry, sitting on Brock's other side, blond and blue-eyed like his father, stands.

"Great. Let's go." I head to the pool table and pick a cue stick from those mounted on the wall.

Of all my cousins, I'm probably closest to Henry. Though he's eight years my junior, he's nearest in age to Donny and me. Plus, we have something in common. Neither of us carries any actual Steel blood. He's Uncle Bryce's kid from his first and very short marriage to a Las Vegas show girl. Aunt Marjorie adopted him after she married Uncle Bryce, but he still sees his birth mother every now and then. Donny used to have a major crush on her, fake tits and all.

"Go ahead and rack," I tell him.

Henry expertly racks the balls. "Eight ball?" he says.

"Sounds good." I don't give a fuck what we play, as long as it gives me something to do so I'm not trying so hard *not* to stare at Ashley and Brendan.

I chalk my stick. "You racked. I'll break."

Henry nods, and I take position to break the triangle.

"I'll play the winner."

My stick scuffs the felt. Ashley's voice. Fuck.

"Nice shot," she says sarcastically.

"Where's your date?" I ask gruffly.

"At the bar."

"Shouldn't you be with him?"

"What do you think he is? My mother? I feel like some pool."

Henry hands her his stick. "Three's a crowd, obviously."

Ashley shakes her head. "No, go ahead."

"You remember my cousin Henry," I say. "Henry, Ashley White."

"From the pool party," Henry says. "Nice to see you again."

"You too." Ashley beams a smile at him.

And I want to punch my favorite cousin's face in.

"Tell me something. Who's the better pool player? You or Dale?"

"We both suck," Henry says with a wink.

Oh, yeah. I really want to punch him now. Since when is

Henry such a flirt? He has a girlfriend, for God's sake.

Henry and I don't suck, of course. I wouldn't try to play pool in front of Ashley if I weren't good at it. Which pisses me off all the more. I'm gripping my stick hard enough to break it in half.

Easy, son.

Words from my father. Words he's said to me so many times over the years.

Words I need now more than ever.

Focus, Dale. For God's sake, focus.

I breathe in and exhale slowly. Then I push my stick against the ball at the apex of the triangle and break them expertly.

Nicely done. Thank God. Fucking up in front of Ashley isn't a top priority at the moment.

The two ball slides into the far right corner pocket.

"Nice," Henry says. "Looks like you're solids."

I nod and regard the layout of the balls on the table. I have a couple of options, one of which is a sure thing. The other isn't, but it would be an amazing feat if I could pull it off.

Damn.

Normally I'd go for the more difficult shot. But with Ashley watching...

Fuck it.

I change for no one. Not even Ashley White. I move around the perimeter of the table, getting into position.

"So seriously, who's the better pool player?" Ashley asks Henry again. "You or Dale?"

"We're pretty evenly matched," he says. "Brock's better than both of us."

Great. Henry had to mention Brock. Nice move to throw off my concentration.

I position my stick between my fingers, eyeballing the shot. I nudge the stick backward slightly. Then again. And I shoot—

"Brock!" Ashley calls. "I hear you're the one to beat at pool."

My stick grabs at the felt, and I barely touch the cue ball.

Fuck it.

Brock ambles over to the table. "Dale, man. What the fuck?"

"Can't get them all the time," I say, trying to sound nonchalant.

"You could make that shot in your sleep," Henry says. "What gives?"

"Some of you were talking," I say. "It messed with my concentration."

"We talk all the time when we play," Brock says. "Nothing shakes you up."

He's right.

Except apparently now he's wrong.

Ashley White shakes me up.

I set my stick against the wall. "Your shot," I say to Henry.

CHAPTER TWENTY-ONE

Ashley

Dale doesn't meet my gaze, but still, I feel the daggers he's shooting at me. They're bright red and full of rage, and they emit the spiky melody of a ghostly violin.

What did I do?

I called to Brock while Dale was making his shot, but Henry himself said they always talk while playing.

Or maybe it was the fact that I called to Brock, Dale's cousin who's shown a marked interest in me.

Or maybe it was because I'm here at all.

I'm the one who barged into Dale and Henry's game. Perhaps I shouldn't have.

But in all honesty? I wanted to be near Dale.

I *still* want to be near Dale.

In his presence, his good-looking cousins, Brendan, and all the other men in the bar become invisible to me. Only Dale exists—Dale with his leonine mane of blond hair, his eyes like emeralds that sparkle and sing joyous holiday music.

And Dale with his husky deep voice that coats me in the red-black warmth of a fully ripened Syrah.

But I've succeeded only in pissing Dale off.

I don't seem to have any middle ground with him.

Either he's angry and wants nothing to do with me, or he's

all over me, telling me he wants me more than anything.

And the reality is that it doesn't matter to me.

Whether he's angry or horny, I want to be near him. My heart cries out for him. I'm so hopelessly in love that I can't bear it.

I can still leave the internship. The thought hasn't left my mind. But I'm not a quitter. I've never been a quitter. My mother taught me that much. She never quit, and eventually she got us off the streets.

I never quit either, and I graduated high school with honors and gained a college education for my efforts.

This internship is an opportunity, and never once have I turned down an opportunity.

Besides, leaving the man I love isn't truly an option for me.

My feelings for him are so strong, so intense, that I'm not sure I can even exist outside his presence anymore.

I chuckle to myself. I sound ridiculous. I don't need a man to make my life complete. I need no one but myself. I proved that a long time ago.

But need... This elemental need I feel for Dale... It's something so foreign to me.

Can I live without him?

Yes, I believe I can.

But it will be an empty life. As if the other half of my heart is missing.

I may need to adapt, though, because Dale may want me, even need me...

But he'll never, ever love me.

My heart wants to shatter at the thought.

I wipe my mind as best I can and return my attention to

the game. Dale is shooting again, and this time he's much more focused. I stay quiet. I don't want him blaming me for missing another shot.

I catch Brendan's grin out of the corner of my eye.

Of all the people in this bar, he's the only one who knows the truth of my feelings. He's smiling. An encouraging smile.

I'm happy that I haven't hurt him. His feelings for me are friendship and nothing more. Or at least they will be now, and he seems okay with it.

But he can't help but notice Dale's indifference toward me.

I return his smile, though halfheartedly. He lifts his eyebrows as if he's asking me a question. Do I want to be saved? Do I want him to intervene?

I shrug.

Within a minute, he's at my side. "Don't let it get to you," he whispers. "If he doesn't come around, it's his loss."

I smile weakly once more. Sure, his loss. I don't even disagree. The bigger problem, though, is that it's also my loss. A loss I have no interest in bearing.

Dale stays focused and completes the game, dunking all the solid balls and then the eight ball.

Henry hands me his cue, smiling. "Looks like you're up."

Damn. I *did* say I'd play the winner.

I'm not bad at pool, but Dale's better. Just by watching one game, I can already tell.

I draw in a breath. Here goes nothing.

Brock smiles. "I'll take the next winner."

"Changed your mind about playing, I see," Dale says to Brock. Then he racks the balls and turns to me. "Ladies first."

I nod and position myself at the foot of the table, my heart thundering against my rib cage.

Come on, Ash. Concentrate.

I execute a perfect break, after which I shoot two stripes into nearby pockets.

My third shot is... Well, it doesn't exist. Dale or Brock might be able to make something out of this mess, but I can't. I finally decide on a bank shot but I miss, sending several balls scattering even farther.

"Nice try," Brendan says.

Those daggers Dale is shooting with his eyes? Brendan is their target now. Does Brendan know? Does he care? He seems his jovial self.

Dale picks up his stick and makes three shots in a row with perfect form.

As he eyes his fourth shot, I'm tempted to say something. *You can do it!*

But that would cause him to lose focus, and then he'll shoot more invisible daggers at me, which I don't want.

He finally decides on a shot, and though his form looks perfect to me, he misses.

I can't help smiling, though. His flub has lined up some perfect shots for me. In fact, if I play this right...

I may be able to finish the game if I can get the eight ball where it needs to be.

The first three shots are easy. The thirteen in the left side pocket, the fifteen in the right side, and then a bank off the bumper to send the nine into the far corner.

Two striped balls left. The first is easy. Straight into the side pocket with little effort.

Only two balls lie between me and victory—the twelve and the eight.

Problem is, the eight is in the path of the twelve.

I can make this shot. I've done it before. But do I want to beat Dale?

For God's sake. I've never dumbed down in my life, and I'm not about to start now. Besides, I may miss the shot. But I'll give it my best effort.

I lean my stick against the table for a moment and stretch my arms, intertwining my fingers and cracking my knuckles. Not the most ladylike, but I don't care. Then I pick up my stick, replenish the chalk, and take aim.

The trick is to hit the cue ball with enough force to jump over the eight ball and propel the twelve into the pocket. If I execute it properly, the eight ball will be lined up for the same corner pocket.

Here goes nothing.

I will myself not to tremble and line up the shot. Just the right amount of pressure, and—

Crap. Too hard.

All three balls, including the cue, land in the pocket.

Scratch.

Normally a scratch gives Dale a shot from anywhere on the table.

But not this time.

Because I drove both the eight ball and the cue ball into the pocket, it's a forfeit.

Dale wins.

He wins after pocketing only three of his balls, while I pocketed six of mine. Seven, if you count the twelve that went in with the eight and the cue.

"Nice job, cuz." Henry pats Dale's shoulder.

Dale doesn't smile. He doesn't say thank you to Henry.

He only shoots more daggers.

I raise my eyebrows. How can he still be angry with me? He won, for God's sake. Two games in a row.

"I want a rematch," he says to me.

My jaw drops. "Why? You won. Why would you want a—"

"A forfeit doesn't count. It's not a win."

"Official rules say otherwise, bro," Brendan says.

"Fuck the official rules," Dale says. "We're playing again."

"Maybe I won't play," I say adamantly. Though I have no reason not to play.

Brock steps up then. "I'm playing. I said I'd take the winner. Remember?"

"You can take the next winner," Dale says, his voice more even-toned than his demeanor suggests.

"He can take *this* winner," I say, handing Brock my stick. "And that's you."

I turn, trying my best to remain composed, and head back to a bar stool. I sit next to Talon, who smiles.

"What happened to you?" I ask.

"Accident in the orchards today."

Looks like a punch to the face to me, but I won't press it. "I'm sorry."

"Nothing that hasn't happened before," he says. Then, "Don't let Dale get to you. He doesn't like to take the easy way out of anything."

"But he won fair and square. I screwed up the shot."

"It was a hard shot."

"I've made shots like that before. I didn't do it on purpose."

"Of course you didn't. That's not what he's thinking."

"I'm not the kind of woman who does that kind of thing."

"No one thinks that." He signals Maryanne, the bartender.

"You want something?" he asks me.

I shake my head. "I had two glasses of wine with dinner. I'm fine, thanks."

He nods and orders a Peach Street bourbon. He takes a sip and then turns back to me. "Did you and Jade have a nice time last night? I hear Lisa's place is something special."

My cheeks grow red-hot. My dinner with Jade. How much does Jade tell her husband?

Does he know how I feel about his son?

I look down at the wooden floor, hoping a giant hole will open up so I can hurl myself in.

No such luck.

Finally, I reply, "It was nice. The food was great."

"I like Italian. Darla doesn't make it very much. My sister makes great Italian, though."

"She's a chef, right?"

"Yeah. Marjorie. Married to Bryce." He gestures to the silver-haired man sitting a few chairs down.

"Right. Henry's dad."

"Yes. You're doing great. In no time you'll be able to pick all of us out of a crowd."

"Does Marjorie work at a restaurant?" I ask.

Talon shakes his head. "It was always her dream, but with four kids, she decided to concentrate on her family and let the rest of us sample her amazing cooking."

"It's a shame she never got to live out her dream."

"Who says she hasn't?"

"Well, you just said . . . "

"Once she married Bryce and adopted Henry, she got pregnant about a day later with David. Two years later, she got pregnant again with the twins."

"That's a lot of kids close in age."

"It is, but my sis is a great mom."

I nod. In the corner of my eye, I see Dale, his mouth in a thin line.

He's staring straight at me.

CHAPTER TWENTY-TWO

Dale

My dad will never betray me. I know that as well as I know the feel of my pool stick between my fingers, as well as I know the Syrah vineyards that are my true home.

Still, as he sits chatting with Ashley, I wonder.

Will he tell her how I feel about her?

Why do I even ponder this? My father's word is as good as gold.

And it dawns on me, as if lightning is striking my brain . . .

Part of me *wants* him to tell her.

Part of me wants her to know.

Because maybe, if she knows, she'll return my feelings.

But I've been around the block enough times to know that women don't respond to the way I've been treating Ashley. Women like to be cherished.

And though I do cherish her, I'll never show it.

Sure, I can fuck the daylights out of her. I have, and I hope to again. But I'll never tell her how I truly feel. Not only do I fear she won't return my feelings.

I also fear that she *will*.

Already my emotions have bubbled to the surface, and it takes all my strength to contain them. If she shares them? I'll erupt.

That won't be pretty.

Sure, the good part of it will be wondrous. I'll be in ecstasy.

Until the bad part comes out.

And it *will* come out.

It's the duality of nature. Of life.

My dad understands. And now I know why. So maybe the answer lies with him.

Or maybe it lies with my mother.

My beautiful mother, whose only crime was that she wasn't the mother I loved and missed.

The mother who left Donny and me home alone after school while she worked.

That's how . . .

The masked men. The vile-smelling van where we rode, blindfolded, for days upon days upon days. Somehow we got to the island off the coast of Jamaica. I don't remember how. On a plane? In a boat?

I still don't know.

We were most likely drugged.

When we arrived, starving, dehydrated, and covered in our own piss and shit, I remember thinking nothing could be so horrible.

I was wrong.

★ ★ ★

"Get in there, you little fuckers."

The man was masked, of course, and he threw Donny and me into a large shower with several other children.

"Take off those shit-stained clothes and clean yourselves."

I looked around for a bar of soap, to no avail.

Donny was crying, tears running down his cheeks—-the round cheeks of a little boy. Mine had only just begun to slim down as puberty headed my way. I wasn't there yet, though. Only a few hairs had sprouted in my pubic area, and they were soon shaved off by one of the minions.

I grabbed my brother and held him close to me. "Don't cry," I said. "Never let them see you cry."

They were empty words, and it was a command Donny couldn't obey.

He continued to cry.

During the next few months, he cried a lot. We were left with so little water, I often wondered how he was still able to produce tears.

We shed our dirty garments and got clean as best we could under the lukewarm water.

It was our last shower until Dad rescued us.

A few minutes later, we were hustled out of the shower, given ragged towels to dry ourselves, and then each given a large gray T-shirt. It was a man's size, and Donny's hung well below his knees. Mine did not. It barely covered my ass, but I had nothing else.

Donny gripped my hand tightly. "What's happening, Dale? Where's Mommy?"

I had no answer for my brother.

It seemed Mommy had forsaken us.

We were led to a door, where one of the kids with us was thrown into a room.

Then another door, and another of the masked minions grabbed me. "In you go," he said, his voice eerie.

"No, Dale!" Donny cried.

"Shut the fuck up," the minion said sharply.

"Please," I said. "Don't. Let him come with me."

The masked man smiled through his ski mask. Creepy, how I could see only his lips but no cheeks and nose. It was a smile of deception, a smile like a snake hissing in a whisper, "Be careful what you wish for . . . "

"Fine." He threw Donny into the room with me, my brother crying out as he landed on his knees.

Donny didn't know at the time, but I soon figured out the reason behind the sly smile of the masked man.

This wasn't the minion helping us.

This was the minion starting to break us.

Horror would descend, and more horrific than anything done to me would be watching it happen to my little brother.

★ ★ ★

"You going to shoot, or what?"

Brock's voice shocks me out of my trip back in time.

I quickly scan the pool table. I'm solids this time, and only two balls remain. Brock missed his last shot, but only one striped ball is left on the table for him to sink.

It's a close game, and Brock is admittedly a better pool player than I am. I beat him about half the time, though, due to my focus. Brock tends to lose focus . . . especially when pretty girls are around.

I can do it this time. Two easy shots await me, and then, if I plan the second shot just right, I'll have a straight line to the eight ball.

Ashley's eyes are on me.

I don't look toward her, but I know. I feel her gaze, and I can't allow it to trip up my focus.

I make the first shot with ease.

Then the second.

Ashley still watches me, and my groin tightens. Fuck. I love her. I want to sink this shot for her. Show her I'm as good as Brock.

I steady my hand and put the cue stick in position. I aim, sliding the slick stick through my fingers once, twice, three times, and then—

Lust whirls through me. Lust I can't control. Except it's not lust. It's love. It takes me over, swirls through my head and gives birth to the rage I've tried so hard to suppress.

My cue stick digs into the table and I miss the shot.

Brock wrinkles his forehead, makes his shots, and in the end, sinks the eight ball.

He wins.

I hope it's a shallow victory for him, as shallow as mine over Ashley.

I played a good game, and I should have won. Indeed, I *could* have won.

But no longer.

The monster inside will never let me rest.

It's eating away at my focus, and soon it will destroy what I've worked so hard to build.

Those walls around me are crumbling.

Crumbling.

And I'm no longer safe from the chaos.

CHAPTER TWENTY-THREE

Ashley

A lump forms in my throat as Brock wins the game against Dale. Dale was so close. That eight ball was an easy shot, but he blew it.

"He's going to be pissed," I murmur to Talon.

"Dale? Nah. He doesn't care much about pool."

"He's good at it."

"Dale's good at a lot of things. He's a virtuoso pianist, for example."

Right. He told me he played. He neglected to say he was a virtuoso. "Oh?" I say.

"Yeah. He's a creative type, like Ryan and Marj. Joe and I didn't get that gene."

"Where do you suppose Dale got it?" Then I clasp my hand to my mouth. "I'm sorry. I didn't mean . . ."

"It's okay. Dale's adopted. We all know that." He takes a sip of his drink. "Honestly, we don't know. We never met his real parents, and Dale and Donny didn't know a lot about their mother. They knew nothing about their father."

"I guess one of them must have had creative gifts," I say. "Or maybe it's nurture, not nature."

Talon laughs. "If that were the case, Jade and I would be creative, and neither of us really is. Diana is, in an analytical way. That's why she's drawn to architecture, I guess. Donny and Bree are more logical than creative."

"I suppose that makes Donny a good lawyer," I say absently.

Talon nods. "And it makes Bree very handy in the orchards as well."

I turn and look toward Dale once more.

And I hold back a gasp.

He's gone.

I quickly scan the bar. Maybe he went to the men's room.

Back at the pool table, Brock is racking the balls once more, and Henry is chalking his stick. The two of them are setting up for another game.

"He's probably outside," Talon says to me.

"Who?"

He chuckles. "I know you're looking for Dale. He needs to leave enclosed spaces sometimes. Especially after losing a game he should have won."

"Why does he like the outdoors so much?" I ask.

Talon sighs. "That's something you'd have to ask him."

I nod. "I doubt he'd be forthcoming if I asked him anything personal like that."

"Probably not." Talon swirls the bourbon in his lowball glass. "But you never know. The right woman can work miracles. I should know."

I meet Talon's gaze. His words are enigmatic. Is he talking about Dale? Is he talking about me? Is he talking about himself? Jade? All of us?

I open my mouth to ask for clarification, but no words leave my throat.

Talon finishes his drink and sets his glass down on the bar.

"I should get home. Got an early morning."

"Yeah. Me too." I stand.

"Need a ride?" he asks.

I shake my head. "I have the car you guys lent me. I drove here to meet Brendan for dinner, and it's been hours since my last drink. I'm good."

"Okay. Dale and I came together, so I'd better see where he went off to. See you at home." He rises and walks out of the bar.

I heave a sigh.

Then, after thanking Brendan again for the lovely evening, I leave the bar as well, walking the short distance to where the car is parked on a side street.

And I gasp.

Dale stands against the car door.

The distance between us seems to grow as I walk my normal pace. How can he be getting farther away?

But my perspective is playing tricks on me, and in an instant I'm standing a mere foot away from the object of my desire.

I'm momentarily at a loss for words, and of course, Dale doesn't deign to speak to me.

Finally, I say, "Your dad is looking for you."

He doesn't reply.

I clear my throat. "Did you hear me?"

"I'm not deaf."

"Then... aren't you going to go find your dad? He said you guys came together."

"My dad's a big boy, and so am I. We don't need to check in with each other. He'll go home if he can't round me up."

"But then how—"

"I've got several family members inside the bar, any of whom can give me a ride home. But I don't need any of them."

"You don't?"

"No," he says, "because I'm going home with you."

My heart thumps wildly.

"But I live—"

"For Christ's sake, Ashley. We're going to my place."

"But Talon said he'd see me at home."

Dale shakes his head. "You're a big girl too. You don't need my father's permission to go with me."

"That's not what I meant."

"Good. Now unlock this fucking car."

I pull the fob out of my purse and click it. My whole body is throbbing from his nearness. From his Syrah-colored voice. From the thought of what he'll do to me at his place.

But he could just mean I'm to drive him home and then leave.

I draw in a breath. Whatever he means, I'll deal with it. One way or another. For now, I'll assume he just wants a ride home.

"Get in," I say.

He takes the fob from me. "I'll drive."

I shake my head. "You've been drinking. I haven't."

"I had one glass of wine, Ashley. You've seen me drive after drinking more than that. Besides, you drank with Brendan. *Latour.*"

His tone is . . . I'm not sure what it is.

"That was hours ago. I haven't had anything since."

"Impressive move," he says, "for Murphy to serve you such an elegant bottle."

"Was it? To serve an *almost* doctor of wine one of the best wines out there?" My tone is sarcastic.

"To pretend he knows shit about the grand crus."

"He's a bartender," I counter. "He has to know about wines."

"He knows about wine, all right," Dale says. "How to choose the right wine for the right woman."

"Is that such a bad thing?"

"Only from where I'm standing." He waves the key fob and opens the passenger door. "Get in."

CHAPTER TWENTY-FOUR

Dale

I'm heading into the chaos. I know this, yet I can't stop myself.

I want Ashley.

Brendan may have shared an expensive bottle of wine with her, but I'll share my body with her. I have to. It's no longer an option for me.

My love for this woman may be the only thing that can keep the monster at bay. If I focus on the good side of what's coming out, maybe the bad will stay buried.

Even I don't believe that, but at least it may delay its release. I have to believe in something.

Denying myself what I want from Ashley will only quicken the process. I have to do what I can to stay sane.

This woman drives me into a frenzy. Somehow I allowed her in, allowed her to start breaking the structure I've built around my heart—the structure that, up until now, has been unbreakable.

I drive her in silence to the guesthouse.

She turns to me. "I need the keys now."

"Oh?"

"To . . ." She clears her throat. "To get home. Er . . . to the main house."

"You're not going to the main house."

"But . . . I have work tomorrow. It's late."

"And I'm your boss. I say you can go in late if you need to."

Already I know she'll be at work bright and early, even if she doesn't get a second of sleep tonight. That's who she is, and it's part of what I love about her.

Why did I have to meet such a wonderful woman? I have no right to her. No right to screw up her life.

None of that matters, though. I'm going to take her anyway. I'm going to take her because I need her.

I love her.

I don't labor under any delusion that she could possibly return my feelings. In fact, she'll never know my feelings. I won't let her in on that weakness.

I've seen what loving a woman can do to a man. It can knock down every wall until a man is nothing more than a puddle of emotion.

For most men, that isn't a problem. Their emotions don't take over. For me?

I'm different.

I've hidden so much inside for so long, and now it's roaring to get out.

I'll control it as best I can, but I need Ashley to do that.

I need to touch her, kiss her, fuck her brains out. I'll let the good take over for as long as I can.

I fear it won't be long enough.

She meets my gaze, her blue eyes sparkling. "All right, Dale. Let's do this."

We walk side by side to the front door, and I punch in the key code.

Penny jumps up to greet us, and Ashley laughs and drops to her knees, showering my dog with affection.

Ashley on her knees.

How well I remember the first time I saw this image, how I imagined her sucking me.

How, when I actually experienced that pleasure, it was even better than I imagined.

"Come on, Pen." I walk through the foyer to the kitchen and open the glass door. Penny eagerly bounds out into the starlight. I walk out onto the deck and look up.

It's a clear night, and though the miracles of the night sky aren't as clear here as they are in the vineyards, they're still spectacular.

There's such beauty in the night. In the darkness.

I've always seen it.

But darkness harbors demons as well. Demons I don't want in my mind right now.

Tonight is for pleasure. For lust, desire, passion.

For love.

Ashley walks outside and stands next to me. "So gorgeous," she says.

I simply nod, and then I turn to her, her lovely face illuminated by the sparkling sky. I cup her cheek, her skin like silk beneath my calloused fingertips. "So gorgeous," I echo.

She sighs, a soft sound that eases its way past her lips and into my soul.

I love you.

How I long to say the words.

But she won't return them. How can she, when I've been such a dick to her?

Besides, if I let the utterance pass my lips, I'll lose what little resistance I have left.

And then all hell will break loose.

She brings her arm upward and places her hand on my own. The warmth of her cheek and the warmth of her palm hug my hand, and the emotion that passes through me is something I've never felt.

It's love, yes. Desire, most definitely.

But it's something more. Something so pure I can't define it.

I'll take her gently tonight. As much as I want to continue what we started that night at the Carlton—and I will—first I need to have her slowly. Carefully.

I remove my hand, taking hers with me, as the truth dawns on me once more.

I don't know *how* to love her.

I know how to kiss her, and I know how to fuck her.

But those tiny reflections of affection—like holding her small hand in my own...

I don't know how to do any of that.

And I don't know how to make love to her the way I want to at this moment.

"What's wrong?" she asks.

I shake my head. "You should go."

She lifts her eyebrows, her lips quirking downward into a pouty frown. Then she shakes her head. "Fine." She turns.

I grab her shoulder and turn her back to face me. "I don't know how to do this, Ashley."

"We did pretty well before."

She's right about that. But that night was borne of jealousy and lust. The love came later, afterward, when I realized the depth of my true feelings.

That was when the monster in my soul broke his bindings and set me on this course.

I itch to touch the soft skin of her cheek once more. I long to caress her, show her my true feelings.

Then there's the pure physical—the lust I can't control. My dick is already hard inside my jeans, and all I've done is feather my fingers over the skin of her cheek.

She meets my gaze. "Kiss me."

And without thinking another thought, I cup both her cheeks, lower my head, and take her lips.

Not gently.

Not the way I wanted to only moments ago.

But fiercely, jamming my tongue into her mouth and drinking of her. Of the drug that soothes me like no other. She returns my kiss, our lips sliding together, tongues tangling. I pull her close so that only the millimeters of our clothing separate us.

We kiss and we kiss and we kiss—

Until she breaks free with a giggle.

I regard her sternly.

"It's Penny. She's tickling my legs."

My dog is dancing around us, her tail swiping over Ashley's ankles.

This won't do. I love that silly mutt, but she's not going to stop me from having what I want.

"Let's go in." I grab Ashley's arm—not gently—and lead her through the door and back into the house, shooing Penny to stay outside for a while.

"A shame to waste such a beautiful night," Ashley says.

"It's more comfortable inside."

She arches one eyebrow. "Since when do you think that way? Aren't you the most comfortable outside? Among your vines?"

I can't deny her words, but at the moment, I'm thinking only about getting inside her, taking my pleasure, and I'm not excited about doing that on the hard wooden deck.

I pull on her arm, again not gently, and lead her to my bedroom.

My green comforter is crumpled on top of my bed. My bed only gets made twice a week, when the housekeeper comes. My mom used to insist I make my bed every day, but I never saw the point. I'll just mess it up again in the evening. Once I moved to the guesthouse, I stopped that stupid chore.

Now, for some ridiculous reason, I wish my bed were made. I don't want Ashley to think I'm a slob.

She doesn't seem to notice, though. She takes the lead and pulls me into her embrace. "Tell me what you want," she says softly.

What a loaded question that is. I want to be free of the demons I carry. I want to cherish the woman I love without baggage. I want to give her everything she deserves.

I want to make slow love to her. Gentle love to her.

But that ship sailed earlier.

I'm not capable of any of that.

"You know exactly what I want," I say. And though she doesn't know the whole of what I desire and can never have, she at least knows my momentary needs.

Her.

I want *her*.

"Tell me," she says. "I want to hear you say it."

I lean down to show her—

She backs away. "No. In words, Dale. Tell me. Tell me what you want."

I love you.

Those damned words again!
Never will they pass my lips.
I want to kiss every inch of your beautiful body, find solace in your heart.
I want... I want... I want...
"You," I finally say. "I want *you*."

CHAPTER TWENTY-FIVE

Ashley

"Will you make love to me among the vines?"

My words surprise even me. Dale just told me he wants me, and I could be kissing him right now. Feeling his hands on my body, undressing me. His lips on my hard nipples. We could be a tangle of limbs on that messy bed of his, and I'd be in heaven.

Why do I choose this moment to push something he'll never agree to?

"Not tonight," he replies. "Tonight I take you here. In my bed."

In my bed. Were any more delicious words ever uttered? Especially in that red-wine voice? The color swirls around me, cloaking both of us in its darkness.

Something dark lives in Dale. I sensed it the moment I saw him, but never was it more clear than that first night when he showed me the vineyards.

If only he could embrace everything about himself and learn to love what's right in front of him.

Not me, though I want that more than anything.

No. That person he sees in the mirror each morning. Because though he's brilliant and talented and he knows all this, something in his sense of self is missing.

Something inside him is broken.

I want so much to heal that part of him. It's not his heart, I feel certain. He's made no bones about the fact that he's pretty inexperienced in ways of the heart, but that's not the issue.

He's broken somewhere else.

And he's broken deeply.

I gaze into those mesmerizing green, symphonic eyes. So much to see in them.

Les yeux sont le miroir de l'âme.

The old proverb I learned long ago in French class. *The eyes are the mirror of the soul.*

I see lust and desire in those green orbs, but I also see sadness. Perhaps even some hopelessness.

I cup his stubbly cheek, let my fingertips scrape over its roughness—a roughness that seems so natural in Dale.

"What are you thinking about?" I ask.

I expect him to say, "fucking you," or "nothing," or something else that won't tell me anything.

For a while, he stays quiet as I continue to thumb his cheekbone.

Then, "I'm thinking about how I'll never have what I truly desire."

I stop my eyes from widening.

How do I respond to such an enigmatic statement? My body is throbbing, reacting to his nearness. I drop my gaze to his crotch. The bulge is still there. He hasn't lost his desire for me. So why open this can of worms?

He doesn't pester me for a reply. Good, because I don't have one.

Finally, I say, "Does anyone truly get what they ultimately desire in this life?"

I'm waxing philosophical, which isn't my intention. But it's a valid question.

He sighs. "I believe my parents have. At least my father."

"Not your mother?"

He breaks our gaze and looks at the floor. "I believe she wants a different kind of relationship with me."

I slide my hand from his cheek to under his chin and nudge his head upward to meet my gaze once more. "She adores you, Dale."

"I know that. And I adore her. But... she always wanted us to be closer."

"Then be closer with her. You have that power."

He shakes his head. "Actually, I don't."

My body is still prickling with desire for him, but I don't want this conversation to end. I'm willing to forego the sex I yearn for if it means Dale will open up to me, which he seems on the verge of doing.

"You do," I say. "You have the ultimate power over who you choose to be."

He scoffs. "I've heard all that before, Ashley, and it's not true."

"Of course it is."

He sighs and brushes my hand from his face. "You're so young. So innocent."

I stop myself from guffawing. Young, sure. I'll take it. Innocent? Not in this lifetime. You don't grow up homeless and retain innocence for long. And sexually? I'm no innocent there, either.

I'm not sure what to say to his comment, so I simply smile.

"My mother and I... I don't know why it's the way it is. We've both gotten used to it over the years. I've talked at length to—"

I trail a finger over his forearm. "Why did you stop so abruptly?"

"I don't talk about this. To anyone."

"You just said you've talked at length—"

"Shut up!" He rakes his fingers through his mane of honey hair. "Just shut the fuck up, Ashley."

"But you—"

He slams his lips down on mine. My lips are parted, and he dives in unapologetically.

Gone is questioning Dale.

Now he's punishing Dale once more. This kiss is raw and angry. Oh, it's full of desire and passion as well, but at its core, I feel rage. Red rage. Not the silky dark red of Dale's low voice.

This is bright red. Raging red.

He's angry. At me? At himself? At the world?

My guess is all three.

I care. I care so much, but the thought is fleeting as I melt into the kiss. Yes, it's hard. Yes, it's angry.

But it's also firm and drugging and perfect in the most precious way.

Though I'm not angry, I press into the kiss, giving as good as I get. Our tongues tangle and duel. Our lips slide together. Our teeth clash.

The red rage merges with the burgundy that surrounds Dale always. What results is a clash of color so vibrant that it takes over my senses. Takes over my libido.

It forces me to take the lead, and I break free from the passion to inhale a desperate breath.

"Bed," I say breathlessly.

He pushes me down onto his mattress. "Take off your fucking clothes."

One day, I hope Dale will undress me seductively. Make love to me slowly.

Tonight is not that night.

Though I want to go slowly, make him wait to discover each additional inch of my flesh, I can't. I grope at the garments binding me, releasing myself from them as quickly as I can, until I sit naked atop his bed, his green comforter cool against my bottom.

But not for long. The fabric heats from my body, and soon I'm sitting on lava.

Dale lowers his eyelids slightly, and a growl vibrates from him.

I open my mouth to demand he undress as well, but then shut it quickly. I want him to stare at me, to rake his gaze over every square centimeter of me. All that I have is his, and I want him to see it.

See all of me.

If I could open my chest and let him look into my heart, my soul, I would.

I lay myself bare to Dale Steel.

I'm his. His and his alone.

But he chooses not to take the time I wish him to. Instead, he spreads my legs, eyes my pussy with hunger in his green eyes, and then he unzips his pants and frees his cock.

Before I can give it the adoration it deserves, it's inside me, and Dale is pumping.

Hard. So hard.

I'm wet, so he slid in with ease, but my nipples ache for his attention. My clit yearns for his mouth.

He's still clothed, his shirt abrading my nipples with delicious friction. His pubic hair does the same for my clit, and

I'm nearing a climax way before I want to.

I can't hold back, though. Not with Dale. He invades all my senses, and an orgasm rises almost of its own accord.

Colors drape over me, and music swells in the background. The spicy taste of our kiss lingers on my lips, and his green eyes bore into mine.

Is it the joyous green caroling?

The burgundy silk of his low growls?

The red rage of his body driving into mine?

Everything. It's a psychedelic kaleidoscope. A rainbow of passion.

He thrusts and he thrusts, harder each time, his dark-red groans the torrent melody around me.

I love you. Dale, I love you so much.

Will I ever be able to share with him my true feelings?

Those feelings that grow stronger every moment?

The thought of being without him is more than I can bear. I close my eyes as the peak draws nearer.

One more thrust against my clit—

I erupt. Words leave my mouth and hang in the swirl of color around us. I can't tell you what the words are. They're jumbled phrases of lust and passion. Of want and need.

And I take a giant leap into paradise.

CHAPTER TWENTY-SIX

Dale

Yes! I'm coming, Dale. So good! Fuck me. Fuck me harder!

Her words ignite a hotter fire in my loins. I'm harder than ever, and I plunge into her faster and faster, letting her feed the emptiness in my soul.

She fills me. With her beauty, her laughter, her brilliance.

Everything about Ashley White propels me further into orgasmic bliss.

I've never felt like this before. I fear I never will again.

I hold back, making it last as long as I can. Don't want it to end. Never want it to end.

But her orgasm milks my cock. Squeezes against me like a fist encased in a fur-lined glove. She's a perfect cast for me.

And though I long to hold on . . . To make it last forever . . .

I thrust.

Once more.

Then give her everything. Everything inside me. So much more than my seed. I give her my heart, my soul, my deepest darkest desires.

And I know I'll never be the same.

When I finally turn onto my side, I'm still hard despite my soul-burning climax. My jeans are like a rubber band around my thighs, and I struggle out of them. I need freedom. Freedom from my clothes so I can touch all of Ashley with all of me.

Once I remove my boots, socks, and jeans, I tackle my shirt, nearly shredding it to get it off my back.

Then I lie next to her.

Her eyes are closed, and she looks like an angel. Blond hair in disarray on the comforter, almost like a halo. Her cheeks are pink and her lips red. And her body—flushed all over as if painted with the petals of a red rose.

I touch her warm hand, and she entwines her fingers with mine.

I don't even know how to hold your hand.

It's easier now. Her hand, so small next to my own. I massage her thumb with mine.

If I can learn to hold her hand, can I learn to do the rest of the stuff she wants? The rest of the stuff she deserves?

Because she deserves everything.

And I want it. I want it more than anything.

Dare I hope?

Dare I risk everything?

She turns then and snuggles her warm body next to mine. "Mmmm," comes from her throat.

Something foreign cascades over me. It's more than love, or it's a love I've never felt before.

Everything I feel for Ashley is brand-new to me, but this . . .

This is something so pure . . . That thing I can't describe . . .

It wants to fill the emptiness inside me. It wants to bring the darkness into the light.

But I resist.

How can I not? I don't know how to be the man she wants me to be.

I don't think I'll ever know.

But as she snuggles against me, and as I grow harder once again, I vow to try.

I brought her home wanting to make real love to her, and I ended up fucking her. I let my rage take over, and I ended up taking her hard and fast.

When a soft snore escapes the back of her throat, I smile without meaning to. She worked hard in the vineyards today, and then she had a dinner date—damn Brendan Murphy—and then a game of pool. It's late. No wonder she's asleep.

Maybe in the morning.

Maybe I'll make love to her then.

★ ★ ★

But I don't.

I end up in the vineyards.

I leave Penny at home with Ashley. I don't want Ashley to wake up alone.

She sleeps soundly as I untangle myself from her body and quietly dress.

Now I'm in my special place, where I do my best thinking.

I lie, encased in my sleeping bag, not inside a tent but under the starlight. I memorized all the constellations decades ago, and now I see them in pictures. Images of what they're meant to represent. Tonight, Cassiopeia stands out. The beautiful self-absorbed queen, who nearly sacrificed her own daughter to Poseidon's sea monster and then fought with Hera, only to be banished to the sky.

Her husband, Cepheus, then begged Zeus to let him go with her, and now they both live in the sky, eternally bound.

A self-absorbed queen and her whiny king.

Two very damaged souls who are now happy in the starlight.

Myth, of course, but what are myths but stories to teach valuable insight?

If those two souls can find true happiness, can't anyone?

Do I, as Ashley suggested, have the power over my own happiness?

Aunt Mel and other therapists have said the same words over the years. I've always brushed it off. I'm content, and I can live with contentment. True happiness always eludes me, and I recognize my own part in that elusion. My fear of letting the good out because of what will ultimately come barreling with it.

It's already here, and the day will come when I can no longer contain it.

It was the rage that kept me from making love to Ashley the way I wanted to. And it's the rage that will ultimately take her away from me.

Which is why she must leave now. Of her own accord, before I ruin her. Before I do something she'll never recover from.

I can't live with that, and neither can she.

I sigh. She'll be angry when she wakes up alone in my bed, and rightly so. I didn't leave any bills on the nightstand this time. Her car is in my driveway, so there was no need.

No way will she give me another chance after this, and though I want to be with her more than anything, to leave her is the most selfless thing I can do.

It's for her. Her happiness is more important to me than my own.

I'll do anything to make her happy.

Anything.

CHAPTER TWENTY-SEVEN

Ashley

I wake up tousled in Dale's comforter. I reach for him . . . and find only an empty bed. Penny sits beside the bed, her tongue hanging out.

I pet her soft head. "Morning, girl. Where's your daddy?"

I rise and pad to the bathroom. Afterward, I walk out, still naked, and put on the shirt Dale was wearing last night. I want to feel the soft cotton and wrap myself in his scent.

But it's not on the floor where he left it.

Okay. Maybe he's just anal about his laundry or something . . .

Except he's not. He's not into tidiness or his bed would have been made.

So maybe he just put the shirt back on. After all, his jeans are gone as well. He went out to the kitchen to start some coffee . . .

But his boots . . . They're also gone.

A lump rises in my throat, and I instinctively look toward the night table. Nothing except a box of tissues and an old-fashioned clock radio. It's six a.m. Dale's an early riser, but this is ridiculous.

He's gone.

He left me again. Alone. Alone in his fucking house. Alone with his dog.

She's probably hungry. "Come on, Penny," I say, leaving the bedroom and heading toward the kitchen. "Let's get you some breakfast."

Take care of the dog. That's what I'll do. It'll keep my mind where it needs to be. Keep the tears at bay that are already threatening to pool in the bottom of my eyes. I check the pantry for a bag of kibble or something, but he must be out. Now what? I open the refrigerator. A plastic container sits on the top shelf. It's marked Penny.

Dale makes his own dog food?

Warmth and love threaten to flow into me, but I stop them. He's crossed the line this time, leaving me alone in his own home. I grab the container and pour two cups of its contents into Penny's stainless-steel bowl. While she gobbles down her food, I refresh her water.

Once she's done, I open the back door to let her out, but I go out with her to check the gate. I'm not going through that again.

She does her business, and I bring her back inside. Then I dress quickly and head back to the main house.

I enter quietly, hoping no one will notice me, until—

"Is that you, Ashley?"

Jade's voice. My cheeks are hot as hell, and I know I must be about twelve shades of crimson. But I can't ignore her. "It's me." I walk into the kitchen.

"Grab some coffee." She smiles, gesturing to the pot on the counter. "Oops. Sorry. I mean orange juice. Darla's off today."

All I really want to do is go to my room and cry my eyes out, but I can't be rude to Jade. None of this is her fault. I paste on a smile as best I can, grab the juice out of the refrigerator, and pour myself a glass.

"Where's Talon?" I ask.

"Already in the orchard. Harvest is a busy time around here, as you know."

I nod and sit down next to her.

"Can I make you some breakfast?"

God, no. If I eat I may puke. "No, thank you," I reply.

She doesn't drop her gaze from mine, but she says nothing more. Is she waiting for me to explain why I'm coming in at six a.m.? She'll be waiting a long time.

Finally Jade speaks. "Talon says he had a nice conversation with you last night at Murphy's."

I nod. "Yeah. Your husband's a good man."

"He is that." She sips her coffee. "Listen, Ashley—"

I gesture her to say nothing more. "I can't. I can't . . . talk about it."

"About Talon? I was just going to say you don't have to be embarrassed about this morning. You're an adult, and we understand that."

"I . . . uh . . . " Shit. Now what? "Thank you."

"Talon goes a little bit crazy when Diana or Bree stay out late, but I've convinced him they're adults now. It's hard for a father of girls."

I nod again. "I'm not his daughter."

"No, but he feels responsible for you while you're here."

"That's sweet of him."

"That's just who he is. He's a protector."

"Dee told me how he saved all those people in Iraq."

"He did," she says. "He didn't get the recognition he deserved."

"Why?"

She smiles. "He didn't want it."

He didn't? There must be a story there, but Brendan's words edge into my mind. The Steels seem to have a lot of secrets. Have they truly covered stuff up? And if so, why?

I'm curious, but not that curious. Right now, I feel mostly empty. I have no desire to look into the Steels' history. And I certainly have no desire to go to work, where I'll see Dale.

But I don't have a choice. I've committed to this internship for three months, and I'll honor my commitment. But damn, I'm not even a month in.

I quickly drink the rest of my juice and stand. "I need to get ready for work."

Jade sets down her coffee cup. "Please, Ashley. Sit down."

Oh, God. I don't know what's coming, but I know it'll be uncomfortable. I sit.

"Do you want to talk?"

I shake my head. Already the tears are threatening once more, and if I speak, I'm afraid I won't be able to contain them.

"All right. Just listen, then."

I nod.

"Talon and I talked briefly this morning, and we agree there's something you should know."

I raise my eyebrows. "Oh?"

"Yeah. Dale won't tell you, and I don't want you to mention this to him, but his father—his birth father—recently reached out to him."

My heart drops. Not just because of what Dale must be going through, but because of what my mother recently told me about my own father a few days before Dee and I left for Colorado—information I buried inside because I couldn't deal with it. I filed it in the Scarlett O'Hara file. Things to think about tomorrow.

"Really? I thought . . . "

"I know. Dale never knew him. Didn't even know his name. He just appeared out of nowhere."

"Why?"

"We don't know, really. The first thought that entered all our minds is that he wants money, but he hasn't asked for any. Still, though, we aren't sure his motives are pure."

"I see. I understand."

"Anyway, Dale took a DNA test, and the man is definitely his father."

"And Donny's?"

She nods. "Yeah. We had a DNA test done on the boys after the adoption. They are full-blooded siblings."

"Wow. I had no idea."

"Dale isn't ever real forthcoming with people, but Talon and I wanted you to know, in case you've noticed that Dale is more"—she twists her lips—"distant than usual."

Distant? Try downright apathetic. Aloof. Eremitic, even. Leaving me alone in his home after we made love was one for the books. My guess is he wound up in the vineyards. Alone. Secluded. Because he couldn't stand sleeping with me. Thank goodness I was there to take care of the dog.

"He hasn't opened up a lot about his father," Jade continues, "but that's Dale's way."

No kidding.

"But a mother knows," she says. "He's not himself."

"He seems about the same to me," I can't help replying.

"I suppose he would. He hasn't been welcoming to you, and I'm very sorry about that."

"I'm fine," I say, lying through my teeth.

"You're not fine. You and I both know how you feel about him."

"You haven't told..."

"Talon." She shakes her head and smiles. "No. I haven't. Some things are better left between girlfriends."

"Thank you."

"What you say stays between us," she replies, "and I expect the same."

"Of course. Absolutely." After all, she didn't rat me out for basically breaking into Dale's home and nearly losing his dog.

"Then listen to me when I say that my son needs you, Ashley. Perhaps more than he knows."

"That's kind of you to say, and no doubt you know Dale better than I do, but his actions say otherwise."

She leans forward and pats my hand with her own. "His actions *always* say otherwise."

"Then how...?"

She smiles—kind of a sad smile. "I've told you before. A mother knows."

CHAPTER TWENTY-EIGHT

Dale

I make it into the office by eight, after showering at home and feeding Penny. She picked at her full bowl. Ashley must have fed her.

She was gone when I got home.

Not that I expected her to be there.

She's not in the office, either, and I *did* expect her to be there. Maybe she went home and went back to bed.

That doesn't sound like Ashley, though. I get up and walk down the hall to Uncle Ryan's office. I peek inside the open door. "Hey."

"Hey, yourself," he says.

"You seen Ashley this morning?"

He nods. "She came in and said she'd prefer to work in the vineyards today, so I sent her off."

I inhale. "Okay. That's surprising."

"Did you have something else in mind for her today?"

"Well . . . we've got the lunch and tasting today. I've been working with her on the wines."

"Hmm, she didn't mention that. I can send someone out to the vineyards to tell her to come back."

"No, it's okay. I can handle things."

"I wasn't planning to be at the tasting today," he says, "but if you need a hand, let me know."

"Will do."

Anger creeps along my spine. But is it anger? I mean, what did I expect after I left her alone at my place last night?

This isn't like Ashley, though. She wouldn't walk out on a tasting. Would she?

Perhaps she just forgot.

In which case, it's my job, as her boss, to remind her of her obligation.

I head out to the parking lot and get into my truck. To the vineyards I drive. Most of our harvesters are working on the southern vines today. The Merlot and Cabernet Franc. I pull into a spot and walk toward the workers.

"Hey, George," I say to the foreman.

"Hey, Dale. What can I do for you?"

"I'm looking for my intern. Ashley. She was working out here yesterday."

"Yeah, yeah. She does good work for a beginner."

"Glad to hear that." Of course I expect nothing less from Ashley. "I'll just go find her."

"Wait. She's not here today."

I lift my eyebrows. "She's not? Ryan said she was working the harvest."

"Not here," George says. "She never checked in with me."

"That's puzzling."

Except it's not, really. Already I know where I'll find her.

"Thanks, George," I say. "See you around."

"You too. Have a good day."

I walk back to my truck and drive to the northern vineyards, specifically to the area where I can access the Syrah. Autopilot. I'm pretty sure my truck could find its way here by itself, I come here so often.

I left here only a couple of hours earlier.

I pull into the gravel parking area and stop abruptly, skidding a little.

Yeah, I'm angry, but I have no reason to be. Ashley has reason to be angry. I do not.

I walk into the vineyards, my feet instinctively taking me to my own special place.

And there she stands.

Ashley.

My Ashley.

Not my Ashley.

She doesn't turn toward me, but in her sweet voice, she says, "I figured you'd come."

I don't respond.

Still not looking at me, she continues, "It's beautiful. Paradise, even. I understand why you're drawn here."

"You don't," I say.

"Oh, I do." She finally turns and meets my gaze. "Do you think you're the only person in the world who's had it rough?"

I stiffen. Ashley knows nothing of my first ten years on this earth, and I'm not about to clue her in. "I never said I had it rough."

She shakes her head, chuckling softly. "Dale, a person doesn't become such a recluse without having a tough time."

"Tough time, huh? You've talked on more than one occasion about my privilege."

"Have I?" She chuckles again. "I suppose I can't help myself. I've had to scrape my fingernails to the bone for everything I have in life, so I guess I'm a little envious of those born to privilege."

I clear my throat. "As you know, I wasn't born to it."

"True." She turns from me and stares at the vines heavy with fruit. "When do we start harvesting the Syrah?"

"Soon."

She turns back to me, her blue eyes stricken with something I can't identify. "That must bother you."

It does, but how would she know?

"I mean," she continues, "this is your special place. And for weeks you'll have strangers in here, defacing your vines."

"The fruit needs to be harvested. Especially this year. This vintage will be our first old-vine Syrah."

"Still," she says, "it bothers you."

I can't deny her words. I don't even try. Though harvest is my favorite season, when the workers descend into the Syrah vineyard, it's tough for me. My sanctuary is invaded, and I have nowhere to go to find the solace I crave. But I make do. I head into the mountains, usually, each weekend, and camp alone, building a fire to keep warm and relaxing in the fresh open air.

But Sunday evening I return, because it's harvest time, and I'm needed here.

Ashley looks to the east, toward the majestic Rockies. "You can find peace here, Dale, but is that all you need?"

Peace? I've never found peace, though the vineyards are the closest I've ever come.

She goes on, "Are you happy alone?"

"Alone? Have you forgotten what a huge family I have?"

Her soft chuckle echoes once more. "I didn't say lonely. But you can have hordes of people around you and still be alone. You don't let anyone in."

"That's not true," I counter. "And this isn't your business anyway."

"Isn't it?" She turns away from the view of the mountains and meets my gaze again. "I believe I've opened myself up to you more than I have to any other person in my life."

I open my mouth to respond, but she gestures me not to. Just as well, as I'm not sure what to say anyway.

"I don't say that lightly," she continues. "I'm not like you. I'm close to my mother, and I'm close to my friends. I've opened up before, but not like this."

I inhale slowly, my flesh ever aware of her body close to mine. Fog enters my mind. But not gray fog. It's more like the steam rising from a lake after the first snowfall. Freakish in its beauty.

"I suppose I shouldn't be surprised that you're not answering," she says.

"You didn't actually ask a question."

Again, the soft chuckle. "You're right. I didn't. So I will now." She looks back toward the mountains. "Is this better? Better than making love with me?"

A brick hits my gut. A loaded question if there ever was one, and I know the answer. But I can't share it with her.

"Ashley—"

"No," she interrupts me. "I don't think I want to hear the answer."

"Then why did you ask the question?"

"Beats the hell out of me." She shakes her head. "You were here this morning, weren't you?"

I don't respond. Not even a nod.

"I'll take that as a yes. I have no idea what time you left your place. I was sound asleep. It was the best night's sleep I've had in a long time, Dale, and it was because I was happy. Really happy. But you weren't, were you?"

I *was*. I was ecstatic. Which terrifies me. Again I don't respond.

She sighs. "So I came here. I came here to take in the beauty of this place. The magnificence. Because it *is* magnificent. No doubt. But more than that, I wanted to see what *you* see when you look at these vines. I wanted to find out if they offer something that I don't. Something more joyful and profound than the lovemaking we've shared." She pauses a few seconds, inhaling and exhaling several times. She closes her eyes and then opens them. "My senses are more acute than most, as you know. My sounds have colors, and my colors have sounds. I can sometimes taste music, and once I actually felt a certain song caressing my body as if it had phantom fingers that reached out from the notes. I've got all my senses on high alert, Dale. Every one of them—by themselves and intermingled. And you know what? It's amazing here. It's tantalizing and awe-inspiring. But it's nothing compared to making love with you."

CHAPTER TWENTY-NINE

Ashley

There.

I did it.

I made the ultimate confession to him.

Well, maybe not the ultimate. That would be those three little words that I feel so profoundly but know Dale will never return.

Already I know he won't answer. Or if he does, it will be something douchey.

I stare again at the vines, at the gorgeous clusters of black grapes nearly ready to drop to the ground. I reach out and hold a cluster of fruit in my palm. It's warm to my touch on this sunny day.

Dale inhales. Yeah, he just held back a gasp. Does he think I'd actually harm his precious Syrah? He doesn't know me at all.

"Let go," he finally says.

"Of the grapes?"

"Yes."

"Fuck off, Dale. If you think I'd hurt these grapes, these vines—"

"No," he says. "Let go, so I can kiss you."

I drop my jaw open and move my hand back to my side.

"Are you kidding me? After you left me alone at your house? You think you can—"

His lips come down on mine. Hard.

Hard and feral and perfectly beautiful.

I open. How can I not? I just confessed to him that making love with him was better than the peaceful beauty of these vineyards.

I wasn't lying.

He probes me with his tongue, and I respond, melting into him. It's a primal kiss, a kiss born solely of nature, and it's fitting that we're surrounded by nature's own beauty.

Yes, he left me again.

But God, I love this man. His kisses, his arms around me, his hands caressing my shoulders, my neck, my cheeks. I love all of that. But mostly I love *him*. His good heart and his tortured soul.

Why can't he be with me? Why can't he get past whatever boundary he's built within himself?

I may never know the answer.

Still, I've promised myself that I'll take what he's willing to give, and at the moment, that's a passionate kiss. I urge him on with my own desire. My body responded to his presence the second he arrived, and now I'm as ripe as the grapes I was holding mere moments ago. My legs weaken, but Dale's strong and muscular body steadies me.

I never want this kiss to end, but like all good things, it does.

But I don't end it.

He does. He breaks away from me and gasps in a breath.

I stare at his face. His beautifully masculine face with his structured jawline and high cheekbones. His clear green eyes that are heavy-lidded and smoldering. And that mouth, those full lips that are even fuller from the kiss.

Last night, I asked him to make love to me here. Among these vines.

I now realize that can never happen.

To Dale, these vines are sacred, and making love here would taint them in some way.

To me? It would make them all the more sacred. But that's because I'm in love with Dale. He won't feel that way because he's not in love with me. Does he even understand love? I've never been in love before, but I understand what I'm feeling. How can you mistake the feeling of passion and wonder and all-encompassing desire and yearning?

"Dale?"

"Yeah?"

I swallow, gaining courage. "Have you ever been in love?"

He widens his eyes. No longer are they heavy-lidded, but still they smolder. Nothing for a moment. A moment that seems like a decade. He's not going to answer. Can I blame him? It's a very personal question.

"Only once," he finally says.

This time *I* widen my eyes. Definitely not the answer I was expecting. Dale Steel has been in love? When? And with whom? But I don't ask. He won't tell me, and part of me doesn't want to know, anyway.

"Same here," I say.

With you. How I long to say the words. But I can't. He won't return them, and that will be too painful to bear.

He clears his throat. "Ashley, the tasting . . . "

I whip my hand to my mouth. How could I have forgotten? "I'm so sorry! What time is it?"

"It's ten thirty."

"Oh, good. We have time. I can't believe I forgot. I'm not usually like this."

"It's okay."

"It's not, though." Sure, he left me alone in his house after we made love, but it's no excuse to slack off on my work. We talked about this tasting all yesterday.

"Come on," he says gruffly. "I'll drive you back."

I nod and walk next to him as we leave the vineyard. He opens the passenger door of his truck, and I climb in.

To the tasting.

I'll kill it like I did the last one.

I won't let myself think about the woman Dale Steel was once in love with.

★ ★ ★

I enjoy the lunch part of the tasting immensely. The tasters are all good-natured and ask a lot of questions, and not a one is young enough to drool over Dale like last time. All are middle-aged couples and a few are in their golden years. All lovely people.

Older couples probably also have more money to spend on wine. It should be a good tasting businesswise.

That part doesn't matter to me, but Dale will be pleased.

Dale pastes on his "tasting face" and responds to the customers as well. The smile—the smile I long to see more often—plays on his lips as though it's more natural than I know it to be.

The tasting proceeds without consequence, and as I predicted, we sell a lot of wine, mostly Dale's table blend, which pleases him.

"You can go on home," he says to me afterward. "It's been a long day."

"I'm fine."

"Please, Ashley. Go. I've got this."

He looks away from me, seeming to focus on the order forms while employees shuffle cases of wine to the tasters' cars in the lot.

Does our time together truly mean so little to him? He wants me. That much is obvious. But he doesn't seem to have any genuine need for me, and he certainly doesn't love me. Relationships have been built on less.

I bring as much courage as I can to the surface and meet his gaze. "Dale, are we going to even try?"

"Try what?" He continues scanning the papers in front of him.

"To . . . " I swallow. "To be together?"

He looks up. "Ashley . . . you don't want to be with me."

I lift my eyebrows. "What?"

"You heard me." He drops his gaze back to the matter in front of him.

Yeah, I heard him, but I didn't expect those words. I expected something snide or douchey or, more likely, no answer at all.

You don't want to be with me.

He's so wrong.

"Isn't that my choice to make?" I reply.

He scoffs. "Last I heard, I have a choice in the matter as well. You're not the only one in this relationship."

A tiny sliver of hope dances in my heart. Relationship. He used the word *relationship*. Of course, he could simply be talking about our working relationship. He probably is. But maybe not. Maybe, in *his* eyes, we have something more.

"Dale, please look at me."

He inhales and lifts his gaze from the paperwork. "I've got to get this done."

"No, you don't. Have you forgotten I've done a tasting with you before? You didn't touch the paperwork after that one."

"Maybe the employee who usually does it is out today."

"I'm not buying."

He sighs, which turns into a soft growl. Such a light touch of his voice, and already I'm enrobed in the gorgeous color of Syrah.

"Ashley, I don't know how I can make this any clearer. We can't be together. We can *never* be together."

Though his words aren't unexpected, an arrow pokes my heart anyway and tears threaten to pool in my eyes. I sniff them back. "Tell me why," I demand. "Tell me why and I'll never bring it up again."

"Because," he says, "you deserve better."

CHAPTER THIRTY

Dale

I don't expect my response to stop her incessant questioning. If that's what I wanted, I could have said something else.

I don't love you and I never will.

We're too different.

I find you repulsive.

All of which are complete lies.

What I said, though? That's the truth. She *does* deserve better.

She's silent for a few minutes, and I can't read her expression. Total poker face.

Finally, she says, "What if I think you're the best? That there's no one better than you?"

I scoff softly. "Then you're deluding yourself."

"Bull. You're brilliant. You're a hard worker. An ethical worker. Already I've learned as much from you as I have from my best professors. Your love for your work is unequaled. You're amazing, Dale. If you let me in, I'll show you how amazing you are."

I inhale slowly. "Ashley, you've got to let this go."

But she won't. I already know this, because I already know her. This woman goes after what she wants, and right now her goal seems to be me.

"Why should I let it go?"

"Because you said if I told you why we couldn't be together, you'd never bring it up again."

Gotcha.

But it won't matter.

"I don't accept your response. I want to know why you think we can't be together. Your answer has nothing to do with you and everything to do with me. You've decided, according to some ridiculous rules inside your head, that I deserve better. I reject that. No one knows better than I do what I deserve."

"You deserve the best," I say.

"And I think he's sitting in front of me."

I rake my fingers through my mass of hair. "Fuck it all, Ashley. Why can't you just let this go?" I stand and push the papers on the table aside. A few of them float to the floor.

"Because you're the best," she says, her lips trembling a touch.

God, those lips. I would give my fortune for one taste of those lips alone. What is the matter with me? How did I let this happen?

"I'm so far from the best," I say, advancing toward her. "I'm a mess on the inside. Not a mess. A disaster. A fucking disaster."

"Let me in," she says bravely. "Let me in and I'll help you."

"You can't! Why won't you just listen to me?"

She stands and faces me, her blue eyes burning like a thousand suns. "Because I love you, damn it. I *love* you!"

My legs weaken, and I grab the edge of the table for support. Those words. Those fucking words. My heart is full yet empty. Full because I love her so much. Empty because I know I can't return her love the way she deserves.

I want to. I want to more than anything.

I learned long ago, though, that wanting something is never enough.

I slump into a chair.

She sits next to me and takes my hand in her own. "You don't have to say it back. Maybe you don't feel it. Maybe you do. It doesn't even matter in the long run. I didn't mean to blurt it out like that, but now that my feelings are out in the open, I'm not sorry they are." She caresses my palm with her thumb. "I've got a little over two months left here. I'll work hard for you. I'll be the best intern you've ever had or ever will have. I promise you. But I also want to spend time with you. For the time I have left. Then I'll leave, and if it's what you want, you'll never hear from me again."

God, that's so far from what I want. But the idea has merit. We can be together. Spend time with each other. And it's all transitory. I can hold back because I know it's not permanent. Maybe, just maybe, I can let those amazing emotions flow and still hold back the abhorrent ones. After all, it's not forever. It's for two months. She'll be gone by Thanksgiving.

I look into her sparkling blue eyes. They're full of wonder and hope. She's so full of life! I want to sink inside her skin, to *be* her. To feel what she feels, love the way she loves. Because that's what this wonderful woman deserves.

"Please, Dale." She trails a finger over my jawline. "I want to know you."

Know is a scary word. She already knows me in the biblical sense, and that's not what she means, anyway. She wants to get inside me, figure me out. Love me.

As much as that appeals to me, I can't let it happen. For her sake as well as for mine. More for hers, because when I consider her well-being, it trumps my own. Big time.

But maybe… Only a little over two months…

Maybe I can let myself be happy. Happy enough that I can hold the other shit back.

Then once she's gone…

I'll explode.

But only *I* will have to deal with that. Ashley will be back in California and won't bear witness to who I truly am.

I don't know if I have the strength to pull this off, but I can't turn down what she's offering. I don't have the inner fortitude.

I love her. And I want her.

So I'll take her.

For two months, I'll take her. I'll cherish her.

I just hope I have the strength to let her leave when I'm done.

I stand and pull her up. I cup her cheek and gaze into those amazing eyes. "All right, Ashley. Until your internship is over. But no longer."

A smile splits her gorgeous face. "It won't interfere with my work. I swear to you."

"I know," I say. "And one more thing."

She lifts her eyebrows.

"No more Brock. And no more Brendan Murphy. If you want to be with me, you have to be *only* with me."

"I didn't sleep with either of them."

A wave of relief sweeps over me. Not that I thought she did, but I'm happy to know for sure. "I'm glad."

"Dale…"

"What?"

"I do love you."

How I yearn to return her vow. My lips part, and the words lodge in my throat.

I love you too, Ashley. I love you more than I ever thought I was capable of loving another person. I ache for you. Adore you. Would gladly stop a bullet for you.

But the confession stays locked inside me.

Instead of answering with words, I lower my head and press my lips to hers.

My body responds instantly, and I want to take her with a kiss so powerful she'll never recover.

I hold back, though. If we're going to do this for two months, I have time. I have time to explore her slowly, the way I've longed to. Slowly and sweetly. I pull back and meet her gaze.

"Tonight," I say. "My place. We'll have dinner."

"And you won't leave me again during the night?"

"No." I trail my finger over her plump lower lip. "I won't."

I mean the words. I mean them with all my heart.

I just hope the darkness in my soul doesn't force me to make them a lie.

CHAPTER THIRTY-ONE

Ashley

After a shower and a change of clothes, I arrive at Dale's place at six thirty on the nose. He opens the door, and the spicy scent of tomatoes and basil wafts toward me from the kitchen.

"You're cooking?"

"Did you think dinner would make itself?"

"No, I . . . You told me you got your start with wine by cooking. I'm not sure why I'm surprised."

"I still love to cook," he says. "I just don't have a lot of time for it. Plus, when it's just me, it seems a waste to go to all the trouble."

I nod. "I'm honored you're going to the trouble for me."

"It's not trouble."

"You just said—"

"I know what I just said." He sighs. "I never say the right thing, Ashley. If you want to be with me, you should probably just expect that."

His tone is so . . . resigned. Am I forcing him into this? He should sound happy, not resigned. Even the color of his voice is different. It's more of a Pinot Noir instead of the dark burgundy of Syrah.

This isn't the Dale I want. I want the passionate Dale. The angry Dale. The Dale I fell in love with.

He's in there—hiding inside that beautiful body. I'll just have to coax him out.

"Can I help?" I ask.

"Can you toss a salad?"

I chuckle. "I think I've done it once or twice."

He nods to the bowl of greens on the counter. "Have at it. Homemade vinaigrette is in the fridge."

I whisk past Dale, our bodies touching slightly, and a wave of desire pokes at me. Dinner, first. Dinner and conversation. Maybe I'll get to know him a little better.

Then later...

I'm so ready, I'm about to burst into bloom.

The cool air from the refrigerator does little to take the edge off my aching loins. I grab the bottle of vinaigrette and get back to the task at hand.

"How much dressing do you like?" I ask. "Light, medium, or heavy?"

"However you like it is fine."

"I prefer medium." I pour on some of the vinaigrette and toss the salad. "Smells great. What are we having?"

"Linguine frutti di mare," he says. "I thought you might be missing seafood."

And oh my God, I love him even more.

"I hope you don't mind seafood with a red sauce," he says.

"Not at all."

"Sometimes I make it with a garlic and white wine sauce, but I prefer my basil marinara."

I inhale. "It smells amazing."

"The secret is the tiniest pinch of caraway along with basil, thyme, and garlic."

"No oregano?"

"Not in this version. Oregano is too harsh. It overwhelms the seafood." He pauses a moment. "Did I just divulge my secret ingredient to you?"

I chuckle. "The caraway?"

"Shit." He shakes his head. "I'm not sure I've even let Aunt Marj in on that secret."

"How did you discover it?"

"What the hell?" he says. "In for a penny, in for a pound. Aunt Marj uses a pinch of anise in one of her red sauces, which I like, but I always felt it was just a bit too much. I did some research and tried caraway, and it gives it the same tang, only without the touch of licorice."

"Interesting."

"Do you cook?"

"A little. I'm pretty good with most seafood. I've perfected cooking cod without drying it out."

"That's a tough one. As you can imagine, I don't cook a lot of fish. So maybe you'll prepare your cod for me sometime."

Happiness explodes inside me. He means it. He really means it. We're going to try this for the rest of my internship.

And maybe . . . just maybe . . . he'll want to keep going.

But I can't push. Jade's warning is forever engraved in my mind. If I push him too hard, he may shrink back from me forever.

"I'd love to cook for you sometime," I say. "But I don't have a kitchen at my disposal."

"You'll cook here, of course." He stirs the sauce.

I smile. "All right. That will be fun. Though I'm wondering if I can get fresh cod here in Snow Creek."

"Hmm," he says. "Probably not. So we'll go to Aspen. Fresh fish is flown in daily."

"Aspen?"

"Yeah, you've heard of it, right?"

"Of course. But it's so—" I stop myself. Affluent was the word that came to mind. Aspen, where all the Hollywood celebs go when they want to get out of LA. So of course they go to mini LA in the Rockies.

"So what?"

"Nothing. I was thinking it's expensive."

"Ah... My privilege again. The Steel family has several properties in Aspen, each with a full kitchen. I thought you could cook for me there. Unless it's too privileged for you."

"No," I say.

"You don't want to go to Aspen?"

"No, that's not what I mean. I mean, no, it's not too privileged for me." I shake my head. "This isn't going the way I want it to at all."

"Face it, Ashley. We come from two different worlds. I don't think that's a problem, but you seem to."

I shake my head again. "I don't. I don't at all. But Dale, this is so different from what I'm used to. I'm sorry. I'm so sorry. I love that you want to share your place in Aspen with me. I love that you want me to cook for you. I just... This is all so new to me, and I guess I'm having a hard time processing it."

To my utter surprise, he turns away from his cooktop and touches my arm. Sparks shoot through me.

"It's okay," he says. "I understand."

CHAPTER THIRTY-TWO

Dale

Even *I'm* surprised at my reaction.

But I do understand.

I was only ten when I came to the ranch, and it was difficult to comprehend its magnitude at first. Difficult to comprehend just how rich my new family was.

"Thank you," she says softly.

"I said I'd try this, Ashley. I'm bound to stumble a few times. More than a few times, to be honest. I've never ... "

"Never what?"

"Done this before."

She wrinkles her forehead. "But you said you were in love once."

I frown and look back at my sauce. Yes, I said that. I was talking about *her*.

She presses, "If you were in love, didn't you have a relationship? Go on dates? All that stuff?"

I clear my throat. "Maybe my love was unrequited."

She huffs. "I can't believe that."

I turn the heat down to low on the sauce and go to the refrigerator. "You were right. Fresh seafood isn't readily available in this small town, but I managed to find some frozen sea scallops and large prawns. That will be our frutti di mare."

"Sounds delicious. Most frutti di mare includes squid, which I personally find kind of rubbery. But Dale . . . "

I turn to face her. "I said I'd try this, okay? I want to. But you can't pepper me with questions all the time. Yes, I've been in love once. That's all I'm going to say for the moment."

She nods, her lips trembling slightly.

I expect her to fight me. To continue her interrogation.

But she stays quiet for a few minutes. I sauté the scallops and prawns in olive oil and garlic until they're cooked through— only about ten minutes. Overcooking will ruin them and make them rubbery, which Ashley apparently doesn't like. I actually agree with her on the squid, though I like the flavor.

I turn to the next burner to check on the linguine. It's perfectly al dente, so I turn down the heat and then pour it through the colander sitting in the sink.

I plate the linguine quickly, topping each with a generous portion of the sautéed scallops and prawns and then a half cup of marinara. I garnish with a few fresh basil leaves.

A loaf of Ava's fresh Italian bread already sits on the table, along with a bottle of Italian Barbera d'Alba.

"Have a seat," I tell Ashley.

She complies, and I slide a plate of food in front of her.

"Smells heavenly." She gestures toward the wine. "No Steel wine tonight?"

"I thought you might appreciate something different. We do make a great Italian blend, but there's nothing quite like a Barbera d'Alba with tomato-based foods."

"I agree."

Not that I expected her to disagree. I'm right. I uncorked the bottle earlier to let it breathe. I pour a tasting portion into her goblet. "What do you think?"

She swirls it in her glass and smiles. "Is this a test?"

"Of course not. But I'm interested in your opinion."

She sinks her nose into the glass. "Mmm. Dark cherry, violet, and"—she sniffs again—"our previous conversation about caraway and anise notwithstanding, I'm getting a touch of licorice." She takes a sip and holds it in her mouth a few seconds before swallowing. "Not very tannic but a lovely acidity. I'm getting mostly the dark cherries again, with a little lavender and violet on the finish."

I nod.

"How'd I do?" she asks.

"I told you. It wasn't a test."

"I know, but your opinion means a lot to me."

"Okay." I fill her glass and then my own. Then I take a taste. She's right on target. I'm getting everything she said. I swallow. "I agree with you. The only thing I'll add is a little vanilla on the finish. In fact . . ." I take another taste. "Make that bourbon vanilla."

She takes another sip. "Yeah, it's subtle, but it's definitely there. I can't believe I missed that."

"I've been tasting wine a lot longer than you have. You may have the education, but there's no substitute for actual experience."

Oddly, she doesn't argue the point. In fact, she nods.

"You're right," she says. "I've learned a ton at school, but it's mostly theory. Sure, we've done some tastings in lab settings, but the real world is different."

She doesn't even know the truth she speaks. My real world—which she sees as one of riches and privilege—holds secrets I may never release.

I wash the thought from my mind. I made a promise to

Ashley and a promise to myself. I'll be with her during this internship. For two more months. I'll hide the beast inside me as best I can. To be with her. To have her. To let my heart feel what it wants to feel.

If I start thinking about the dark secrets I hide, I won't get very far with those promises.

I gesture toward her plate. "Dig in. I want to know what a coastal girl thinks of my attempt at seafood."

"I already know I'll love it." She twirls linguine on her fork and then spears a piece of scallop before bringing the utensil to her mouth. Her eyes widen as she chews and swallows. "It's wonderful. I've never tasted anything like it."

My cheeks warm. I know I'm a great cook. Aunt Marj has sung my praises for years, and she's a better chef than those in most of the finest restaurants. But to hear the praise from Ashley's pink lips means more to me than my aunt's most formidable compliment.

My lips nudge. I want to smile. Why am I holding back? I feel good, so I should smile. After all, I made that promise to Ashley and to myself. Yes, I need to hold back on emotion, but this is just a smile. What can it hurt?

I let my muscles go as she takes another bite, and her eyes widen once more.

She swallows. "Wow."

"I'm glad you like it."

"I do. It's delicious. But the 'wow' was for that gorgeous smile on your face. I'm not sure I've ever seen you smile like that."

I know she hasn't.

"You should smile more often," she goes on.

"I'm just glad you like the dish."

She returns my smile with her own dazzling one. Unlike me, Ashley smiles a lot, and every time it's better than the last. Her whole face lights up, and my heart wants to leap out of my chest.

"Are you going to eat?" she asks.

My plate sits in front of me, the food still untouched. I've been entranced by her smile. I pick up my fork and swirl pasta onto it. "I've eaten this at least a hundred times."

"But never with me." She smiles again.

True words. I bring my fork to my mouth and savor the goodness of the linguine frutti di mare. The flavors dance on my tongue.

And damn, it's never tasted better.

CHAPTER THIRTY-THREE

Ashley

Dale doesn't talk much more as we finish the pasta, but that's okay. I'm used to him being quiet. All I care about is that he's here, I'm here, and we're going to be together for the rest of my time in Colorado.

It's not forever, but it's a start.

And in the end, if three months are all I have of Dale Steel, it will be enough. One day with this man is better than a century with any other.

What if I don't want to let him go at the end?

I brush off the thought and secure it in the Scarlett O'Hara file in the back of my mind. I'll think about that tomorrow. More likely, in two months.

Dale refreshes our wineglasses and gestures to my empty plate. "Would you like some more?"

"Maybe just a little."

He takes my plate and refills it with a half portion, his own with a full. Then he replenishes our salad bowls as well. These Steel boys all love to eat. They work so hard they can probably put away four thousand or more calories a day. I'm going to have to watch it while I'm here. Very easy to overeat all this delicious food.

When we finish our second helpings, Dale clears the

table. "I didn't have time to make dessert," he says. "But I have some homemade brown sugar vanilla ice cream that Aunt Marj made."

"Sounds great. I'd like to finish my wine first."

He nods.

I lift my glass. "We didn't toast."

"I guess we didn't." He picks up his glass. "*Salute.*"

I smile. "Cheers in Italian. Appropriate for the meal, but I was thinking more along the lines of 'to us.'" I clink my glass to his.

His expression tightens.

Oh, Dale. You're still fighting this.

His silence goes on for a few seconds that seem like days. Until finally—

"To us."

His voice is low and rich, its burgundy color saturating me.

He means it. He really means it.

We both take a sip. I want desperately to probe him with questions about his unrequited love. Who wouldn't love Dale Steel? I yearn to break down his walls, get inside him, help him see the wonder of all he is.

Don't push. I've gotten this far, and I can't ruin it. Even though Dale is trying, part of his countenance is still rigid. Any mistake on my part, and our whole deal could be off.

This man means everything to me, and I can't risk losing what he's offered.

I smile, take another sip of my wine, and set the glass down. "Tell me something about yourself," I say.

He widens his eyes. "Like what?"

"I don't know. Anything. I know very little about you."

"I'm sure Dee filled you in."

"Just on your personality. How you're a little hard on people sometimes."

"And I suppose you agree with her?"

I can't hold back a laugh. "I'd say it was an understatement. With regard to me, anyway. Then I see you during tastings, and you're smiling and jubilant."

"My job at tastings is to sell wine. You should understand that, given your sommelier aspirations."

"I do understand that, but you prove that you do have people skills, despite what Ryan says."

"I do. I believe I've told you before that I bring them out when necessary."

"Tell me why."

"Why what?"

"Why do you only bring them out when necessary?"

He takes a sip of wine. "There's no simple answer to that question, so I'll answer another. You want me to tell you something about me. Something you don't know. Here goes." He inhales, exhales slowly. "My favorite color is blue."

That's what I get? Granted, I didn't put any limitations on the question. So I'll roll with it. "Really? That's surprising."

"Why?"

"Because I've never seen you wear blue. You wear black or green. I think you wore a white shirt one time."

"I look good in black and green. They both bring out the color of my eyes."

"You'll get no argument from me there. You have the most beautiful eyes I've ever seen. I'm puzzled, though."

"Why?"

"Because you seem almost… I don't know. Like your looks don't matter to you."

"My looks aren't who I am."

"Exactly my point. So why do you wear colors that show off one of your best features?"

He takes another sip of wine.

Ha! He can't answer. I'm loving this.

Finally, "I guess I don't know."

"It's okay, you know. Everyone wants to accentuate their best features. It's simply . . . human."

"Except my looks . . . " He stares down at his wineglass.

"What?"

He jerks his head back up. "Nothing. All's fair now. Your turn. Tell me something about yourself."

I take a sip, draining my wineglass. The smooth Barbera is like silk on my tongue. I want to open up, tell him everything about my past. Let him inside me the way I want to be inside him. But it's too soon for that. I feel it in my bones.

"Okay," I say. "My favorite gemstone is the garnet."

Then my heart thuds. Did I just tell him my favorite gemstone? Is that going to sound like I'm gunning for a gift of jewelry? From this man who doesn't love me? Who wants me but is only willing to commit to me for two months?

Should've gone with the whole favorite color routine.

I totally wasn't thinking.

He stands and takes our empty wineglasses to the sink. "Coffee?" he asks.

I open my mouth to remind him I don't drink coffee, when—

"Sorry. You don't drink coffee."

"No."

I guess the gemstone conversation is over.

He starts a pot of coffee, for himself, I presume, and then

turns to me. "Come with me. I want to show you something."

"Okay." I stand and follow him to his bedroom, trying not to think about how I woke up here alone.

He walks to his large chest and opens the top drawer. He pulls out a large velvet jewel box and opens it, showing it to me.

I gasp. Nestled on the black velvet is a garnet necklace. Three strands of tiny gems put together in a woven pattern so that it looks almost like rope. It's beautiful and unique, like nothing I've ever seen.

"It was my mother's," he says. "My real mother. Her name was Cheri."

I drop my mouth open. Is this the same man who told me Jade was his real mother? His language perplexes me, but only for a moment, as I can't draw my gaze from the beautiful piece of art in the velvet jewel case.

"There wasn't much to recover from the house after her suicide. We don't have any photos of her, and there wasn't much of value, so most of it went to charity when the Steels adopted us. But a few things remained. This is one of them."

"It's amazing." Garnets, despite their beauty, aren't overly expensive, so it's not unusual that Dale's biological mother would have a piece such as this. I reach out and touch it, running my fingers over the tiny facets.

"It's not worth much," he says. "I had it appraised a while back."

"Garnets are my favorite, but they're considered only a semiprecious stone," I say. "I guess that shows you about my taste."

"You have impeccable taste in wine."

I laugh. "I like what I like. To me, a garnet is more beautiful than a diamond."

"Because it's the color of red wine," he says. "Of a dark Syrah."

Funny that I never considered that angle. I just adore the deep red. But he's right. It's the color of Syrah.

The color of Dale's voice.

He takes the piece from the box. "Turn around."

"Why?"

"I'm going to put it on you."

My jaw drops. "Dale . . . "

"I've never seen it on anyone. I certainly never remember my mother wearing it. And my other mother—Jade—never wore it either. She kept it for me and gave it to me when I turned eighteen."

"And you never let anyone wear it? Not even the woman you were in love with?"

"No. Now turn around."

I'm trembling. Actually trembling, as I turn around and pull my hair off my neck.

He clasps the necklace, his fingers warm against my shivering flesh. The piece is heavy and cool against me.

I turn toward him. "Well?"

He smiles. "Now I have."

"Now you've what?"

He draws in a breath, his forehead wrinkling. Then he relaxes—as much as Dale can relax—and his lips nudge into a smile.

"Now . . . the woman I love has worn it."

CHAPTER THIRTY-FOUR

Dale

Those words took courage.

Every freaking ounce inside me.

I didn't plan to say them. I didn't plan to show Ashley my mother's necklace.

But when she mentioned garnets, how could I not?

And now she knows.

Ashley knows I love her.

That she is the person I meant when I said I was in love once.

Still *am* in love.

She doesn't speak. Her gorgeous blue eyes are wide, her pink lips parted. I want to kiss her senseless.

I lower my head—

"Dale."

"Yes," I say, my voice raspy.

"Are you telling me . . . ?"

I sigh. "I didn't intend to say it, Ashley. I didn't intend for you to ever find out. But the necklace. Placing it around your beautiful neck. Then looking at you. You, wearing this creation of wine-colored gems . . . I had to tell you. Had to let you know that I love you."

"I . . . Dale, I . . . " She pauses. "Please, tell me you're not playing around. That's not fair."

I lower my eyelids slightly. "Do you really think I'd kid about something like this?"

"Then . . . when you said . . . "

"Yes, when I told you I've only been in love once, I was speaking of you."

She clasps her hand to her mouth, and her eyes glisten.

"Tears?" I say. "Please, no tears."

"They're happy tears." She melts into my arms.

I embrace her. Hold her as close as possible given our clothing.

And I hope I haven't just made the biggest mistake of my life.

"I love you so much," she says against my chest. "So much. I didn't ever think it was possible to love someone the way I love you."

I kiss the top of her head. "Me neither."

She pulls back a little and fidgets with the clasp of the necklace. "Thank you for letting me try this on. It's the most lovely thing I've ever had around my neck."

I brush her fingers away from the clasp. "Keep it on. It's yours."

"No, I couldn't."

"Ashley, no matter where we go from here, whether this works or it doesn't, that necklace was meant for you. No one else can possibly wear it."

She fingers the garnet rope. "Are you sure?"

"I'm not sure of a lot of things," I say, "but I'm sure that this necklace is meant for you."

She parts her lips as if to say something.

"Don't," I say. "I still can't promise anything beyond these two months."

"But if you love me—"

I touch my fingers to her lips. "Ashley, sometimes love isn't enough."

"Love is always enough!"

I shake my head. "I've committed to the rest of your internship. That's all I can do."

"Dale . . ."

"Please, don't push this."

She drops her lips into an O. "Push. You can't be pushed."

"Can anyone? But that's not what I mean. I want this. I want you. And yes, I love you. I tried not to, but you crept inside my heart. I never meant to tell you."

"I don't understand that. Love is something that should be shared."

"I never thought love was in my future," I say.

"Love is in everyone's future, Dale. Everyone is worthy of love."

Worthy? That's not the issue, though I'm not sure how to describe to her exactly what the issue is. Not without baring more than I'm willing to.

"Two months, Ashley," I say. "Two months. That's all I can offer."

She reaches behind her and unclasps the necklace. "Then I can't accept this." She hands it back to me.

"Yes, you can. I want you to have it."

She shakes her head. "I'd give it more meaning than it has. You should keep it. You may"—she pauses, gulping—"find someone else you'd rather give it to."

I won't. No one else will ever wear this piece. It's Ashley's. It's stunning on her, but that's not the reason it's hers and hers alone.

It's hers because I'll never love this way again. Not in this lifetime or any other.

The love I feel for her came quickly, like an arrow to my heart. Like a vise around my soul. It sneaked into me when I let my guard down for a millisecond.

I won't let that guard down again.

"It's yours," I say simply.

"No." She closes my hand around the garnets.

I place the necklace back into the velvet box. Whether she takes it into her possession or not, it's hers.

It always will be.

"Maybe someday you can give it back to me," she says. "If we choose to go beyond these two months."

I simply nod. Is there harm in letting her think there's a chance? Perhaps there is, but I can't help myself. I want to please her. Her happiness means more to me than anything.

Even my own.

Oddly, I'm not being altruistic. Happiness has never been in the cards for me, and I accepted that long ago.

If it were, though, Ashley's happiness would trump my own. Absolutely. I know this without question.

Which means I'm truly in love.

God help both of us.

CHAPTER THIRTY-FIVE

Ashley

Giving the necklace back to Dale was the most difficult thing I've ever done. I don't say that lightly, as I've gone to bed hungry and cold more often than I prefer to think about.

I remember those times as if they were yesterday. Such is the life of a synesthete. We're stuck recalling even the most horrid points in our past because of the overwhelming sensory detail of each one. Senses make memories, and since my senses overlap, I remember almost everything.

So yeah, I recall with every sense I have those horrid times during my youth.

And still, I can say with utmost certainty that giving that necklace back to Dale was the hardest thing I've ever had to do.

I don't even have to consider the reason. It's love, of course. The love I feel for Dale is unlike anything I've ever experienced, and if it ends, I'll break inside.

The necklace, though beautiful, would be a reminder of the love I'll carry forever for a man who couldn't ultimately commit to me.

That's why I can't keep it. Not now. Perhaps not ever.

I'll hold out a glimmer of hope, though.

He loves me. He truly loves me, for he wouldn't lie to me.

Maybe, just maybe, he'll want to commit after these next two months are over.

Over. God. That word. It slides into my heart like a greased blade.

Dale places the velvet case back in his top drawer, and then he turns to me, his eyes unreadable. "The necklace is yours, Ashley, no matter what."

I open my mouth to speak, but he gestures me to stay silent.

"Whether you and I are together now or in the future, the necklace is yours. I feel it deeply in my bones. It's meant for you. No one could look as dazzling in it as you do. My mother certainly couldn't have."

"Your mother must have been beautiful," I say.

"She was, in her way."

"What does that mean?"

"It means I don't really remember much about her physical attributes. I told you once that Aunt Mel had me draw a picture of her, which helped a little, despite my nontalent for drawing. She had brown hair and brown eyes."

"She must have been beautiful," I say. "Look at you and Donny."

"She didn't have green eyes," he says, his voice monotone.

"Green eyes are a recessive trait," I tell him. "A brown-eyed person can produce a green-eyed child."

"You took genetics?"

"No. Anatomy, to fulfill a general science requirement in undergrad. But I figured that was common knowledge."

"Is it?"

"You didn't know?"

"I knew. My father told me long ago, when we were still kids. Still, I always assumed the green eyes had come from my birth father. You know, since Donny and I both have them and our mother didn't."

"Oh." He knows his birth father's eye color because he met him recently. Jade told me, and I can't break her confidence. "Well, you never know."

"I suppose not." He stares at the open door of his bedroom that leads back out to the hallway. His voice, still wine-red, sounds wistful, like a breeze is carrying the vivid color away from him.

Away from *us*.

Crap. This is my fault. Dale opened up to me. Admitted his love for me. Gave me a beautiful gift that I shoved back in his face.

I'm totally screwing up.

I touch his forearm. "Hey. Dessert?" I attempt a smile.

"Sure."

We walk together back to the kitchen. Dale opens the door to the deck, and a panting Penny enters. I give her some well-deserved ear rubs.

Dale serves up the ice cream. "Want to eat it outside?"

"Sure."

He grabs a cup of coffee for himself and a glass of water for me. I take the dishes of ice cream and follow him outside, Penny at my heels.

A small table awaits us. I set the dishes down as Dale holds out a chair for me.

"Thank you," I murmur.

The mood is ... different. I've majorly fucked up, and I know it.

This man—this man who I love more than life itself—said those coveted words to me. *I love you.* He said them. Said what I feared I'd never hear from his firm lips. Then he gave me a beautiful gift.

Which I refused.

I've made a train wreck out of what could have been a perfect evening.

I swirl my spoon around the edge of my bowl, capturing a bit of the ice cream. I bring it to my mouth.

Vanilla and brown sugar creaminess explodes across my tongue. No color or sound. Just the flavor. No surprise. My senses go on hiatus sometimes if I'm upset.

And I'm definitely upset.

Not with Dale. He's just being Dale.

I'm upset with myself.

Dale doesn't eat. Just lets the ice cream begin to melt in his bowl.

I raise my eyebrows at him. "It's delicious."

"Aunt Marj never misses."

"Does she make a lot of ice cream?"

"During the summer. This is her last batch for a while."

I nod. "Aren't you going to eat?"

"Maybe. I don't have much of an appetite."

I smile halfheartedly. "You did eat two helpings of linguine."

He scoffs softly. "That has nothing to do with it."

"Dale . . . " I reach forward and grab his hand. "I'm sorry about the necklace. I just . . . "

"I'm not upset about the necklace, Ashley."

Did you mean it? When you said you loved me, did you mean it?

I say this inside my head, knowing if I let the words blare out I'll ruin everything.

Dale wouldn't say something he didn't mean. I need to accept this man for who he is and not push him.

The warmth of his love has turned to chills, and not from the ice cream.

"Then what's wrong?"

"Nothing. Nothing is wrong."

More chills. I swallow the ice cream in my mouth and then stand. "I should go."

He lifts one eyebrow. "So that's how it's going to be, then?"

Penny paws at me, and I pet her soft head.

What am I supposed to say now? *Don't push*, Jade told me. But what else am I supposed to do?

Then I realize the answer is within me, and I just made a fatal error.

I'm ready to run off just because I'm confused.

I can't help a soft chuckle. I've been confused since I met Dale Steel. Did I really think that would change once he said he loves me?

"What's funny?" he asks.

"I am," I reply truthfully. "I'm funny, because I just did the one thing that makes sense in this situation, except that it doesn't, because you're not like anyone else I've ever met."

"Care to elaborate?"

"Sure, since you've admitted to me on more than one occasion that you don't have much experience with relationships."

"That's not true."

I lift my eyebrows.

"I have *no* experience with relationships," he says.

I laugh. Seriously just laugh aloud.

"*Now* what's funny?" he asks, clearly not amused.

"No. You're just... you. You're so fine tuned to the last detail. You don't like subjective words like lusty or exuberant when you taste wine. Fine. I get it. You have no experience in relationships. I shouldn't have said you don't have much."

"No, you shouldn't say something that isn't accurate. I have *no* experience, Ashley. *Nada.* Now get on with what you want to say."

My God, this man will be the death of me. Please let it be a good death. "I want to say that I'm sorry. I don't want to leave, and I shouldn't have said I'd go." I inhale, exhale slowly. "I'm not going anywhere, Dale. If you want me to leave, you're going to have to literally carry me out of here."

He stands, closes the gap between us.

Then he lifts me in his arms.

And my heart crumbles.

I should really be more careful what I say to this man.

CHAPTER THIRTY-SIX

Dale

Ashley is light as a feather in my arms.

I know what she's thinking. She expects me to carry her back to the main house. It would serve her right for her attempt to manipulate me by telling me she was going to leave, but I don't want her to leave.

So I carry her...

I carry her to...my bedroom.

I set her on the bed—not gently. She stares at me with wide blue eyes.

"Surprised?" I ask.

"A little, yeah."

"I don't respond well to manipulation."

"But I wasn't—"

"I'm not saying you were consciously trying to manipulate me."

"Good, because—"

"For God's sake!" I rake my fingers through my hair. "Listen. Just *listen*."

She nods, her pretty pink lips trembling.

"I didn't mean to tell you how I feel," I say, pacing. "I meant to take those words to the grave."

She opens her mouth, but I dart arrows at her with my

eyes. She presses her lips together abruptly.

"I'm going to finish this, Ashley, if it kills me." *And it just may.* "I'm not sure when I fell in love, but I swear to God, I feel like there was never a moment of my life when I didn't love you. That makes no sense, of course, since we just met, but it's my feeling. You're going to ask why I wouldn't tell you. The only answer I can give you is that you deserve better than me. And don't tell me I'm the best there is. I get that you think that, but it's just not true. You're looking through your infatuated glasses. Rose-colored glasses. Syrah-colored glasses, or whatever you want to call it. It's so fucking far from true."

I want to say more.

I want to tell her about the demons that live inside me, eating my flesh from the inside out.

I want to tell her how as a young boy I was used and abused, saw things no child—hell, no adult—should ever see. Heard things no one should have heard. How there were times the stench of my own waste made my eyes water, how the cries of my brother made me ache inside as if I were being punched in the stomach again and again with no end in sight.

I want to open up to her, let her see the real me.

I won't.

I've already decided I won't, because if I do, all hell will be unleashed. I'll succumb to the chaos inside me, and then I won't be able to control anything anymore.

But a new reason has dawned. I won't open up, because if I do, Ashley will run away screaming.

She'll no longer love me.

And I can't bear that.

I promised her two months.

I'll give her two months.

"Take off your clothes," I say through clenched teeth.

"Dale..."

"Did I tell you to speak?" My voice is darker and more commanding than I mean it to be.

Does she see the red color? Or has it turned black?

I feel black at the moment. Even Ashley, who's a shining light for me, doesn't penetrate the dark opacity. I'm going to have her, and it's not going to be nice.

Or soft.

Or gentle.

Her blue eyes are wide, those dark-brown lashes forming a semicircle on their upper halves.

God, such beauty. Sparkling eyes, full pink lips, rosy cheeks. And a dusty blush over her chest.

She trembles as she fumbles with her T-shirt at the waist.

"I'm waiting," I say with a growl.

She lifts the shirt over her head, revealing a white lacy bra.

I hold back a gasp and adjust my groin. I'm already hard and aching.

I'm angry. Not at Ashley, but at myself, for thinking I could do this. The darkness drapes over me like a phantom's cloak.

I'm all in now, and it's going to happen. I'm giving her two months if it kills me.

"Take off your bra," I say, raking her over with my hungry gaze.

She complies, more slowly than I'd prefer, but the white lace ends up on the floor where she tosses it.

"Your jeans now."

She tugs off her sandals first and then unbuttons her jeans. Slowly again.

"Faster," I say on a low growl.

She stands and shimmies out of them, taking her white bikini panties with them. Then she sits back down on the bed where I planted her in the first place.

Her beauty beguiles me. Those sweet tits that fit in my palm so perfectly, her pink nipples already erect. Her concave abdomen, and then her pussy. Bare tonight. Bare and beautiful and hiding the gems I've grown dependent on.

"Are you going to get undressed?" she asks, her voice slightly timid.

I narrow my eyes. My cock is so hard I could slice a brick with it. "Quiet," I say more harshly than I mean to.

Ashley is flushed all over. She's responding to my harshness.

Which makes me even harder, if that's possible.

I unbutton my shirt slowly, determined to make her squirm the way she made me squirm.

One button.

Two.

Three.

I pull it out of my waistband.

Four buttons.

Five.

She sucks in an audible breath and opens her mouth.

I gesture her to be quiet as I finish the shirt, slide it slowly over my shoulders, and let it fall to the floor.

My boots are next. I've been wearing cowboy boots for twenty-five years, and I know how to get out of them quickly.

Then my jeans. God, they're uncomfortable. So much for the slow burn. I shed them rapidly and free my aching dick.

Ashley sucks in another breath. Fuck, she's beautiful, that warm rosy glow, those sparkling azure eyes, the ashy blond hair falling over her milky shoulders ...

I don't want to wait.

One day maybe I'll be able to take her slowly, as I've dreamed of.

But not this day.

Not this moment.

No gentle love tonight.

I lunge toward her, claiming her lips as I shove my cock into her heat.

She's ready for me. Always so ready. Sweet and silky and wet in the most luscious of ways.

She gloves me, and I sink into her perfection. Her paradise.

And I know, in my heart of hearts, that I'll never find anyone who feels like Ashley White.

CHAPTER THIRTY-SEVEN

Ashley

His sandy chest hair abrades my hard nipples as he pumps into me. If it's possible, he's even harder than normal, larger than normal.

He fills every empty spot inside me, and as he pumps, his pubic bone torments my clit, and I race toward the top of the mountain.

I cry out as I come, and then I come again.

Dale is fucking me harder than he ever has before. It's an angry fuck. A tormented fuck. A lusty and exuberant fuck.

All those feelings . . .

All those colors . . .

It's the dark red of Syrah, but kaleidoscoping around the main color are emerald green, bright red, and black.

A translucent veil of black.

Dale.

All the colors of Dale in this one amazing meeting of our bodies.

I come again, and then again, my body responding to him in a way it never has before.

"Damn, Ashley," he rasps. "Damn it all to hell!"

His words taunt me. He's still angry. Angry and passionate and full of lust.

It's always been this way with him, but another layer has formed.

Love.

Dale's love.

And mine.

My climax has transcended to another level. Another whole plane, where only Dale and I exist. The two of us—our bodies, hearts, and souls morphed together into one. One ultimate being made of love and light.

And darkness.

Always the darkness with Dale.

I embrace it. I embrace all that is the man I love.

And with the next climax, I soar even higher.

"Fuck, Ashley," he says again. "Fuck it. I love you!" He slams into me just as I break into one last orgasm.

Together we soar across the sky, lighter than air.

"I love you too," I cry. "I love you so much!"

Our love floats around us, the color of soft pink. It covers everything else—the burgundy, the green, the red, and the black.

For one single moment, the blush of our love takes over.

I meet Dale's gaze. Strands of blond hair stick to his forehead and cheeks with perspiration. I push one back over his forehead and then trail my fingers over his strong jawline.

His lips are parted, and they tremble a bit. Only a bit.

"I love you," I say softly.

He closes his eyes and inhales, as if he's savoring my words. Then he opens them, and his eyes are green fire. "I love you too. God help me, but I do. I love you so damned much."

He rolls off me and then onto his back, his legs dangling off the side of the bed. He stares at the ceiling, his lips still parted.

I snuggle up next to him and breathe in the scent of him mingled with the musky fragrance of our lovemaking.

"Will you be here in the morning?" I can't help asking.

"Yes," he says. "I promised you two months. I'll give you two months."

I sigh and kiss his shoulder. It's not what I ultimately want, but it's something. It's more than he was willing to offer even yesterday.

I'll take it, I say to myself.

And even as I drift off to sleep, I try not to think about how difficult it will be to leave him in November. Already I feel as though I've lost a piece of my heart.

★ ★ ★

My phone buzzes at six a.m.

For a moment, I'm disoriented. Then I remember. I'm in Dale's bed. At Dale's place. And...

"Damn it!" I say out loud.

I'm alone in this big bed once more.

Anger rushes through me. But no time for that. I scurry into my clothes. I have to get back to the main house and get ready for work.

I should have known better than to trust Dale Steel.

Was he lying when he said he loved me as well?

I stomp out the door of his bedroom and down the hallway. I'm breathing hard, the rage pumping through me. Then I smell...

Bacon? Eggs? I turn into the kitchen, and—

"Hey, sleepyhead."

Dale's dreamy Syrah-laced drawl wraps me in warmth.

He's standing at the cooktop, bare-chested and glorious, wearing only lounge pants. My breath catches at his gorgeousness.

"You're here," I can't help saying.

"Where else would I be?"

Myriad answers to his question exist, but I exercise control over my snark. He promised me he'd be here, and he is. Not only that, he's making breakfast.

"I poured your juice." He nods to the table.

Sure enough, a tall glass of OJ awaits me. "Thank you." I pick it up and take a sip.

"Not fresh squeezed," he says. "We don't get a lot of fresh oranges here in the fall. Sorry."

"It's delicious."

"Getting used to concentrate?" he asks.

"Contrary to your apparent belief, I drink a lot of concentrate at home. It's cheaper."

"You don't juice your own?"

I take another sip. "Don't own a juicer."

He turns toward me, his eyebrows raised. "Really? A Cali girl like you?"

"I'm not a vegetarian, either, as you've probably noticed. And clearly I have no problem poisoning myself with alcohol."

He smiles a little at that one. "You probably know all the health benefits of wine."

I nod. "I live by them."

He turns back to the cooktop. "How do you like your eggs?"

"However you like them is fine. I'm not picky."

He looks over his shoulder. "I want to know how *you* like them, Ashley. I want to make them for you."

I smile. *Who are you and what have you done with Dale Steel?* I say only, "That's sweet of you. Scrambled, please."

"You got it."

A few minutes later, a plate of eggs, bacon, and whole wheat toast slides in front of me.

"Thank you."

"Just wait." He gestures to a mason jar. "Try some of that on your toast."

"What is it?"

"Try it and see." He pushes the jar toward me.

The color is a lovely smoky orange. I spread some of the jam on my toast and take a bite.

"Oh my God!" I say with my mouth full. Lively peach scatters over my tastebuds, followed by cinnamon, cloves, and something I can't quite identify. I let it sit for a moment, tasting the jam as if I were tasting wine. It's pepper. Subtle pepper. Maybe white pepper?

"I take it you approve?" Dale says.

I chew my toast and swallow. "That's delicious. Did you make it?"

"Not guilty," he says. "That's Aunt Marj's creation. Her spiced peach preserves from last season. She hasn't made this year's batch yet."

"I doubt she can improve on this." I take another bite and swallow more quickly this time. "Is that really white pepper I'm tasting?"

"It's crushed pink peppercorns, actually," he says. "The flavor is similar, but they aren't actually true peppercorns. They're berries from the Brazilian pepper tree. The taste is lighter."

"Pink pepper, huh? Is there anything you don't know

about spices and cooking?"

"Not a lot. The pink is a more subtle flavor that doesn't overwhelm the peaches and other spices. It just adds a light zing."

I can't help a laugh. "Zing? What's that mean, Mr. Don't-Be-Subjective?"

"It means a sharply piquant flavor," he deadpans.

I shake my head, still chuckling. "I'll never win with you, will I?"

Dale doesn't reply. He says simply, "Just enjoy your breakfast, Ashley. We have a big day today at work."

I slather more jam on my toast as I realize I haven't even touched my bacon and eggs. The eggs look perfectly scrambled, too, just the way I like them. I have to eat them. He made them especially for me.

"Oh?" I bring a forkful of eggs to my mouth.

Light and fluffy and perfect with a touch of butter, just as I knew they'd be. I can't help a satisfied, "Mmm."

"You approve?" he says.

"Wow. Yes. Best eggs I've ever eaten." I'm not even embellishing.

"Good. Yeah." He clears his throat. "We're beginning the harvest of the Syrah today. I figured you'd want to be involved."

"Your vines," I say softly.

"Yes." He looks down at his plate.

"I imagine you like to be there. To . . . "

"To what?"

"I don't know. Protect your vines?"

He smiles slightly. Just the thought of his vines makes him happy. "Sort of. They're vines. They're part of our business. They have to be harvested. Harvest is my favorite time of the year, honestly. But . . . "

"But those vines are special."

He nods. "Yes, more special this year because we're producing our first old-vine Syrah."

"Right. You told me."

"I need to make sure none of the fruit is harmed."

"But your harvesters know what they're doing," I say. "I've been with them the last few days."

"They do." He offers no further explanation.

He doesn't have to.

The Syrah vines are special to him. More than special.

He's part of them.

He loves them.

And I wonder—only for an instant—if he loves them more than he loves me.

CHAPTER THIRTY-EIGHT

Dale

I both love and hate Syrah harvest.

Ashley won't understand, and I don't expect her to. Harvest, when we capture our bounty. This year's Syrah is so beautiful, so perfect. And while I want to take the fruit from the vines—want to make those beautiful grapes into magnificent wine—still I resist inside.

But it's the circle of life, as it is with any living thing. Because those particular vines are my sanctuary doesn't change that.

I just like to be there. Exist next to those vines as their fruit is taken from them.

Watch over them, in a way, like they watch over me the rest of the season.

Until winter, when they're dormant. I still sleep with them, but it's different. They're alive but hibernating.

Winter is hard for me.

I push the thought aside.

Winter isn't here yet. This is autumn. Harvest time. And Ashley.

Two more months of Ashley before I fade into the cold cloak of winter.

She takes the last bite of bacon, rises, and takes her empty plate to the sink. "I have to stop eating like this. I'm going to gain a ton while I'm here."

Her body is perfect, and honestly, if she gained weight? She'd still be perfect to me. I fell in love with her, not with her body. With her vibrancy. Her exuberance. Her light. A few pounds won't change those fundamental things about her.

I think about how to respond to her, when my phone buzzes. Hmm. I don't recognize the number. I excuse myself and take the phone into my office.

"Dale Steel."

"Mr. Steel, this is Dr. Montgomery from Woodrow Rehab Center in Grand Junction."

Is that where Floyd is? I never asked Dad. "Yes, good morning."

"I'm your father's physician."

Not my father, but whatever. "Yes, what can I help you with?"

"I'm sorry to have to tell you this, but he's had a myocardial infarction."

"A heart attack?" Why doctors can't just speak English is beyond me.

"Yes."

"How is he?"

"He was transported by ambulance to St. Mary's. I'm sorry, but that's all I know right now."

On the first day of Syrah harvest? *Really, Floyd?* "I'll contact the hospital," I say to the doctor. "Thank you for letting me know."

"You're welcome. We'll hope for the best."

"Thank you. Goodbye." I end the call.

Now what? I have to deal with the dumbass who fathered

me after I just told Ashley we have a big day. Only one person can help me. Dad.

I return to the kitchen, where Ashley is loading the dishwasher. Her ass looks delectable in those jeans...

But no.

So much else is going on now.

I owe Floyd Jolly nothing. Not a damned thing. But his doctor called *me*, which means Floyd put me down as an emergency contact. Not my father. Not my brother. Not anyone else.

Me.

His firstborn.

He may be dead already, for all I know. But if he isn't? Can I let him die alone?

"Ashley..."

She turns to face me. "Yeah?"

What am I supposed to say to her? She knows nothing of my birth father, that he showed up a few weeks ago. A big part of me doesn't want to pour out the story now.

But another part of me *does* want to.

I'm already hiding so much from her—so much that I'll never be able to reveal.

Can I reveal this tiny bit?

It's not a secret, really. Mom and Dad know. All the aunts and uncles know. Probably all the cousins. Dee may have already told Ashley, for all I know.

"Have you talked to Diana lately?" I ask.

"Just yesterday, actually," Ashley says. "She loves her boss and all her coworkers. They're letting her take the lead on one of the committees."

"Good. That's good." I clear my throat. "Did she tell you

anything else? I mean . . . about me?"

"No. Why would she?"

"You want some more juice?" I ask, heading to the coffeemaker for a fresh cup.

"I'm fine. I need to get back to the house to shower and change."

I nod, taking a sip of my coffee and pulling out a chair for her. "Sit."

Her eyes widen, and not in a good way.

She thinks I'm going to end things. I can see it in her face. But she doesn't know me well yet. I promised her two months, and I don't break promises.

She inhales and then exhales slowly. "Give it to me straight."

Yup, that's what she thinks. "I'm not breaking up with you."

She drops her mouth open, a squeak escaping. "You're not?"

"No, Ashley, I'm not."

She sighs, visibly relieved. "What's up, then?"

"I have to go to Grand Junction today."

"So you won't be going to the harvest?"

"No. Not today, anyway. I'll be there tomorrow." God willing.

"Okay. What do you want me to do, then?"

"You can work the harvest if you'd like, or I can have you shadow Uncle Ry or one of his associates. Uncle Ry stopped working the harvest last year when he decided to retire after this season. He might be tasting the barrels. He does that once a week. You'd like that."

"I would," she says, "but I'd rather be with you. What's

going on in Grand Junction?"

"I'm not going there on business."

"Oh." She looks down at the table.

"So you can't go along," I say, "but...I want to tell you why I'm going."

She looks up and meets my gaze. "Okay. I appreciate that."

"My...uh...birth father showed up a little while ago."

Her eyebrows rise, but only a touch.

"That's why I went to Grand Junction. To meet him, and to have a DNA test."

"And...?"

"He's legit. Well, he's my father." Legit is another question altogether. "Anyway, he had a heart attack early this morning."

Her hand flies to her mouth. "I'm so sorry, Dale."

"I'm okay. I don't have any feelings for him. He's blood, but he's not family."

She nods.

"But I'm his emergency contact, obviously, so I need to go see to his affairs, if there are any."

"Did he...die?"

"I don't know yet. He was transferred to the hospital. That's all I know."

"You need to call the hospital."

"I will. I wanted to tell you first."

My words surprise even me. Not that I have any feelings for my birth father, but telling Ashley something about myself—no big secret, but more than I've ever even thought about telling her before now—took precedence.

Her cheeks flush that adorable pink. "You wanted to tell me? Something?"

"Don't act so surprised."

"You're usually such a closed book."

She has no idea. "I was pretty open last night, I think."

Her cheeks pink further. "When you said you love me."

I don't respond.

"Can I go with you?" she asks.

"Why would you want to?"

"To support the man I love," she says. "Why do you think?"

Surprisingly, I don't hate the idea. But... no. I need my father with me. He's the only one who...

Who understands.

Except maybe he doesn't. I still don't know any details of what befell him. And it occurs to me.

Never once has Ashley mentioned *her* father.

Perhaps she's the one who will understand better than my father, who *knew* his father.

Do I dare ask?

"Ashley..."

"I won't get in the way," she promises. "I just don't... I don't want you to be alone, is all."

I draw in a breath. "Ashley, you've talked about your mother. Tell me about your father."

She bites her lower lip.

"Ashley..."

"I don't talk about him."

"I understand. But if you want to go with me, I need to know if..." I shake my head. "Oh, hell. It doesn't matter anyway."

"You're right," she says. "My father doesn't matter at all."

Her countenance is... different. Her usual vibrancy has taken a vacation. I want to press her, but how can I? Knowledge of my birth father notwithstanding, I've shared so little of who

I truly am with this woman. For her own good as well as mine.

"You may come with me if you'd like," I say, surprising even myself.

More of a surprise is that I actually want her there. By my side. I have no emotional attachment to Floyd Jolly, but he's still a part of me. A physical part of me the way Talon Steel isn't.

She smiles, her vibrancy returning. "I'll go to the house and shower. When do you want to leave?"

"In an hour, if possible."

"Sure. No problem." She stands and drains the last of her juice from her cup. "I'll be back before then. You should call your brother." She gives me a quick kiss and then runs out the back door and up the pathway.

She's right. I need to call Donny. And I need to call Dad. But first, the hospital.

To find out whether my father is dead or alive.

CHAPTER THIRTY-NINE

Ashley

I sprint—even wearing sandals—to the main house.

I shouldn't feel so jubilant, given that a man has had a heart attack and is in the hospital, but if this is the catalyst that can bring Dale and me closer, I can't help feeling pretty good.

Laced with the joy, though, is the fact that I didn't answer his question about my own father.

Not that I owe him any explanation. He's pretty closed off himself. But he did ask, and I didn't answer.

I try not to think about my conception. In fact, until a few weeks ago, I thought my father had died when I was young.

Which isn't wrong. He did die when I was young. When I was two, to be exact.

My father died in prison.

But that's not the story my mother originally told me. I heard a story about how he died in a car accident, leaving us destitute, and several years later, we ended up on the streets.

It was a big fat lie, but when I learned the truth, I understood why my mother told it.

Recently, she sat me down and told me I had a right to know where I came from, and I'm still numb about the truth.

I haven't let myself think about it. Until now.

Dale asked about my father, and the truth is—

My father was a rapist.

A serial rapist.

I'm a product of a rape.

Think about it tomorrow.

My mantra when it comes to unpleasantness, but I have to face it. Dale asked me about my father, and I owe him the truth.

My mother was right to tell me, but it's not something I want to talk about.

To anyone.

Especially not the man I love.

I don't want him to see me as tainted in any way.

Not that I feel tainted. I'm the same person I always was. I know that, and I truly feel that inside. My mother may not have been able to give me much, but she gave me enough love for two parents. And she may think I have my head in the clouds for chasing a career in something as bourgeois as wine, but still she loves me and always will.

I reach the main house.

"Done," I say aloud.

I'm done thinking about the rapist who fathered me. He was caught, and he got what was coming. Prison isn't kind to rapists. He was beaten and killed, among other things. An eye for an eye, apparently.

Done thinking about that now. I'll consider telling Dale tomorrow.

I walk into the ranch house through the back door. "Hey, Darla."

Darla looks away from her rolling pin. "Miss Ashley, good morning."

"Anyone home?"

"Mr. Talon has already left for work. Miss Jade is getting ready, I think."

"Okay, thanks."

Just as well. I don't particularly want to explain where I've been. But maybe I should explain where I'm going.

I walk toward my bedroom as Jade emerges from the master suite at the end of the hall.

"Good morning, Ashley," she says.

My cheeks warm. She's not stupid. She knows I didn't spend the night here. Better to dive right into what's happening now.

"Jade, I'm glad you're still here. Dale's birth father had a heart attack, and I'm going with him to Grand Junction. I thought you should know."

Jade goes still. "Oh my. Is he okay?"

"We don't know. Dale's calling the hospital. I'm just going to shower and change, and then we're heading out."

"I should go talk to him," Jade says, smoothing out a slight wrinkle in her blazer.

I nod. "He's at home."

"I have to be in court in an hour." She sighs. "I'll call Mary. My son comes first."

"Mary?"

"The assistant city attorney. She should be in by now. Thank you for telling me."

"Of course."

She waves absently as she rushes the other way, cell phone already at her ear.

I enter my bedroom and hope I didn't just make a fatal mistake. Dale may not want to talk to his mother.

★ ★ ★

Freshly showered and clothed in jeans and a silk blouse, I knock on Dale's back door. Penny spies me through the glass, panting.

"Hey, girl," I say.

A few seconds later, Dale clomps into the kitchen and opens the door. He looks . . . uncomfortable.

Which probably means Jade is still here.

"Is your mom here?" I whisper.

He simply nods, his expression stoic. Crap. He's probably angry with me.

Jade whisks into the kitchen then. "Ashley, good. You're here. I'll let you two be on your way." She steps onto her tiptoes and kisses Dale's cheek. "Call me later, honey."

"I will," Dale says. "Have Dad call me when he can."

"Absolutely." She walks out the back way and up the trail to the main house.

"I'm . . ." I begin.

"What?"

I'm sorry I told your mom? I can't say that, because I'm not really sorry. She had a right to know.

"Nothing."

"Let's go," he says, petting Penny.

I eye her water bowl. It's nearly empty. "She needs water."

Dale rakes his fingers through his disheveled hair. "Right. I was going to fill it up and then my mom showed up." He picks up the bowl.

"So . . . your mom . . ." I say.

"Means well," he says, setting Penny's bowl down.

She eagerly laps up some water.

I'm not sure how to respond. Luckily, I don't have to.

"Let's go," Dale says.

We head out and get into his truck. He's quiet Dale now. Stoic Dale. Which means it will be a long, silent ride to Grand Junction.

I settle in.

CHAPTER FORTY

Dale

I turn on the radio to listen to news of the fires. Colorado is a desert climate, and fire happens nearly every year. This year, we've just come out of a drought, so it's a little less worrisome, but a few days ago, a big blaze started in the Pine Gulch north of Grand Junction. So far, Steel Ranch isn't in danger, but we have to stay ahead of the game by having all information.

Dad and his brothers are really good at keeping their land free from anything that could kindle a wildfire, but we still have to watch carefully. This year, with such a great grape crop, I'm determined nothing will be an issue.

Plus, it keeps me from having to talk to Ashley.

A half hour with my mother drains me. She's wonderful, I love her, and she means well, but... Sometimes she just tries too hard.

By the time she showed up at my place, I'd already called Dad and filled him in, and then the hospital. Floyd was still alive as of then, though he was in the ICU and no one had any information on his prognosis.

Finally, I turn off the radio and fill Ashley in.

"At least he's alive," she says.

I don't know how to respond to that. Honestly? I don't really care if he's alive or not.

Except that somewhere, deep inside, a little part of me does. Yeah, he's a jerk for abandoning Donny and me, but his DNA lives inside me. He's a part of me. And frankly, if he's prone to heart attacks, that's something I need to know. Now I'll at least have half of my parental medical history, and I'll have to minimize my risk of heart attack.

I can't help a soft scoff at that thought. I eat a lot of beef. That's a lot of saturated fat. Of course I also drink a lot of red wine, which lowers cholesterol. At least some expert said something to that effect once. Who knows what to believe?

Finally, I pull into the hospital and hand the truck off to the valet. Ashley and I go inside, where I query the volunteer on duty. Armed with my father's whereabouts, I lead Ashley to the elevator that will take us to the floor that houses the ICU.

Ashley grabs my hand and entwines her fingers through mine.

I soften a little. Her small hand is engulfed by my large one, but at least I know how to hold it now. It gives me comfort. Not that I need comfort at the moment. Or do I?

The elevator dings, bringing us to the floor. She and I walk hastily to another volunteer.

"I'm here for Floyd Jolly."

"And you are?"

"Dale Steel. He's my birth father. I'm his emergency contact, apparently."

"Just a moment, please." She taps her fingers on her keyboard. "He's under Dr. Larson's care. I'll buzz her to come out and talk to you as soon as she can."

"Is he . . . still alive?" I ask.

"As far as I can tell, yes." The volunteer smiles. "So that's good news."

I nod. I guess it's good news. All those years of tamping down all my emotion, and now I don't have a clue how to feel about this man. My birth father. My abandoner.

Ashley tugs on my arm. "Let's sit. Do you want anything? I can find you a cup of coffee somewhere."

I don't want any coffee, but it will give Ashley something to do so I won't have to talk. "Thanks. That would be great."

She squeezes my hand before dropping it and walks out of the waiting area.

I plunk down on a chair. A display of magazines sits on the table in front of me. *Cosmopolitan.* Yeah, no thanks. *Woman's Day.* Nope. *Esquire.* Still a hard no, though it's better than the other two. No *Agriculture Weekly*? No *Food and Wine*? I sigh and grab my phone. I can at least catch up on emails.

"Mr. Steel?"

I nearly jump out of my chair when a woman holds out her hand.

"I'm Dr. Larson."

I stand. "Dale Steel. How is Mr. Jolly?"

"It's lucky you got here when you did," she says. "Any later and he'd already be in surgery. He has two coronary artery blockages, and he didn't respond to other treatment, which means we need to do a triple bypass right away."

I inhale. "I see. And what is his prognosis?"

"Most patients do quite well, but I won't lie to you. There are risks."

"What kind of risks?"

"Bleeding, infection, memory loss. Sometimes kidney issues or stroke."

"I see." My tone is apathetic. I don't know how to feel. I *can't* feel.

Ashley walks toward us carrying a large paper cup. "Any news?"

"Doctor, this is my . . . friend. Ashley White."

Ashley holds out her hand. "Nice to meet you."

"My pleasure," the doctor says. "I'll let Mr. Steel explain what's going on. I need to get to the OR." She pulls a mask over her face and rushes through the double doors out of the waiting area.

Ashley hands me the coffee. "What's going on?"

"Triple bypass surgery," I say in a monotone.

Her eyes widen. "You okay?"

"Yeah." I sit back down and place the coffee on the table in front of me.

Ashley sits next to me. "How long will he be in surgery?"

"I don't know."

"She didn't tell you?"

"I didn't ask." I should have asked. If my true father were in there, I'd have researched this on my phone and asked all the right questions.

Ashley fiddles with her own phone. "Looks like between three and six hours."

I sigh. "There goes this whole day. You don't have to stay if you don't want to."

"Are you kidding?" Then she frowns. "I mean, you're my boss, so if you want me to get back and work, I will."

"Do what you want," I say.

"I want to be with you." She grabs my hand once more. "You shouldn't be alone here."

"My mom offered to take the day off and come," I say. "I told her no."

"What about your dad?"

"I told him no as well."

That response seems to surprise her. "Then I'm definitely staying. I get that this guy's a stranger to you, but you shouldn't be alone."

Her words have a tone I can't quite place.

Then her vibrancy returns. "You can dock me a day's pay. Except that I'm not paid. So I'll be happy to work late the rest of the week. Or work this weekend. Whatever you need."

I let out a scoff without meaning to, knowing I should keep the following thought to myself but saying it anyway. "I never thought we needed an intern. You're superfluous."

It's not untrue. We *don't* need an intern. We never did. Still, now isn't the time to bring that up. Ashley is here, and I love her. If Uncle Ry never offered her the internship, she and I wouldn't have met.

Which may have been best for both of us.

Definitely best for her.

She drops my hand and picks up the copy of *Cosmopolitan*.

Yeah, I fucked this up. Again.

CHAPTER FORTY-ONE

Ashley

I admit it. I'm a *Cosmo* girl. The magazine is like crack to me. I can't resist the juicy stories written by readers about their most embarrassing sexual encounters. More than once, I've considered submitting one of my own. My sexual past is filled with embarrassing stories. Like the time during the summer before my sophomore year of college. I hooked up with a UPS guy one Saturday afternoon while my mom was working. I was in my room reading when she got home.

She knocked on my door and stuck her head in. "I'm home," *she said. "I brought takeout."*

I closed my book. "Sweet. I'll be right down."

She gazed downward for a split second and then said, "Sounds good. Be sure to pick up that candy wrapper on the floor."

Candy wrapper? I hadn't been eating any candy. I jumped off my bed and—

"Oh, shit," I said aloud.

The dude's condom sat on the middle of my floor.

At that point in my life, I was already pretty experienced. I always practiced safe sex, and never once did a guy fail to take care of his used condom. I thought it was something they all did. After-sex etiquette, or whatever. Apparently not this guy.

Yeah, I never saw him again.

I grabbed a tissue and disposed of the *candy wrapper* in the trash can.

My mother never mentioned it again. She was probably relieved to know I used condoms.

I always thought that story might be good *Cosmo* fodder.

Today, though, I stare at the words without reading them. They may as well be written in Swahili. The letters blur together and make no sense to me. I shuffle through the pages of the magazine, trying to find something that might take my mind off Dale's cross words, when I come across an article that piques my interest.

"When He Won't Open Up."

I tilt the magazine away from Dale so he can't see what I'm reading. Not that he's even looking my way. I'm trying to give him the benefit of the doubt. His birth father is in the middle of open-heart surgery. That's a big deal for anyone. Not sure how I'd feel if it were my own birth father, the serial rapist, but...

God, both Dale's and my lives are fucked up in their own way.

I read the title again.

"When He Won't Open Up."

I doubt the article is talking about an adopted guy whose birth father is in the middle of cardiac bypass surgery. Still, I'm here for the duration, so it's worth a read.

First point—Be direct.

Well, duh. Can I be any more direct with Dale?

Second point—Open up to him about something.

I'm a freaking open book.

Except...

About my childhood.

About my father.

I read no further. It's all fluff anyway.

For someone who prides herself on being an open book, I'm kind of sealed shut about those two areas. I don't even let myself think about the father thing.

Dale holds his phone, but he's not reading what's on the screen. Rather, he's staring into space. Is this a good time? Maybe if I tell Dale about my childhood, about my own birth father, he'll open up. If not? At least he'll have something else to focus on for the next several hours.

I lightly touch his forearm. "Dale?"

"Hmm?" He doesn't turn to look at me.

"I want to talk to you."

"About what?" Still not looking at me.

I squeeze his muscled forearm. "Look at me. Please."

He sighs and turns toward me. His green eyes are unreadable. They don't show sadness. They don't show anger. They don't show fear. All emotions that would be normal when a parent is having life-threatening surgery.

But this man isn't a parent to Dale. Only biologically.

Just like my own father.

"What is it?" he asks.

"I want to tell you something about myself."

"Sure. What?"

"I ... My father ... "

"You said you don't talk about him."

"I don't, normally. But I'd like to tell you what I know. And about some other things."

"Okay." His tone softens a little, and the burgundy fills the air and seems to float around me in a protective cloak.

I clear my throat. Here goes. No shoving it back inside

the Scarlett O'Hara file. "When I was old enough to ask, my mother told me he died in a car crash when I was a baby. She made do as best she could, but eventually we were evicted from our apartment because she missed so much rent."

"I'm sorry." He takes my hand. "You told me you've gone to bed hungry before. I'm sorry about that."

"Yeah. Hungry. Sometimes cold and hungry. Other times sweltering and hungry. San Francisco can get up to a hundred degrees in the summer."

He squeezes my hand to the point it's uncomfortable. "Wait. Are you telling me...?"

"That I was homeless? Yeah, that's what I'm telling you."

"Ashley, baby, I'm so sorry."

I melt. Seriously. Right into butter on the uncomfortable waiting room chair. *Baby*. He's never called me any kind of endearment.

Baby.

Baby.

That voice that enthralls me.

But I can't stop now. I'm opening up to him in hopes that he'll open up to me.

"Yeah. I mean, we stayed in shelters when we could, but we also lived in a tent sometimes."

"Fuck," he says.

I clear my throat. "Anyway—"

"How did you eat?"

"Well...sometimes, we didn't. Other times, my mom would get a day's work here or there, and her employer would send home food for us. There was a guy in Chinatown who owned a restaurant. He'd give me rice and lo mein if I went in. Every now and then someone would give me a half-eaten sandwich or something."

"You ate leftovers?"

"Yeah. I even dumpster dived a few times. Not when my mother was around. She hated that. She's a classy woman. Being homeless didn't change who she is."

"It shouldn't."

"It didn't. She was determined to find her own way and get us out of there. She never resorted to prostitution or selling drugs, like a lot of homeless people do. And she was determined no one would touch me. Ever."

As a mother should be, of course. But when I found out about my father and what my mother had been through at his hand, I truly understood her determination.

"She sounds amazing."

"She is." I force a laugh. "She agrees with you about my oenology degrees, though."

"Oh?"

"Yeah. She wanted me to go to trade school right out of high school so I could start making money. She didn't want me ever to be in the situation we were in when I was a kid."

He smiles. Sort of. A half smile.

I'll take it.

"But I worked my ass off in high school and got great scholarships and grants. The fact that we had virtually no money helped a lot. There's a ton of college money available for those who really need it."

He says nothing.

Of course, he never needed it. Didn't matter anyway, since he didn't finish college. I want to ask why, but that's a question for another time. This is about *me* opening up. Not pushing him to open up.

"I read all the time. I still read a lot, but not like when I was a kid. When you grow up without TV and everything, books are your best friends."

"Books?" he says.

"Yeah. Books. You do read, don't you?"

"Not much. I mean, not for a while. What's your favorite book?"

"*Kidnapped.*"

Dale goes rigid. Over a book?

I'm not sure what to do, so I say, "Anyway, back to my ... "

"Your what?"

I draw in a breath. "My father. Back to my father."

"You said he died."

"Yes, and he did, in a way. But before I came here, my mother told me the truth about him. He's dead."

"I'm sorry."

"Please. Don't be." I draw in another breath. "I don't let myself think about what I'm about to say, Dale. It's something I'd rather forget. In a way, I wish my mother had never told me, but I understand why she did. We have to know where we come from. We have to keep ourselves from making the same mistakes as our parents. Not that I'd ever do what my father did ... "

He brings the back of my hand to his lips and kisses it gently. A sweet gesture, and I think I fall in love with him a little bit more, if that's even possible.

"It's okay," he says. "Tell me."

CHAPTER FORTY-TWO

Dale

Homeless.

Ashley was homeless.

When she told me she sometimes went to bed hungry, I never imagined . . .

My sweet Ashley.

She's opening up, probably hoping I'll do the same.

Unfortunately, she's going to be disappointed.

"My father wasn't a good man," she says. "He died years ago. In prison."

I lift my eyebrows. For some reason, though, I'm not overly surprised. A person doesn't "not talk" about a parent if he or she is a paragon of society.

"I'm sorry," I say again.

"I didn't know the man, and once my mother told me the truth about him, I'm glad I never knew him."

"You mean he was a criminal."

She clears her throat. "Yeah. And what he did. To her."

A bad feeling lodges in my stomach—kind of like I ate some rank food and the acid is trying to digest it but can't.

A feeling not unlike . . .

I shake my head to clear my thoughts. "Ashley, what did he do?"

Her neck moves as she swallows slowly. "He raped her, Dale. And I'm the result."

That acidic lump in my stomach balloons into nausea that threatens to prick its talons through my flesh.

Ashley's mother and I have something in common, then. I don't want to go there, but I can't help thinking about it.

This beautiful woman—this woman I love more than anything—only exists because a criminal forced himself on her mother.

What must it be like to go through life with a child of a rape? Did she remember the horror every time she looked at Ashley? Beautiful Ashley?

Ashley has nothing but good to say about her mother, though. Clearly, then, her mother loved her daughter more than she hated her rapist.

An amazing woman. Well, she had to be to raise such a wonderful daughter in such horrific circumstances. Homelessness. Hunger. Trauma.

And I know what all of those feel like.

I can probably relate more to Ashley's mother than I can to Ashley herself.

But Ashley will never know. Ashley can't ever know those things I keep so bottled up inside.

I've let enough out already.

Ashley gulps again. "Are you going to say anything? Please tell me I haven't made a mistake by telling you this."

I rub my thumb into the palm of her hand. "Of course not. I just... I hate the thought of you ever being cold or hungry. And your mother... What she went through..."

I can say no more without letting negative emotion overwhelm me, and I'm already on that perilous edge, sitting here while my degenerate of a birth father has life-threatening surgery.

I know how I feel, yet I don't know how I feel.

"Thank you," Ashley says softly. "I just wanted you to know."

I don't want any secrets between us.

Those are the words she doesn't utter but that I hear plain as day anyway.

But secrets ... Some secrets aren't fit for conversation.

Some secrets have to stay buried forever.

I open my mouth but am saved from talking by a nurse approaching us.

"Mr. Steel," the young woman says, "Dr. Larson sent me to tell you that Mr. Jolly's surgery will take longer than expected."

I wrinkle my forehead, wondering what I should be feeling. "Why is that?"

"We found an anomaly in his cardiac anatomy. His aortic valve has a deformity."

"Didn't you do an echocardiogram?"

"Of course, but it's a minute deformity that wasn't detectable. The doctor has to repair it before she can complete the bypass."

"Did this deformity contribute to his heart attack?"

"There's no way to know that without testing. Mr. Jolly isn't in any further danger. The surgery will just take longer."

"How much longer?"

"Probably several more hours."

"You've already been in there for two."

"This is a complex surgery, sir."

"I understand that. But—"

Ashley takes my hand. "How much longer?"

"Probably at least four hours. Possibly five."

"All right. Come on, Dale. We should get some lunch."

"That's a good idea," the nurse says. "Make sure reception has your number so they can call you if anything comes up, but otherwise, it's a waiting game at this point."

Things jumble in my head. What does this mean for me genetically? If he has a heart deformity, do I?

I open my mouth to ask, but the nurse turns and walks back through the double doors.

Fuck.

More shit to deal with.

"You need to eat something," Ashley says again.

"Not hungry," I grumble.

"Doesn't matter." She tugs on my hand. "Let's go."

I sigh. Why not let her take charge? I sure as hell don't know what to do at this point. My father abandoned me. If he hadn't, maybe Donny and I wouldn't have been sitting ducks that horrible day.

Now the asshole may have given me a heart deformity.

What next?

Yeah, pity party for me. It's not my style, but what the hell? The man lying with his chest cut open fathered me.

I should feel something.

But I feel nothing. Absolutely nothing.

If he dies on the table, I won't shed a tear.

If he doesn't, I'll probably never see him again.

"Come on." Ashley tugs once more.

I relent and allow her to lead me out of the waiting area.

CHAPTER FORTY-THREE

Ashley

After dragging Dale out of the hospital and to a nearby sandwich shop, I stood over him while he ate his roast beef on sourdough and drained a full glass of iced tea.

He fought me at every step.

We're back in the waiting room now. After four hours of excruciating silence—Dale didn't ask me any more about my father, and he didn't volunteer any information about his own past—we just got word that the doctor will be out soon to talk to us.

"Dale."

I jump at the voice.

It's Talon.

Dale stands. "Hey, Dad. You didn't have to come down here."

"I'd've been here sooner, but I had meetings that couldn't wait. I see you haven't been alone. Thank you, Ashley."

"It's no problem," I say. "This is where I want to be."

Talon smiles at me. Does he know? Did Jade tell him I didn't spend the night at home?

Get over yourself, Ash. None of that even remotely matters.

"We all appreciate it," Talon says. "Any news?"

"Actually, yeah," Dale says. "The doc should be out soon to talk to us."

Dr. Larson steps through the double doors.

"Here she comes now," I say.

"Mr. Steel," she says to Dale.

"How is he?"

"He's doing pretty well at the moment." She eyes me and then Talon.

"Sorry," Dale says. "This is my father, Talon Steel, and you met my friend Ashley. It's okay to speak in front of them."

"Certainly," the doctor says. "As you know, your father—er, Mr. Jolly—has an abnormal aortic valve that we had to replace while we were in there. That's part of what took so long. He's recovering in the ICU, where he'll be for the next few days. He's still unconscious, which is normal. We keep heart patients intubated for several hours after surgery, and we keep them pretty sedated as well."

Dale's lips move slightly, but nothing comes out, almost like he doesn't know what to say.

Talon steps up then. "Can we see him?"

"I can let one of you in if you'd like," Dr. Larson says, "but he won't know you're there."

Dale shakes his head. "It's okay. Let him rest."

Dr. Larson nods as she hands Dale a card. "Here's my information if you have any other questions."

"How long will he be here?" Talon asks.

"At least four days, possibly longer. Then no driving or heavy lifting for two months. He'll get all of that information in his discharge instructions. Will one of you be staying with him?"

Dale lifts his eyebrows. More like makes them nearly fly off his forehead.

"We'll see that he has adequate care," Talon says.

That seems to satisfy the doctor. She nods and then turns back toward the double doors, disappearing through them.

Suddenly I feel like a very visible third wheel here. The air is thick, and I'm almost suffocating. "Since you're here now," I say to Talon, "I think I'll find my way back to the ranch. I don't want to miss another day of work tomorrow."

"Nonsense," Talon says. "I'll book all of us into the Carlton for as long as necessary."

"Dad, I don't think—"

"No argument," Talon says to Dale. "This man is responsible for bringing you into the world. The least we can do is let him know he's not alone."

Now I feel really weird. "I came here to work," I say.

"She's right, Dad," Dale agrees. "It's harvest time. Not just for me but for you too. We can't stay here."

I don't want to stay here.

Those are the words Dale really wants to say. I hear them floating on the velvety burgundy of his voice.

Talon stays quiet for a moment, his head cocked as if he's in thought. Finally, "All right, Dale. Take Ashley home. See to the harvest. I know how much it means to you."

"You're not saying . . . " Dale begins.

"Yes. I'll stay here with your father."

"*You're* my father, and the ranch needs you now."

"We've got the best staff in the business," Talon says. "The orchard will get along fine without me for a couple days."

"Dad . . . "

"Did I not just say no argument? Go. Both of you. Someone should be here when the man wakes up."

"The nurse will be here," Dale says without feeling.

Talon's jawline tenses. "You've made your feelings clear.

Go. I understand. But do not attempt to sway me. I will stay here so Floyd is not alone when he wakes up. The man is responsible for bringing two of the people I love most into this world."

"Neither one of us owes him a damned thing," Dale says.

"You do. You owe him your life. Literally. And I owe him for giving me you and your brother."

Dale says nothing.

The words hang in the air, and though I haven't seen colors in other voices since I met Dale and his voice had such an impact, a new shade cloaks me now.

Talon's voice is dark blue—a calming dark blue, like the night sky. It's the voice of authority, and also the voice of a father's love. This man loves his child so much that he also loves the man who's responsible for his existence.

A lump catches in my throat.

Does my mother feel that way about my father? The vehicle that caused her such pain and torment but that also brought me into her life?

I hate what he did to my mother, but other than that, I have no feeling at all for the man.

Before I can contemplate the thought further, Dale grabs my hand. "Let's go."

"I'll call you if there's any news," Talon says.

Dale nods.

"Wait, wait." My thoughts are muddled. Love fills me. Love for Dale. And this man, who just went through surgery . . . This man is responsible for Dale being in the world. Talon's words have made me see everything differently.

I don't know. Maybe I'm overemotional because of the situation. Because of my love for Dale. Because I told him about my childhood. My father. Everything's on the surface now, and I don't know how to deal with any of it.

Except I can't leave.

I feel the same way Talon does. The man in the ICU brought the man I love into this world.

Anyone who loves Dale should be here.

"For God's sake," Dale says. "What is it?"

"I . . . I think I want to stay. I mean, I know I have an internship, and if you want to fire me, I get it. I probably deserve it. But this man . . . Like your dad said. He's responsible for bringing you into the world, Dale, and you know how I feel about you."

Dale pushes his hand through his mass of hair. "Are you both serious right now?"

"It's all right, Ashley," Talon says. "Go with Dale. He needs you more than Floyd right now."

Dale messes with his hair once more. "For fuck's sake . . . "

Talon's words ring true. He'll stay here with Floyd, and he needs me to stay with Dale. To take care of his son. For even though Floyd abandoned Dale and Dale doesn't feel anything for him, he's still Dale's birth father, and Dale is struggling on some level.

Dale always seems to be struggling on some level.

"Go on," Talon says again. "I'll call your mother and tell her what's going on."

"You're right," I say to Talon. "Let's go, Dale."

CHAPTER FORTY-FOUR

Dale

I take Ashley home to the main house.

"Wait just a minute," she says. "I'm going with you."

"Ash, it's late. I'm exhausted. We got nothing done today, and I just need ... "

"Need what?" she asks. "What do you need? I'll do whatever you need me to do."

I need to be alone.

But the words don't make it past the lump in my throat. Because I do want to be alone, but I also want to be with Ashley.

Ashley, who makes my world a brighter place.

Ashley, whose smile could melt a glacier.

Ashley, who, God help me, I love more than my own life.

She continues, "Your father said you need me. I'm not going to let you go through this alone."

"Damn it, Ashley, I'm not going through anything! Just let me ... " I pound one fist on the steering wheel, inadvertently honking the horn.

"It's late," Ashley says softly. "You'll wake up your mom."

"My mom's not asleep yet. Damn!" I pound it again, avoiding the horn this time.

She touches my upper arm. "Hey. Let's go. Penny's bladder is probably about to burst, and she needs to be fed. I'll take care of all that. You need a shower and then maybe a soak in your hot tub."

What I need is . . .

Hell, I don't have a clue what I need.

I turn and gaze into Ashley's sparkling blue eyes. They're tired, but still they dazzle.

"Please," she says. "Let me take care of you tonight."

"You're as exhausted as I am, baby."

She closes her eyes for a split second and then opens them. "I like that. When you call me baby."

My hand, seemingly of its own accord, reaches toward her, caresses her silky cheek. "I'm okay. I don't need anyone to take care of me."

"So? Maybe it's what *I* need. Maybe I need to take care of you."

I chuckle softly, but it comes out more like a groan. "You don't need that."

Those tired eyes light on fire then. Blue fire. "Who are *you* to say what I need?"

I let out a slow sigh. Do I want her with me tonight? Yeah. I do. And it's not because I'm having a rough time, or because I'm worried about my birth father, or because I missed the harvest, or because I'm having a pity party for myself.

I want her with me tonight for one reason and one reason only.

I love her.

I fucking love her.

I maneuver the truck out of the driveway and head to the guesthouse.

Once home, we let Penny out.

"Relax," Ashley says. "I'll feed her. What do you need? A

glass of water? Glass of wine?"

Why do I resist being cared for? That was always part of the issue with my mom. She wanted to constantly hover over me, try to make up for the pain I'd been through. It was a loving gesture, but it wasn't what I needed or wanted.

Ashley's words barrel through my mind. *Maybe it's what I need.*

All those years, did I neglect my mother's needs?

Did she *need* to care for me, and I turned her away at every count?

"Shit," I say aloud.

"What's wrong?" Ashley asks.

"Nothing. A glass of wine would be nice. Thanks. There's an open bottle of Ruby in the pantry sealed with the Vacu Vin."

"I'll get it. I'm going to get you some water too. You're probably dehydrated. I haven't seen you drink anything but coffee and your iced tea at lunch. Go sit down."

I drop into a kitchen chair.

"Not there," she admonishes. "Go to the family room. Sit somewhere comfortable. I'll bring your wine and water in a minute, right after I feed Penny."

Numbly, I obey her. I'm not used to obeying anyone, but honestly? Right now it feels kind of good to have someone else tell me what to do.

It means I don't have to think.

Thinking is overrated, I think.

Then I laugh aloud at my own oxymoron, which makes me realize how fucked in the head I truly am at this moment.

I plunk down on my leather chair and recline it as far as it goes. I close my eyes, listening to Ashley shuffling in the kitchen, preparing Penny's food.

"Hey, sweetie," she says as she opens the door.

Penny's claws tap the floor as she runs to her feast.

Then the pop as Ashley removes the vacuum sealer from the wine bottle. Soft trickles as she pours, and then louder ones for the water.

Sounds. I'm only used to Penny's and my sounds at home. Hearing Ashley's sounds comforts me in an odd way.

And maybe that's not so odd after all.

I've resisted comfort since I came to Steel Ranch. Even when Aunt Mel and my other therapist told me I was worthy of comfort, still I held back.

Chills erupt on the back of my neck.

The reason...

The reason I don't deserve comfort. It's there, hidden in the back of my mind, blurred like a black cancer made of crab-shaped cells that dig their spiky claws into me and don't let go.

This is what I feared.

This...

When I opened up to Ashley, let her awaken me, cherish me...

This...

This is what I risk letting loose on the world.

Emotions curl inside me, but in my fatigue, they stay where they are.

"Here you go, babe." Ashley hands me a tall glass of ice water. "Drink up, and then you can have your wine."

"You sound like my mother," I can't help saying. "I'm thirty-five years old. I want my wine."

"And you'll have it," she snaps, "as soon as you drink some water."

I'm too exhausted to argue. I take the water, intending to

sip it, but it slides like a waterfall down my throat, easing my dryness. Ashley is right. I'm dehydrated. Big time.

"Better?" she says.

I nod.

"Good. Here's your wine."

I sigh. "I think I want some more water."

She grabs the glass. "You got it."

Before I can tell her to stay, she's back in the kitchen refilling my glass. I take a sip of the wine. Its dark cherry and woodiness coats my mouth as I swallow.

Ashley returns with my water and a glass of wine for herself. She sits down on the couch so she's facing me.

How I wish I sat there instead of in my recliner. I could be cuddling her against me, embracing her light and warmth. I drain the glass of water and take another sip of wine.

"Come here," I say.

She rises. "What do you need?"

I set the wine on the end table and grab her hand, pulling her into my lap. "You. I need you, Ashley."

CHAPTER FORTY-FIVE

Ashley

Dale's hard cock pushes against my ass.

I honestly wasn't expecting this. "Amazing what a little hydration can do." I giggle.

"I won't deny that it helped," Dale says, "but I've been hard since we got home."

"Let me take care of you, then," I say.

"You've *been* taking care of me. I wasn't asking for . . . "

"I know you weren't, but you're exhausted and tense. Not a good combination." I climb off his lap and onto the floor and then unbuckle his belt. "I can help you with that."

"Ashley . . . "

"No use fighting me," I say. "I'm in control now."

He groans, the vibration low in his chest—a brown earthy color.

I release his cock and pull it out. He's huge and hard, already a drop of pre-come emerging at the tip. I lick it off.

He sucks in a breath. "Damn."

"What can I do for you?" I meet his gaze. "Anything, Dale. Tell me what you want."

"Suck me. Please."

He doesn't have to ask twice. I take him between my lips, savoring the salty musk of him. He's warm inside my mouth—

warm and huge and beautiful. I slide my lips along his shaft, sucking gently, and then I release him, moving backward until I almost release his cock head.

He groans again, earthy and brown with a translucent veil of burgundy.

A groan that says how much he loves what I'm doing to him.

I slide along his shaft again, slowly, teasing him. More groans. A sigh. Then he goes rigid.

And I realize he doesn't need to be teased right now. He needs release, and he needs it badly.

I grab his shaft in my right hand, using it to increase the friction as I continue to work him with my lips and tongue.

He sucks in a breath. "Fuck."

Yes, it's okay. Come, Dale. Let it go. Release.

I increase my speed, hoping he knows not to hold back. That I don't care about my own satisfaction right now. Only him. Only what the man I love needs.

His breaths become more rapid, and he grabs the back of my head, increasing my pace.

That's it. Let it go, my love. Let go.

When the contractions begin at the base of his cock, I feel them through my whole body. Tiny combustions that increase, increase, increase, until he's holding me in place and filling me. Coming inside my mouth, down my throat.

Using me for his release.

And I'm okay with that. With whatever he needs.

I breathe through my nose as he stays embedded against my throat, still pulsing.

Determination sweeps through me. I'll stay here until he's done. Until he's completely released and relaxed. I love him that much.

A few seconds later, he releases my head, and I slowly slide my lips to his tip, licking him as I go.

"Fuck," he says huskily. "I should have—"

"Stop. This was about you, and I'm fine with that." I stand and hand him his wine.

He takes a sip. "I could fall asleep right here."

"Then do it. Nothing's stopping you."

"But you . . . "

I smooth back his disheveled hair. "I'm not an issue. In fact, I think I'll take my own advice and have a soak in your tub. It's been a long day."

"If that's not the truth." He closes his eyes, his breathing slowing down.

I kiss his lips lightly, grab the empty glasses, and head to the kitchen. Penny is finishing her supper. "Feel like going out for a dip, Penny?" I open the back door, and she scrambles out.

The evening breeze is slightly cool—a perfect night for the hot tub. I haven't been in a tub since my first night here when Dee and I soaked at the main house. I wore a suit that night, but I don't have one here. The tub is adequately secluded, so I shed my clothes.

Goosebumps erupt on my flesh. Crap. I forgot to take the cover off the tub. I grab one corner of it and find it's a lot heavier than I anticipated. With a few breathless moves, I get it pushed to the side. I scurry into the steaming water.

Ah . . . Heaven.

Penny jumps up so her forepaws are on the rail of the tub. I pet her with a wet hand. "Good dog. Such a good girl!"

She jumps down and runs into the yard, chasing some invisible squirrel or rabbit.

I close my eyes and breathe. Just breathe.

Next to being in Dale's arms, this is pretty much the best thing ever.

What a freaking day! How wonderful to finally relax, to let the water soothe me. I flip the switch for the jets and enjoy a massage against my back and shoulders.

Yes, this is what I need. Pure relaxation. Pure . . . solace. Pure . . . paradise.

★ ★ ★

"Ashley!"

I jerk. Someone's touching my shoulder, pulling me out of the hot tub.

"What the—"

"You fell asleep!" Dale shouts. "Do you have any idea how dangerous that is?"

"You . . . What . . . ?"

"You were sleeping. How long have you been out here? Where's your robe and towel?"

"Robe and towel?"

"Yes. A towel. You need a towel or you'll freeze."

I blink my eyes a few times. How long *have* I been out here? It's dark. Really dark. Stars are numerous against the black sky. Penny jingles around Dale's legs.

Towel. I don't have one. I just . . . I just . . .

"I took my clothes off out here. I don't have a towel."

"For God's sake." Dale strips off his shirt and lays it down. Then he pulls me out of the tub and wraps it around me.

I inhale. Salty pine and cinnamon man. My Dale. The best fragrance ever. I moan and close my eyes again.

"Don't ever do that again," Dale is saying. "Promise me."

"Do what?"

"Fall asleep in the hot tub! You could have drowned!"

Finally, I wake up out of my alpha state. "Drowned? I'm a good swimmer, and the hot tub isn't even deep."

"But you were asleep."

"And if I ended up underwater, I'd wake up."

"Still. Please. Never again. Promise me."

"Dale, what's this about?"

"Just promise me, Ashley."

His tone is jarred. He's scared, and I don't know why.

"Babe," I say, "you know this isn't something to worry about. I'm fine."

"Please." Again with the tone. It's fear, and the burgundy color has divided into black and brighter red. Like the parting of the sea. I've never experienced a sound-color like this before.

And I know I need to make this promise to him. If I don't, he'll . . . He'll . . . I don't know what he'll do.

"Okay, I promise. Never again, Dale. I promise I'll never fall asleep in the hot tub again."

He lets out a slow breath. "Good. Thank you."

This is about more than me falling asleep in the hot tub. But I can't ask him. I won't ask him.

Because I'll just be disappointed when he walls himself off and doesn't tell me.

CHAPTER FORTY-SIX

Dale

Donny lifted his head from the kind man's chest. "I'm sorry, Dale. I tried."

"No!" I grabbed my little brother into a bear hug. "No, God. I'm so sorry. I never meant... I'm so glad you're okay. That you're alive."

"But we made a pact."

"It was a stupid pact. We were starving and hurting. But now we're not. I want to live, Donny, and I want you to live too."

★ ★ ★

It *was* a stupid pact, but to a seven-year-old little boy, it was a blood promise between brothers. Donny had tried to drown himself because I told him to. We made the suicide pact when we were captive, when we didn't have any hope left.

And after I...

After I did the unthinkable.

Ending our lives seemed preferable to living the rest of them the way we seemed to be destined to, and after I had...

God, can't. Can't even think it.

So Donny and I made a pact. If either of us ever had the chance to end our own life, we'd take it. We'd escape from the hell we were living. That was all we wanted for each other and for ourselves.

251

Donny was seven, though, and when Dad and Uncle Ryan rescued us, he didn't realize the pact was no longer valid. When Aunt Ruby helped him take a bath and then looked away for just a moment, Donny tried to drown himself in the tub.

Aunt Ruby was a cop back then, and she knew CPR. She resuscitated Donny, and he was no worse for the wear despite being malnourished and covered with bruises and sores from the beatings we both endured.

I've never gotten over how frightened I was that day.

So when I saw Ashley, the woman I love, asleep in the hot tub...

I freaked. I freaked big time.

"Dale"—she cups my cheek after I get her inside and into a warm robe—"what's this about?"

I've kept so much from her, and I'll continue to do so.

But I can give her this much.

"My brother almost drowned in the tub when he was seven."

"Oh!" She melts against me. "I'm so sorry."

"Finding you asleep. It brought it all back. So vividly."

She hugs me tighter and says nothing.

Unusual for Ashley, but I don't need her words. I need only her presence. Her comfort.

And for the first time in a long time, I feel good about opening up.

Really good.

★ ★ ★

The next few days pass in a blur. Ashley and I leave Uncle Ry to do the tastings, and we work the harvest. We work straight through the weekend and are exhausted by the end of the day. Donny visits for one day, to meet our birth father in Grand Junction. He's still in the ICU but is doing okay.

I sleep at home. Not in the mountains, which is usual for me during Syrah harvest, but at home, with Ashley next to me.

And I begin to wonder if maybe I can actually do this. Have a relationship with her.

"Dale?" Ashley says, leaning back in the hot tub after a particularly grueling day among the Syrah vines.

"Yeah?"

"Could I . . . have your mother's necklace back?"

My heart jolts—in a good or bad way, I'm not sure. I will give it to her, though. It's hers. It will never belong to anyone else.

"Of course. I was never sure why you wouldn't take it in the first place."

She sighs. "I guess I was hoping . . . Hoping maybe you'd change your mind and give us beyond two months. But now I want to take things day by day, because each day with you gets better, Dale. Each day I love you more, and even if you can't commit to forever with me, I want the beautiful necklace to remember our time together."

"It was always yours, Ash. I knew it as soon as I placed it around your neck. No one else could ever wear it."

She kisses me on the cheek so hard that I nearly fall over into the water.

"Let's go get it now!"

I chuckle. "All right. I'm turning into a prune anyway." I climb out of the tub and hand Ashley her robe.

We—Penny at our heels—head into the house and back

into the master suite, dripping water onto the hardwood as we walk. I open the top drawer of my chest and find the velvet box buried under my boxer briefs. I open it and finger the necklace.

It's worth all of two hundred bucks. I could buy Ashley something so much more elegant, but this is a gift from my heart.

"Turn around," I tell her, "and lift your hair off your neck."

Easier said than done, as her hair is wet and sticking to her creamy skin. But she manages, and I clasp the garnet necklace around her.

She turns to face me. "Well?"

"You're beautiful," I say. "It was made for you. Now lose the robe."

Slowly, she unties the terrycloth sash and parts the two sides of the white robe, letting it fall from her shoulders into a heap at her feet.

Her pink skin shines with the moisture left from the hot tub, and the garnets around her neck seem to glow from the light that lives within her.

"I've never seen you look more beautiful," I say on a breath.

She giggles nervously. "With my hair all wet and sticky?"

"You look perfect. Perfectly delectable." I stalk toward her—

Only to be interrupted by my phone.

"Damn!" I shake my head. "I'm going to ignore it."

That's not like me, and Ashley seems to know.

"It's okay," she says. "Go ahead. It might be important."

"Nothing's important at ten o'clock at night."

"That's my point. Anyone who bothers you at this hour

will have a good reason. Go ahead. I'd never forgive myself if I made you miss an important call."

Yeah, she has a point. Still, I resist. I've actually felt good the past few days. Telling her about Donny nearly drowning opened up a part of my heart I feared was closed for all time, and the weirdest part? Nothing bad came along with it. Sure, I still have secrets buried inside, but they didn't come roaring out as I feared they would.

I reluctantly pick up my phone. It's not a number I recognize. "Dale Steel."

"Mr. Steel, this is Dr. Jane Forrester. I'm the on-call cardiologist at St. Mary's. I have some news about Floyd Jolly."

"Yeah?"

"I'm afraid Mr. Jolly has developed sepsis."

"That's an infection, right?"

"Yes, a systemic infection. It's uncommon after heart surgery, as we administer antibiotics, but it does happen."

I inhale. "All right. What does this mean for his prognosis?"

"He's running a high fever and his kidneys are failing. We're administering more antibiotics as well as continuing his pain meds. He's on oxygen. But I have to be honest with you. It doesn't look good."

I drop my mouth open.

What am I supposed to feel?

I've felt more in the past three days with Ashley than I've ever allowed myself to feel, and right now, I feel . . .

Not sad, exactly. Not angry. Not happy, of course. But it's definitely something that I can't pinpoint.

Regret? Perhaps a touch. But why? Floyd is the one who should be having regrets.

Resignation? Yeah, that's definitely there, kind of mixed

with the tiny smidge of regret.

"What is it?" Ashley asks softly.

I don't answer her.

"Mr. Steel?"

"Yeah, I'm here."

"We've called in the infectious disease specialist, and we have the internist on call looking at him now. If his kidneys continue to fail, we may have to administer dialysis."

"Okay. I see."

"And there's one more thing."

"Yes?"

"He wants to see you."

I'm not sure why her words surprise me, but they do. "Why?"

"He knows his situation, Mr. Steel. We've been honest with him. His body is weak from his withdrawal and from the open-heart surgery. It's not likely that he'll live."

CHAPTER FORTY-SEVEN

Ashley

In a robotic tone—only a tiny sliver of his dark red shines through—Dale explains to me what the doctor on the phone said about his birth father.

"You should go," I say.

"Not tonight."

"What if he doesn't make it through the night? He wants to see you."

"Ashley, I'm exhausted. I can't do it tonight. I'm sorry if that disappoints you, but I just can't."

Don't push.

Those words have become my mantra with Dale. But a man is dying here. The man who fathered him.

Then again, if my father had lived longer and then asked for me on his deathbed, would I have gone?

Yes, I would have. Out of curiosity if nothing else. Part of me wants to know if the birthmark on my shoulder came from him. Or my full lips. My mother's are thin.

But Dale and I are two different people, and he's already met his birth father. Indeed, he already spent a whole day at the hospital during the man's bypass surgery.

"I understand," I finally say, "but don't you think you should tell your parents?"

He stays silent for a few seconds. Then, "Yeah, we probably should."

My heart jumps. "We?"

He nods. "We. Would you come with me?"

"Of course! Do you think they're still up?"

"Dad will be. He never goes to bed before midnight. Mom is a crapshoot. She might be."

"Then let's go." I grab my clothes and start getting dressed.

"Ashley..."

I nearly stumble as I try to put my leg into my jeans. "Yeah?"

"Thank you."

"For what?"

"For just... I don't know. For being with me."

I stumble toward him with only one leg in my jeans and melt into his arms. "There's nowhere I'd rather be."

★ ★ ★

"The necklace looks lovely on you." Jade smiles.

We're sitting in Talon's office, where Dale just told his parents about Floyd.

I touch the necklace, letting its jewels slide beneath my fingertips. "I'm honored that he wants me to have it."

"I knew when I gave it to him that he'd make it a special gift to someone, and I see that he has."

Warmth coats me. I have Dale's mother's blessing, and that means everything.

"I don't want to go tonight, Dad," Dale is saying to Talon. "I just can't."

"Fair enough," Talon says. "We'll go first thing in the morning."

"What if he doesn't make it?"

"Then he won't make it. You have nothing to feel guilty about, son. But you do need to call your brother."

Dale sighs and messes with his still-damp hair. "I hate to pull the father-son card, but would you do it?"

"I'll call him. I wish he'd stayed another day. Then he'd be here and could see Floyd one last time."

"He may still be able to," Dale says. "We don't know for sure that he's going to die."

"That's true." Talon yawns.

Talon's tone isn't convincing any of us. Dale's birth father's days are numbered. I'll respect Dale's decision to wait until morning. I just hope Floyd can hold out.

"Thanks, Dad," Dale says. "I owe you one."

"You owe me nothing. Fathers take care of their kids. For life." Talon's eyes take on a sadness.

I look to Jade, who's watching her husband, her expression worried.

We walk back to the guesthouse hand in hand.

"Your dad had a weird expression on his face when he said that fathers take care of their kids."

Dale nods. "Yeah, he gets that way sometimes. Usually when he's thinking about his own father."

"The one who died in prison."

"Yeah. No one talks much about him, but it's clear that he wasn't the best father in the world."

"I don't imagine he was, if he died in prison."

"He didn't go to prison until late in life. He barely spent a year there, and he died under mysterious circumstances."

I widen my eyes. "Meaning...?"

"Meaning he was in great health and just died one night.

His heart literally just stopped. No one knows why."

"Well, he was old, I imagine."

"Not that old. In his sixties."

That *is* odd. My father was young when he passed, but I know the reason for his death. He was beaten and violated until his body couldn't take any more. Even now, I can't bring much emotion to the surface.

"That's pretty much all I know about my grandfather," Dale says.

"Why was he in prison?"

"I don't know for sure, but there's some record that he withheld evidence in a federal investigation."

"What type of investigation?"

"I don't know. The records were sealed, and like I said, the family doesn't talk about it. I've talked about it with my brother, sisters, and cousins. We're not even sure if our parents know."

"That doesn't make any sense. They have to know."

Dale gets distant, then. "I think they do. For a while, I wasn't sure, but I recently learned something, and . . . "

"And what?"

"I can't. I don't want to talk about this. Not right now. I'm too tired."

My instinct tells me to push him, but I know better. He's already given me more than I expected tonight and in the last few days. I can't risk what we have.

"Let's go to bed," I say.

"Best idea I've heard all night." Dale takes my hand and leads me to the bedroom.

I don't expect anything, so I'm more than surprised when he grabs me and crushes his mouth to mine.

Exhaustion weighs on both of us, and I feel it in this kiss. His lips don't slide over mine with as much passion as they normally do, yet I feel his desire almost more than usual. As if the kiss is occurring in that alpha dreamland between wakefulness and sleep, and we're cloaked in burgundy translucence.

I don't know how our clothes end up off, but they do, and we're naked, writhing against each other as we kiss.

Dale breaks the kiss and lays me gently on the bed. He doesn't speak, just spreads my legs and buries his tongue between them.

Still in dreamland, still floating in that red-wine cloud. Dale devours me with his lips and tongue, his growls making the cloak around us more vibrant.

I sink into the soft bed, grasping the covers. I'm still in alpha heaven, where climaxes are vibrant and they come quickly.

He nips at my clit, and I soar instantly toward the peak. Almost there... Almost there...

When one of his long, thick fingers breaches my channel.

"God! Dale!" The orgasm breaks me into pieces like shattering crystal. Cracks everywhere, like the jagged glass of a broken mirror. All in a good way as my molecules find their way back together.

Back together, back together, back together.

One. One with Dale because now he's inside me, his cock stretching and burning me, tunneling through me like a baton of fire.

Ashley. I love you, Ashley. Fuck, I love you so much.

The words float around me, encased in silk. Yes, he's saying them, but even so, they fly directly into my mind, as if, for one timeless moment, we're truly one.

Our minds have melded. Our hearts have joined like our bodies.

And still we exist in dreamland, in the Syrah-hued haze.

And still . . .

And still . . .

I'm on fire. At the same time, ice shrouds me. I fly higher, higher, and higher still.

Until . . .

Until . . .

"God, I love you." He thrusts hard into me, holding our bodies together as if they're no longer joined but have fused into one being.

He fills every empty crevice inside me. Everything bad in my life ceases to exist in this one tender moment.

And I know . . .

I know . . .

This won't end after two months.

This won't end.

Ever.

CHAPTER FORTY-EIGHT

Dale

"I need you here," I tell Ashley in the morning.

"I need to be with you," she says.

I called St. Mary's earlier. Floyd Jolly is still alive and still wants to see Donny and me. After a quick call to Donny, I learned he has court today and can't get here. He plans to come tomorrow—if it's not too late.

I want to tell Ashley to come. That I need her. That I need her more than I ever thought I could need anyone.

But—

"This is something I have to do alone."

Truth be told, I don't know how I'll react to seeing my birth father on his deathbed. I'm still struggling with the knowledge of what happened to my real father. Questions. So many questions. Not my father. Not Talon Steel. Strong and muscular Talon Steel. How? And why? And what does my grandfather have to do with all of it?

But those thoughts have to wait. I'm a master of burying things, and I bury this now. It doesn't change anything.

I'm going to face Floyd alone. I've done enough opening up to Ashley for now.

"All right." Ashley finally relents. "Be careful, please. Driving, I mean."

I chuckle softly. "I've been driving for twenty years."

"I know, but you're upset."

"I'm not that upset." Not a lie at all. I'm feeling... I'm not sure what I'm feeling. I can't think about my father and what he went through. As for Floyd... It's an odd sensation to know that one of the two people who made you is dead. When it first happened, I was only ten, and I didn't think about it in those terms. Now? My last link to my body will be gone from earth soon.

The emotion is bleak but not sad. I'd likely feel much worse if Floyd had ever been a true father to me.

"Just come back to me," Ashley says. "Promise?"

I haven't been able to promise her anything beyond the next two months, but I can promise this.

"I'll be back," I say. "Count on it."

★ ★ ★

"He doesn't have much time," the nurse says. "Try not to upset him."

"I have no intention of upsetting him. He called *me* here. He's the one who says he needs to talk to me."

"I understand, just—"

I whisk past her and into Floyd's ICU room. An aide stands next to him, checking his vitals. I clear my throat, and she turns.

"May I help you?"

"I'm here to see the patient."

"Okay. I'm just finishing up here." She makes some notes, walks to the door, and sets the chart in its place.

Floyd Jolly is pale, his eyes barely open. He looks like he's dying. Which he is, literally. He doesn't look my way. Does he remember that he asked to see me?

So I'm surprised when I hear his voice.

"Come, Dale. Sit down."

A chair sits on the other side of his bed. I walk to it slowly and sit. He still hasn't looked at me.

"I'm here," I say. "What do you want?"

Still, he looks straight ahead. "I'm dying."

"I know."

He grunts.

Did he expect me to say I'm sorry? That I wish he weren't dying? I simply have no feelings on the matter. None.

"Why did you want to see me?"

"Can you call me Dad?" he asks. "Just once?"

Really? This is why he called me here? To play the father card?

"No, I can't."

"Please, just once."

My father—my real father—would tell me to do it. To give him his dying wish. But I'm not letting Floyd off the hook that easily.

"Why me?" I demand. "Why not your other son? My brother? Or why not one of the other kids you probably fathered and then abandoned?"

He doesn't reply.

We sit in silence for a few minutes that seem like years until he finally speaks again.

"I haven't asked you for anything," he says. "You have all the money in the world, and I haven't asked you for a penny. I could have used it."

"You speak the truth," I admit, "but I don't owe you anything either."

"You owe me your life."

Shit. Really? My father said that to me after Floyd's heart attack. It's the truth, of course, but I'm not buying. "So you had a climax inside my mother at the right time. You made me. She had a significant part in it as well, and she stuck around. There's a hell of a lot more to being a father than fertilizing an egg."

A few more moments of silence, and I'm about ready to stand and leave when—

"Please."

"For fuck's sake." I push my hand through my hair. "Fine. Dad. You satisfied now?"

A gurgling sound, and then he produces a sputtering cough. I'm about ready to call the nurse when he stops.

"Sorry about that."

"No problem. You want to tell me why I'm here now?"

"Yes. There's a reason why I tried to find you and your brother, and it wasn't about your money."

"All right. I'll give you that much. Though my dad paid for your rehab."

"He did, and I appreciate it. I told him he didn't have to. Turns out I spent all of a day there."

"My father is a great man. The kind of man you'll never be. He takes care of people who matter to him."

"And I matter to him?"

"Apparently."

"He's a good man."

"Yes. I know that. I believe I just said it. None of this is why I'm here. Let's get on with it."

"I don't have a lot of time."

"Which is a good reason for getting on with it." My voice

is tight, full of tension. Yes, I should be sympathetic to the fact that Floyd is dying, but I can't bring myself to be.

"I had an uncle," he says.

"Yeah? I have three uncles. Great."

"It's difficult for me to talk. Just let me get it out. Please."

I huff. "Fine."

"I had an uncle. My father's brother. Your great-uncle. His name was Frederick Jolly."

He pauses then. Am I supposed to say something? He told me to let him get it out. I stay silent.

"He was an attorney in Denver. He was my father's older brother."

"What was your father's name?" I ask, not sure why. For some reason, I want to know my birth grandfather's name. I could have researched it before now, but I didn't, and I want to know.

"Robert. And your grandmother's name was Michaela Johnson Jolly."

"Why didn't you marry my mother?" I ask.

Again, I'm not sure where the question is coming from, except that this man is dying, and I may never be able to find out this information again.

"She didn't want to get married," he says.

"I don't believe you."

"It's the truth."

"You couldn't even remember her name. You couldn't remember *my* name."

"We were together for four years. You and your brother are three years apart. I'm not lying."

"How could you forget our names?"

"The booze and pills," he says. "It fucked up my brain."

"No shit." I shake my head. "Go on, then. Tell me what I came here for."

"So I needed money."

"For booze and pills?"

He sputters out a cough again, and again I think about calling someone, but he gets it under control.

He makes a gurgling noise and then continues. "I was homeless. On my last dime, and I had this rich uncle. Fred Jolly. My own parents were gone."

"Dead?"

"Yeah. They died when I was twenty-five. A year or so before this."

"So you had no one to bail you out."

"I did. I had Uncle Fred."

"The rich attorney. Tell me. What does all of this have to do with me?"

He coughs again, and this time, one of his machines starts beeping.

I can't help an eye roll. This is getting tedious. I don't really care what he has to say. I already gave him his last wish. I called him Dad, even though he doesn't deserve it.

Hell is obviously summoning him. *So take him, why don't you?* I literally look to the ceiling and then realize my folly. Hell, if it exists, is down, not up. I hold back a laugh as a nurse hurries in.

"Mr. Jolly? Doing okay?" She fidgets with the machines. "You bent your arm again. Try to hold it still, okay? I'm going to reset everything."

A few minutes later, she leaves. He coughs again.

Finally, I rise. "I don't have any more time for this."

"Sit down," he commands.

And his voice, when he takes that tone, is familiar to me. It's...

It's so like my own.

Scary as hell.

What's scarier? I sit. I fucking obey the man.

CHAPTER FORTY-NINE

Ashley

After Dale leaves, I walk to the main house. It's Saturday, and though I'll go work the harvest, I want some orange juice, and Dale's out of it. Maybe I'll run into town later today and pick up groceries.

Or is that too pushy?

I've spent the last several nights at Dale's, but I haven't technically moved in with him. My belongings, with the exception of a toothbrush, my skincare routine, and some pajamas—which of course I never wear at Dale's—are still at the main house. I have to go there every morning to change clothes. So far, I haven't run into Talon or Jade since that first morning, which is good. I know I have no reason to be embarrassed, but still . . .

Jade is sitting at the kitchen table reading something on her tablet when I enter through the back. She looks up.

"Good morning, Ashley. When are you and Dale leaving this morning to go to the hospital?"

"He already left. He wanted to go alone."

Jade sips her coffee and sighs. "That's so like him. He never wants any help with anything."

I nod. She's not wrong.

"Have a seat," she says. "There's juice in the fridge."

"Thank you." I help myself to a glass and pour a serving of O.J. I sit down next to Jade.

"How are you?" she asks. "We haven't had the chance for any girl talk for a while."

"I'm good." I take a sip and swallow. "Dale and I . . ."

"Yes, I know. Talon and I are thrilled for both of you."

"But it's . . . He and I, we . . ." I huff out a sigh. "He only committed to me for the time I'm here. That's all he's giving me."

"Is that enough for you?"

"Of course not! I'm in love with him. But it's all he's giving me, so I'm taking it. And before you say anything, I know I'm worth more, that I deserve more."

"Actually"—she smiles—"I know exactly how you're feeling."

"You do?"

She chuckles. "When I was living here that summer, I took every single second I could get with Talon. He treated me terribly sometimes, but I still savored every moment with him."

"I can't imagine him treating anyone terribly."

"He was different then. A lot like Dale, as I've told you."

"Dale doesn't—" I stop.

"Dale doesn't what?" she asks.

"I was going to say Dale doesn't treat me badly. He doesn't. But there have been a few times when his words weren't the nicest."

She nods. "I understand."

"Jade . . ."

"Hmm?"

"I know you don't talk about these things, but maybe if

you can tell me how you were able to finally reach Talon ... "

She inhales deeply, her expression resigned. "I want to tell you everything, Ashley. I do. But the truth is that it's not my story to tell. I will say this much. Don't give up. You're the best thing that has ever happened to my son. I can see how much you cherish him just by your expression when you say his name. He may not know it yet, but he needs you. Maybe even more than you need him."

I run my finger over a drip of condensation on my juice glass. "It always seems what Dale needs most is his solitude."

"Solitude is important to him. It's true. But you've touched something in him. Something I never could, and Lord knows I tried. Something even Talon never could. He's a little less walled-off since you came along, and that's a very good thing."

"How is it a good thing, if solitude is what he craves?"

"Because in the end, we all—including Dale—yearn to belong to something bigger. Being alone can be wonderful. We all need it sometimes, but at the end of the day, we all want to belong to someone else."

"Not Dale," I say.

"He does, and you've begun to prove it. He just doesn't know it yet."

"I don't know whether to feel good or bad about that," I say. "I don't want to change him. I fell in love with him the way he is."

"Oh, there's so much to love in him," Jade says. "So much that he doesn't even know he has to offer. He's brilliant, of course. And genuine. He'd take a bullet for his father or me in a heartbeat. Or any of his siblings. But mostly, somewhere inside him is a soul that needs to heal. I could tell from the first time we talked, Ashley, that you're attracted to that part of him. The same thing that attracted me to Talon."

"How did you get through to Talon?"

"It took time. Though looking back, we met at the beginning of summer and were married during the fall. Crazy, but it seemed longer."

"Dale and I haven't known each other very long either."

"No, you haven't." She sighs, shaking her head and smiling. "I've said this before, but I see so much of myself in you, except that you're more together than I ever was."

"I don't feel very together sometimes," I say.

"No one feels together all the time."

I nod, though I have a hard time believing Jade doesn't feel together constantly. She's a wonderful mother, a brilliant lawyer, and gorgeous as all get-out. Plus she's just nice. Such a nice woman, and I'm privileged to know her.

"Thank you," I say.

"For what?"

"For letting me stay here. For the opportunity you've given me."

"That was Ryan," she says.

"I know. But I feel like you guys all function as sort of a unit, you know?"

She chuckles. "I suppose we do. Talon and his brothers and sister are all very close."

I gather my nerves. "Is that because of their father?"

"In some ways."

"I asked Dale about him," I say.

"I doubt Dale could tell you much."

"No, he couldn't. Just that he was in prison for tampering with federal evidence, and that he died within a year of his incarceration."

"There's a huge story there," Jade says, "and to be honest, I never agreed with Talon and the others to keep it from the kids. Ruby and Melanie agreed with me, but the rest, including Marj's husband, Bryce, wanted it kept quiet. I was outvoted."

"I don't understand."

"Brad Steel was a very good man. He was also a very bad man."

"What about his wife? Talon's mother?"

"She was mentally ill for most of her life."

I touch my lips, remembering what Ryan told me about the Steel Foundation. "I'm so sorry to hear that."

"She lived out her life in full-time care, in a dreamworld where her children were still small. It's very sad."

But Brendan said she committed suicide. Maybe he meant later. "I had no idea."

"I know. We don't talk about it, and as I said, there's a lot the kids don't know."

"I get it." And I do. My own mother didn't tell me the truth about who my father was until recently. "But they're adults now," I continue. "Don't they deserve to know the truth of their history?"

"I wrestle with that. But look at it this way. Do you think Dale is better off now? Knowing his birth father?"

I stare down at my now-empty glass.

I don't know whether the answer to Jade's question is yes or no.

CHAPTER FIFTY

Dale

"Get on with it," I say. "Rich Uncle Fred."

"Uncle Fred was really rich," he says.

"Well, lawyers tend to do well in big cities."

"Oh, he was way richer than most lawyers. He had outside investments."

"Great, great. He was a damned millionaire. Who cares?"

"He wasn't as rich as your father, but close."

I stop my jaw from dropping. Does he have any clue how much the Steels are worth? Because if this guy was close, he was a billionaire. Or close to being one.

"What kind of outside investments?" I ask hesitantly.

"I didn't know at the time, but I found out. They were mostly illegal."

"So your uncle was a crook. So what?"

"I didn't know that at the time," he says, his voice cracking. He begins to pant and then he wipes at his face, knocking the nasal cannula out of his nose.

Beeping again. I stand and look at the machines. His pulse ox is down to eighty. The same nurse scurries in once more.

"Mr. Jolly, you've got to keep this on." She adjusts the cannula. "Are you going to behave yourself now?"

Right, I say to myself.

She looks to me. "Have you finished your business yet? He's very tired."

I move to open my mouth, but Floyd speaks first.

"No, he's not done here."

The nurse sighs. "Very well, but try to stay still, okay?" She whisks back out the door.

"Get on with it," I say, not kindly.

"If I could relive the next few moments I'm going to tell you about, I'd never go to my uncle. I'd live on the streets, die on the streets."

"Maybe it would have helped you," I say. "I know a young woman who grew up homeless, and she's bright and hardworking and the most amazing person I've ever met."

Floyd turns, finally, meeting my gaze. His green eyes are bloodshot and watery, but still I can see myself in them. I see the man who fathered me. The man who once looked a lot like me. Tall, broad, blond.

And now he's a shadow of his former self. Booze and pills will do that.

"You're in love," he finally says.

I say nothing.

"Don't try to deny it. I see that look in your eyes when you speak of your young lady. Don't let her get away, son."

I widen my eyes at his use of the endearment. I'm no more his son than the guy across the hall. Only genetically.

"My personal life isn't any of your business," I say.

"I won't argue with you on that." He turns away and resumes staring straight ahead. "I should get on with it, I guess."

"I really wish you would."

"My biggest regret is that I went to see Uncle Fred that day."

"Biggest? Really? Bigger than abandoning your kids and their mother?"

"Yes."

I shake my head and stand. "Unbelievable. I'm out of here."

"For God's sake, Dale, sit down!"

That voice again. So like my own when I'm angry. When I'm trying so hard to be understood.

So again, I sit. I'll hear him out. He'll be dead soon anyway.

"You have two more minutes," I say, "and then I'm going."

"Good enough." He coughs and sputters once more but gains control. "I went to Uncle Fred for money. I needed a fresh start. I already found a rehab place that would take me, but of course I couldn't afford it. I needed five thousand dollars to get in the door. Once there, I could apply for state funding as an indigent."

"That doesn't make any sense."

"Well, that's what I was told at the time. I was strung out, ready to go through withdrawal, and I believed what anyone told me. So I went to Uncle Fred."

"And your rich uncle told you to take a hike?"

He shakes his head. "How I wish he had. No, he said he'd give me the money, but that I needed to do something for him in return."

"Bartering. Sure. The man wasn't stupid. What the hell could a strung-out alcoholic and junkie have that your rich uncle wanted?"

He closes his mouth and then his eyes. The beeps on one of his machines increase in speed. His heart is pounding rapidly. Why? I have no idea.

Finally, he opens his eyes and turns to gaze at me. Then,

apparently thinking better of it, he cocks his head back and stares straight ahead.

"What did he want from me?" he says.

"Yeah. What the hell could you possibly have that he wanted?"

Another pause that seems to go on for years. Then—

"You. He wanted your brother and you."

Somewhere in the air, words hang and voices echo.

You. He wanted your brother and you.

"So... You're telling me..." No. Can't let the thought form in my mind. Can't. Just can't.

"I told you a lot of his investments were illegal," Floyd finally goes on.

Illegal. Yeah. Immoral. All that shit. But get to the goddamned point!

None of this makes it past my lips. I'm numb. My lips won't open, and if they don't open soon, I may explode on the spot and all the vileness will spew out of me.

Still numb.

Fucking numb.

Somewhere outside of the bubble I'm sitting in, Floyd is still speaking.

Illegal. Trafficking. Kids. Boys especially. Young, good-looking boys. I did it. I told him where he could find you. I sold your brother and you to Uncle Fred for five thousand dollars.

Still numb. Still immobile.

But somewhere inside, smoke is rising. Guts are churning. Rage is tornadoing. It all starts low, and then moves slowly, *andante*, and then begins to *crescendo*.

Finally, I break free and rise, pulling my arms from the invisible chains binding me.

I'm Frankenstein's monster. Alive for the first time.

Finally knowing the truth of my life.

Random. Nothing is fucking random.

No. Just a biological father who needed money.

"Why us?" I cry. "Why not sell your soul to the devil himself?"

"Don't you understand?" he says softly. "I *did*."

"Fuck you. Then only you would suffer for your deed. Donny and I suffered. Do you have any idea what those psychopaths did to us?"

He doesn't speak.

He knows.

He knew then, and he knows now.

"How was fucking rehab, Dad? Was it worth it?"

Still no words from him.

And I know.

I know the truth.

He never went to rehab. He took the money he got for his children and bought more booze and pills.

And he ended up the sorry sight he is now.

"This?" I say. "This is why you dragged me in here on your deathbed?"

"I had to let it go," he says. "Had to erase my sins before it was too late."

"What the hell kind of answer is that? You can't erase a sin, Floyd. The sin already exists. You can ask forgiveness, but you can't erase it."

He closes his eyes. "Will you... Can you... forgive me?"

"You're kidding, right?"

"I didn't go to rehab," he says. "I never got clean. I couldn't. I had to live with what I did. I never forgave myself."

"Then we have something in common," I say. "Because I'll never forgive you either." I stride toward the door.

"Please. Son." His voice is broken and cracking.

"Ask for forgiveness in hell." I open the door and walk out, slamming it shut.

That horror. That perversion Donny and I lived through.

Perpetrated on us by our own father.

I stand outside the door to Floyd's room when the machines start blaring once more. The nurse rushes by me and enters. Seconds later—

"Code blue!" she cries.

I stand against the wall as staffers roll in a crash cart in slow motion. Broken words meet my ears.

BP ninety over sixty. Septic shock. Kidney failure. Arrhythmia.

He's gone.

I know in my heart. He's gone.

They'll try for several minutes to resuscitate him, but he's already gone. In his warped mind, he did what he had to do. He spilled his last secret and begged for forgiveness.

Should I have given it to him?

I'll never know the answer to that.

For I have my own secret. My own reason for needing forgiveness. If I ever reveal it, I'll lose the love and respect of the person I've known the longest.

I can't let that happen.

So I'll take that secret to my grave.

CHAPTER FIFTY-ONE

Ashley

I don't work the harvest. Ryan gives me some paperwork to handle, and since it's Saturday, he lets me go by three p.m. I head to Dale's, let Penny out, and refresh her water. He's still not home, and I haven't heard from him since he left this morning. I send a quick text.

Hey, how is everything? Call me, please.
I love you.

Dale's not a huge texter, but he does usually respond, albeit in very few words. When he doesn't, I assume he's driving home, which means he'll be here soon.

I want to do something special for him. I'm not the cook that he is, but I have a few recipes in my repertoire. I surf through the freezer. Beef, beef, and more beef. If only he had some—

Aha! Fillets of cod buried under a pound of ground beef. Did he sneak it in after I told him I know how to prepare cod?

Warmth rushes through me. He must have. Tonight I'll surprise him with cod à la Ashley. I can make a white wine and butter sauce with garlic and capers. I know he has those two staples in the door of the fridge. As for white wine, I have my choice from his wine cellar in the basement. No fresh vegetables other than salad greens, spinach, and peppers. Sautéed spinach will go nicely with the cod, and I can make a mock rice pilaf with the peppers, brown rice from the pantry, and Dale's myriad spices.

Not perfect, but it will be good, wholesome food that will be ready soon after he arrives.

I head down to the basement to Dale's refrigerated wine cellar. A dry Sauvignon Blanc is my white of choice for cooking. Chardonnay is a little too oaky unless it's not aged in oak, and very few Chards aren't. I choose a wine—not from Steel Vineyards—and head back up to prepare my feast.

A half hour later, Dale still hasn't arrived. My brown rice is nearly done. Do I start the fish now? Fish only takes about ten to fifteen minutes to cook, and there's nothing worse than overcooked seafood of any kind. It gets rubbery and tough. Cod has a tendency to dry out as well.

I look at my phone sitting on the counter. Still no response to my text.

I check the rice. It can go for about ten more minutes.

Ten more minutes.

I pick up my phone to text Dale again, but something stops me.

It's my heart. It drops to my stomach.

"Be careful, please. Driving, I mean."

"I've been driving for twenty years."

"I know, but you're upset."

"I'm not that upset."

"Just come back to me. Promise?"

"I'll be back. Count on it."

He made a promise to me. To come back to me. But some

promises can't be kept through no fault of the person making them.

Images splatter into my mind. Dale slumped over his steering wheel. Blood gushing from his nose and mouth. Glass shards splayed over him. Sirens. Wailing sirens.

"No!" I say aloud. "Just no!"

Then the door. Feet clomping.

"Dale!" I run to him, throw myself into his arms.

And all is right in my world once more.

CHAPTER FIFTY-TWO

Dale

Ashley's in my arms.

She'd comfort me if she knew I needed it, but I don't want comfort right now. I don't know what I want.

Revenge?

The man's already dead.

He sold his children.

He sold Donny.

He sold me.

To a bunch of psychopaths who starved us, beat us, raped and humiliated us. I was ten years old, but to hell with me.

Donny was seven. Still a kid. Still slept with that stupid-ass teddy bear.

I used to give him such grief for it. So much I wish I could take back.

So much I can't even bring myself to think about.

"Hey." Ashley melts against me, hugging me.

She's warm. Warm and loving and familiar.

But I don't want warmth at the moment. I don't want love.

Familiarity?

Even that doesn't sound good.

Normally I'd run to my vineyards to seek something with a semblance of tranquility. But even if I wanted to, I couldn't.

It's harvest time. The vineyards belong to everyone during harvest. Usually I accept this, because harvest is my favorite time of year—when the fruits of our labor begin a new journey.

I want something unfamiliar.

I pull back from Ashley. "We need to talk."

Her blue eyes widen. She's expecting the worst. She thinks I'm going to dump her. It's written all over her face.

She's wrong.

I gave her my word. Two months. I'm nothing without my word. I've gone back on my word only once, and I'll pay for it until the day I die.

"I need a favor," I say.

"Of course. Anything."

"I need you to stay here for a few days. Take care of Penny."

"Well . . . sure. But where will you be?"

"I don't know."

"Dale, what's wrong?"

"Floyd is dead."

"Oh." She presses her fingers to her bottom lip. "I'm sorry."

"I'm not." No truer words.

"It's okay to feel something."

"Oh, I feel something, all right, but it's not even close to sorrow."

She reaches for my hand, but I whisk it away.

"Please," I say. "Stay here. Take care of my dog. There's plenty of food in the pantry, fridge, and freezer. Or you can eat at the main house with my parents."

"Dale, I—"

"Please, Ashley." I rub furiously at my forehead. "For God's sake, don't ask me a bunch of questions I can't answer. Just promise me you'll take care of my dog."

She falls back, her beautiful lips trembling. "Yes, of course. I'll take care of her. Whatever you need. Always."

"Thank you."

"But it's harvest. We're just about to—"

"Damn it, Ashley!" I push my fingers through my hair.

Her eyes widen. "You look . . . "

"What? I look what?"

"Like . . . Like a lion. Ready to pounce on prey."

My dick is hard, all right. It always is when Ashley's around. But if I take her now, it won't be for love.

It will be in anger and rage about something that has nothing to do with her. Indeed, she has no idea what it even is, and if I have my way, she'll never know.

Maybe I'm not fit to live with others. Maybe I need to go somewhere, build a life alone. Live like a hermit. Or a nomad. I can wander the world, see all its sights . . .

I've considered this path before, and as much as it appeals to me in some ways, I've never followed it. I've always thought of others.

And now, I not only have my family to consider, but a woman who . . .

So I won't take the path of least resistance. I won't. But I need these few days, maybe even a week.

I need to go.

"Dale . . . "

"What? For God's sake, what?"

"Running away isn't the answer."

I don't respond. She's right, of course, but what she doesn't know is that I have no choice. I have to run. If I don't, I can't be responsible for what I may do.

"Can you at least tell me where you're going?" she asks.

She'll pester me until I give her something, so I reply, "To the mountains."

"Without Penny?"

"I need to be alone."

"Please, I—"

"I'm done talking about this. Tell my parents not to worry. I'll text Uncle Ry that I'm taking a few days off."

"They'll worry anyway."

"That's on them, then. I'm going to pack."

"Dale!" Her tone has changed. It's angry now. She's going to fight me.

She will lose.

"I've said all I'm going to say."

She whips her hands to her hips. "Well, *I* haven't. I'm not letting you run away like this. Whatever's going on, you shouldn't be alone right now. I'm here for you. That's what you do when you love someone, Dale. You feel their pain with them."

I rub at my temples, trying to ease the throbbing that has erupted. "I don't want you feeling my pain. I don't want anyone feeling my pain. It's mine, damn it! All mine!"

"Bullshit," she says. "I don't buy it. Not for a minute."

"You're not me, Ashley. No one will *ever* be me, so you don't know what's going on in my head. Believe me, you don't want to know." Truth. I don't want to know myself half the time.

"You want a fight?" she says. "You've got one."

"I don't want a fight. You're the one who's determined to fight me on this. I just want to go!"

"What if I block the door?"

I shake my head. Really? This is where she's going? "I'll move you."

"Take your best shot." She walks to the back door and plasters herself against it.

I stalk toward her, lift her into my arms, and—

She wraps her arms around me and kisses me. Hard. Her tongue probing the seam of my lips until I open for her without meaning to.

I can't help myself. I love her. I want her. I need her.

I'm going to take her. Right now in my kitchen. I walk to the island and set her on the granite countertop, our lips still fused together.

I unsnap her jeans and use both hands to slide them, not gently, over her hips. I get as far as her knees. It will be a tight fit, but I don't give a damn.

Our lips still sliding against each other's, I take care of my own jeans and free my aching cock.

With one swift thrust, I'm inside her.

Fuck. So tight, even with her wetness. Her legs are pinned together by her jeans around her knees, which makes for narrow paradise between her legs.

I fuck her hard. I fuck her fast.

I'm concerned only about my own gratification. It's all about me this time. All about me and the broken soul inside my body.

She groans into my mouth, finally breaking our kiss and gasping. "Dale!"

If she tells me to stop, I'm not sure I'll be able to.

She doesn't.

She holds still and lets me take what I need. I fuck her. Just fuck her. And when I release, I bury myself in her comforting body, pulsating into her, grunting.

I love you.

The words don't leave my throat.

I love you.

Still don't.

I love you.

"I love you," she says.

I pull out, then, satiated, and leaving her sitting on the counter, I head to my bedroom where I pack a bag quickly.

Within fifteen minutes, I'm in my truck, en route to . . .

To somewhere else.

CHAPTER FIFTY-THREE

Ashley

Two days later, and Dale is still gone.

He hasn't stopped loving me. I believe it with all my heart. If that were the case, he wouldn't have asked me to stay at his place, to take care of his precious dog.

"It's just you and me, girl." I give Penny a pet on her soft head as I attach her leash and take her to the car. "Let's go find your daddy."

I've been here on the ranch long enough to know my way around. But even if I didn't, I'd still be able to find my way to the Syrah vineyards. That first night with Dale, when he took me, is etched inside my brain as if I was born with it.

Penny sits in the passenger seat, panting, as we make the drive. I try not to think too much, but my mind never fails.

When I try not to think, I think, and I think a lot.

I finger the garnet necklace around my throat. And I think.

"And you never let anyone wear it? Not even the woman you were in love with?"

"No. Now turn around."

I'm trembling. Actually trembling, as I turn around and pull my hair off my neck.

He clasps the necklace, his fingers warm against my shivering flesh. The piece is heavy and cool against me.

I turn toward him. "Well?"

He smiles. "Now I have."

"Now you've what?"

He draws in a breath, his forehead wrinkling. Then he relaxes—as much as Dale can relax—and his lips nudge into a smile.

"Now . . . the woman I love has worn it."

★ ★ ★

I park the car, grab the backpack and Penny's leash, and walk to the Syrah vineyards. The harvesting tools sit at the foot of one of the rows. About half of the Syrah has been harvested. I walk to the little shed Dale showed me that first night.

Of course the shed is locked. I didn't expect it to be open. I don't need Dale's tent and sleeping bag. I won't be here long.

But I need to be here. I need to be here with Penny. And with Dale.

I look toward the mountains, where the sun set an hour ago. Dale is somewhere up there. Alone.

He didn't even take his dog.

"Let's sit, girl." I plunk onto the ground.

If I sit, if I touch this ground that he finds so hallowed, maybe I'll understand why he left. Maybe I'll understand that thing inside him that he can't share with me.

Maybe . . .

Penny lies down next to me, and her body against mine is a warm comfort. I rub my arms to ease the chill.

Dale told me to bring a jacket that first night. Why didn't I bring one tonight? The weather was warm today, but nights are a different story. At least I'm wearing long sleeves.

I grab the backpack and open it. I pull out a bottle of water and pour some into a bowl for Penny. She eagerly takes a drink. I take a drink from the bottle myself, letting the water coat my dry throat.

I won't cry.

I've cried enough tears for Dale Steel.

I gave him all of me. My body, my heart, my soul.

I take another drink and then look up at the sky. So many stars! If possible, I think more are visible tonight than the first night here with Dale.

Except that I was so consumed by Dale that night... His enthralling red-wine voice. His blond perfection. His dark countenance.

I hardly noticed the stars.

Dale still consumes me, but at least I can see the stars now. They're bright and dazzling, and they seem to twinkle. Ha! There's truth in that song from my childhood, "Twinkle, Twinkle Little Star."

"You like those stars, Pen?"

She's not looking at the stars, of course. Her eyes are closed, her head resting on my thigh. Such a sweet pup.

She loves her daddy. If I let her, would she lead me to Dale? How far into the mountains has he gone? I've no doubt Penny could find him, but I won't put her through that. Who knows how long it would take? I'm not exactly a backwoods type of girl.

I sigh and pull the bottle of wine I packed out of the backpack. "Let's have a toast," I say to Penny.

I uncork the bottle and pour a glass.

"Something's missing." I pull the votive candle out of the pack. "Candlelight would be nice, don't you think?"

Yeah, I'm talking to a dog. She seems to understand me though. She licks my hand at the mention of candlelight. I take that as agreement.

I strike a match and light the votive inside its crystal holder. Lovely. The candlelight flickers through the glass, casting diamonds on the ground and vines.

"If only I had a cigarette now," I say to Penny. Then I force out a laugh. I don't smoke. I've never smoked. Though I wouldn't say no to a joint right about now. I gave that up years ago, but sometimes a little herb helps when your world is imploding.

This is a lovely place. Peaceful and tranquil, especially at night, when no one else is around. I understand why Dale finds solace here. What I don't understand is why he won't let me provide what he needs.

"What do you have that I don't?" I ask the vines.

I stop then and I actually listen. As if I truly think they might answer me.

The only response I get is a soft breeze that makes me rub at my upper arms once more.

I sit for a few more minutes, waiting for the vines to say to me what they say to Dale when he's here. To reveal those secrets that give him peace.

To reveal Dale to me.

But as they did the last time I came here, the vines stay silent. They keep Dale's secrets.

I love him. I love him so damned much.

But I don't know how to be with him. Clearly I'm not fulfilling his needs.

"Fuck this." I stand, knocking over the votive holder. "Shit." I quickly pick it up and blow out the candle. Then I let it cool for a few minutes before I throw it into the backpack. I pour my undrunk wine onto the ground, recork the bottle, and pack everything up.

"Let's get out of here," I say to Penny. "I don't know what I was thinking."

I take hold of Penny's leash and lead her back to the car.

Where we drive back to Dale's . . . alone.

EPILOGUE

FIRE ATTACKS WESTERN SLOPE VINEYARDS

The most recent fire to break out in Colorado this fall began on the western slope, igniting remote, rough terrain including juniper and sagebrush outside the small town of Snow Creek.

Several vineyards are in its path, including those owned by Colorado Pike Winery and Steel Acres Vineyards. Grape harvesting has begun, and so far, the fires have had minimal effect. Firefighters hope the recent moisture from thunderstorms will keep the fire from spreading too rapidly.

No evacuations have been ordered, though that could change at any time. Firefighters are blaming a lightning strike for starting the blaze, but fire from campers in the foothills has not been ruled out.

CONTINUE THE STEEL BROTHERS SAGA
WITH BOOK EIGHTEEN

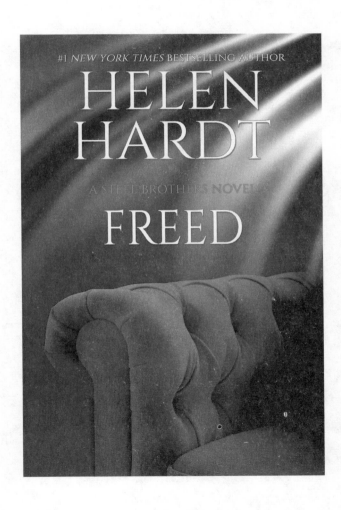

MESSAGE FROM HELEN HARDT

Dear Reader,

Thank you for reading *Cherished*. If you want to find out about my current backlist and future releases, please like my Facebook page and join my mailing list. I often do giveaways. If you're a fan and would like to join my street team to help spread the word about my books, please see the web addresses below. I regularly do awesome giveaways for my street team members.

If you enjoyed the story, please take the time to leave a review on a site like Amazon or Goodreads. I welcome all feedback. I wish you all the best!

Helen

Facebook
Facebook.com/HelenHardt

Newsletter
HelenHardt.com/SignUp

Street Team
Facebook.com/Groups/HardtAndSoul

ALSO BY HELEN HARDT

The Steel Brothers Saga:
Craving
Obsession
Possession
Melt
Burn
Surrender
Shattered
Twisted
Unraveled
Breathless
Ravenous
Insatiable
Fate
Legacy
Descent
Awakened
Cherished
Freed

Blood Bond Saga:
Unchained
Unhinged
Undaunted
Unmasked
Undefeated

Misadventures Series:
Misadventures with a Rock Star
Misadventures of a Good Wife (with Meredith Wild)

The Temptation Saga:
Tempting Dusty
Teasing Annie
Taking Catie
Taming Angelina
Treasuring Amber
Trusting Sydney
Tantalizing Maria

The Sex and the Season Series:
Lily and the Duke
Rose in Bloom
Lady Alexandra's Lover
Sophie's Voice

Daughters of the Prairie:
The Outlaw's Angel
Lessons of the Heart
Song of the Raven

Cougar Chronicles:
The Cowboy and the Cougar
Calendar Boy

Anthologies Collection:
Destination Desire
Her Two Lovers

ACKNOWLEDGMENTS

My poor Dale...

At my very first writers' conference back in 2007, I attended a workshop presented by RITA Award–winning author Linnea Sinclair called *Character Torture 101*. Our assignment was to think of the worst thing that could happen to a character. Then, Linnea said, "Make it worse." I use this advice a lot in my writing, but never more than in *Cherished*. Dale, Ashley, and their love will all be tested in *Freed*.

Huge thanks to the always brilliant team at Waterhouse Press: Jennifer Becker, Audrey Bobak, Haley Boudreaux, Keli Jo Chen, Yvonne Ellis, Jesse Kench, Robyn Lee, Jon Mac, Amber Maxwell, Dave McInerney, Michele Hamner Moore, Chrissie Saunders, Scott Saunders, Kurt Vachon, and Meredith Wild.

Thanks also to the women and men of Hardt and Soul. Your endless and unwavering support keeps me going.

To my family and friends, thank you for your encouragement. Special shout out to Dean—aka Mr. Hardt—and our amazing sons, Eric and Grant.

Thank you most of all to my readers. Without you, none of this would be possible.

Freed is coming soon!

ABOUT THE AUTHOR

#1 *New York Times,* #1 *USA Today,* and #1 *Wall Street Journal* bestselling author Helen Hardt's passion for the written word began with the books her mother read to her at bedtime. She wrote her first story at age six and hasn't stopped since. In addition to being an award-winning author of romantic fiction, she's a mother, an attorney, a black belt in Taekwondo, a grammar geek, an appreciator of fine red wine, and a lover of Ben and Jerry's ice cream. She writes from her home in Colorado, where she lives with her family. Helen loves to hear from readers.

Visit her at HelenHardt.com